THE

PERFECT SEASON

Stephen Roth

Stephen Roth

122 Long Dr.

Stratford, ON

N5A7Y8

www.stephenroth.org

This is a work of fiction. All of the characters, organizations and events portrayed in this novel are either products of the author's imagination or used fictitiously.

Printed in the United States of America

Dedication

Dear Jacob and Noah,

Thank you for the wonderful memories, listening to the cracks of the bat and following you from diamond to diamond, province to province and country to country. Let this book be a permanent reminder of my love for you and the smiles you brought to my face.

Remember – life is like baseball; when you expect a fastball, be prepared to hit the curve.

Love, Dad.

THE PERFECT SEASON

CHAPTER ONE

Cup of Joe

"The benevolence or malevolence of the baseball gods depends on which dugout you sit in, Dad," explained my son, our bantering on America's favorite pastime always bringing a twinkle to his eye. I have yet to discover a better example of perspective.

However, it was an ancient Chinese expression that Charlie put to me that I found profound, a healthy dose of hindsight required to appreciate the clever words fully.

"*He who knows all the answers has not been asked all the questions.*" My failure to revere this philosophical observation empowered life to hoodwink me for a period, although I might have garnered the last laugh.

How was it that my barely teenaged son even considered Confucius's cerebral insight at his pubescent age, let alone offered it to me as advice? Charlie, with his genius-level IQ, allowed the logical in, pushed the nonsensical away, and deposited the ambiguous for later assessment.

Conventional wisdom never quite fit my boy's lens, the lack of synchronicity with our world a burden thrust upon him by the randomness of his inherited DNA. I fear my eventual admiration for Charlie lacked any significant consolation, the

1

well-meaning sentiment overwhelmed by the immense weight positioned on the other end of life's teeter-totter.

Yesterday, a polite conversation with a stranger in the checkout line at Meijer's grocery store at King and Clarke filled the ten-minute wait. The stout man, clearly an extrovert, called upon his friendly disposition to ensure not an instant of silence interrupted our discussion. As we debated the Detroit Tigers' chances of securing a playoff position this year, it became evident the twenty-something fan didn't recognize me.

"Oh, they'll make it. I'm certain of it!" he confidently declared, loud enough that several heads in front swiveled around to investigate the disturbance. With mischievous delight swelling in his sun-kissed face, the man removed a hand from his cart, rubbed the Tigers logo on his ball cap, and then knocked three times on the side of his head before addressing me again, "Knock it, then rocket!"

I responded with two thumbs up, grinning internally, knowing I was partly responsible for the phrase's widespread popularity, four words that had now transcended the game of baseball. Most said it with a wink.

"If only the Tigers had another Charlie Hustle," offered the fellow, nostalgia fueling his shaking head, lament engulfing his hazel eyes; he had no idea he was referring to my late son.

The irony was almost too magnificent to withhold from my new acquaintance, but I refrained; I was in a hurry and knew the admission would extend our chat far longer than the line permitted.

"But you know what Mark Twain said, mister," he announced, extending his hands out, palms to the ceiling, in preparation for his grand pronouncement. "You can only be certain of death and taxes." The chatty guy waited for my response, stretching his neck and pushing his head toward me in search of my approval.

Charlie surely would have corrected the amiable Tigers fan, employing that brilliant brain of his, quickly retrieving the necessary facts from within his mop-topped head. I had heard him do it before—explain that English actor Christopher Bullock first uttered the phrase during a performance in 1716, and that is who should receive proper attribution. The recipient's reaction was always the same, eyes wide open, confused as to who was the adult, while heeding the encyclopedia-worthy statement emanating from a pint-sized body.

I had no appetite to rectify the trivial error. Unlike my son, I could let it go, permit the meaningless inaccuracy to pass without hesitation, without it gnawing at my intellectual duty. However, it struck me, barely shy of thunderbolt-style, that Bullock could have added a third certainty: ignorance—not in the ill-mannered sense, but the unenlightened variety. Death, taxes, and ignorance. Confucius would have agreed, and likely Mark Twain, too, that every last one of us will possess woefully incomplete knowledge when the final curtain is closed—a vast yet unquantifiable deficit. What a disadvantage, I concluded, when attempting to decipher that thorny and complex question we colloquially refer to as the meaning of life.

A day later, Charlie permeated my thoughts while my size-ten feet, comfortably slipped into flip-flops, stepped off the curb and into the intersection of Gratiot and Broadway in downtown Detroit.

I began whistling the tune to my favorite song, "Take Me Out to the Ball Game." My mind silently belted out the lyrics, keeping pace with my cheerfully pursed lips. *Oh, then root, root, root, for the home team. If they don't win, it's a shame. For its one, two, three strikes you're out at the old ball game!* Years ago, I detested the 1908 iconic song, traditionally played in the middle of the seventh inning of a ball game. Oh, how my life had changed since that unfortunate period. Thirty seconds changed everything—my outlook, my relationships, and how I viewed humanity.

The light turned green, and I stepped off the sidewalk, ensuring that I didn't step on the straight white lines of the painted crosswalk. A ballplayer never steps on the chalked lines of a baseball diamond—it's bad luck. Those lines looked similar, and superstition compelled me to avoid them. Peculiar, us humans.

The combined images of a green light and white lines pushed my thoughts to that split-fingered fastball on that fateful day, or as the locals called it, *The Day*. Coach Staub touched his chest, left ear, and then the indicator—his right arm. He then tapped the tip of his baseball cap, the sign to follow. Risky, I thought, given the circumstances, but I was a rookie, and not about to disregard the coach's direction, one foot in the batter's box, fifty thousand fans on their feet, their chants deafening the stadium. At least that's the explanation I had planned for the media, a silent wink and a mea culpa tucked in my back pocket, in the event my lone-wolf decision soured.

I continued north on Broadway, enjoying Detroit's unusually warm September morning, excited to meet my friends. The sun beamed down on me; a gentle wind blew northeast off the Detroit River, strong enough to rustle my brown curly locks. I ran my hand through my hair, the thinness reminding me of the mounting years and the tenuity of life. Bullock's assertion on the certainty of death briefly commanded my attention, quickly shoved aside by a vision of the delicious burger I would be ordering shortly.

A minute later and several steps away from my final destination, the sound of quickly-approaching footsteps from behind caused me to spin around 180 degrees. A young boy, huffing and puffing, hastened upon me with a baseball in one hand and a pen in the other. His flushed face and wide grin were a welcome interruption. Two magical blue eyes exuded excitement; I wondered what he saw in mine. My wife always insisted, "You can't fake a twinkle in the eye."

The boy reminded me of my son, the way he lumbered up to me, his lurching gait providing overwhelming evidence of a body devoid of athleticism. Even the way his red hair flopped over into his eyes and obstructed his vision forced me to take a second look, to ensure I wasn't peering into the eyes of a ghost. But it was his T-shirt that grabbed my attention and violently shook it around, threatening my already-shaky equilibrium. Charlie had the same one, the silhouette of Albert Einstein's face on the front with his famous physics equation underneath: $E=MC^2$.

"Mr. Unger, sir, may I have your autograph?" he asked politely in between gasps for air. The enthusiasm remained in his face as the youngster slowly extended his freckled hands toward me, wonderment stalking him from head to toe. "To Timmy, please, sir."

Timmy, who appeared to be about twelve, handed me an official Rawlings Major League baseball, which I placed in my left hand and squeezed tightly. Staring down at the unblemished ball, my fingertips soon resembled the shade of that magical white sphere. I loosened my grip, allowing the blood to return, memories washing over me, some that I welcomed, and others that were tougher to hold back than a man in rage. After a brief clash between the two, the warm images took control and blanketed the cold losses that I suffered with a wave of goodness.

My left thumb softly massaged the raised red stitching. "Timmy, did you know there are two hundred and sixteen single stitches in a Major League baseball?"

"No, sir, but I do now!" replied the boy exuberantly, nodding his head and maintaining that wide grin of his. He pushed the hair away from his eyes and gazed at me. "I'll never forget it! I'll never forget anything that you tell me! Yes, sir, two hundred and sixteen stitches."

I signed my name and handed the ball back to the eager fan, patting him on the shoulder.

"Thank you, thank you!" Timmy smiled at me, squinting through the sunlight before scrutinizing the ball and my barely legible scribble. He cupped it in both hands, much like one may gently hold a robin's egg, to ensure the fragile shell won't crack.

"You are very welcome, Timmy," I said, meaning it more than he could imagine.

The youngster softly blew on the black ink, intent on preserving a smudge-free signature.

I turned my back and began walking away when the boy called out to me. "I was at that game, ya know, Mr. Unger."

I stopped but did not turn around. Uninvited, the grip of grief appeared, grabbing my shoulders and holding me there, those gigantic hands imposing their will over my mismatched vulnerabilities, as they had done frequently.

I didn't want Timmy to see tears in the eyes of his hero. Calling upon my strength, using all my might, I tugged and tugged on those stubborn hands, finally ripping them off my body, allowing me to inch away.

Timmy piled on, "I want to be just like your son! I mean it!" he hollered while I took two more steps away from the unintentional provocateur.

I stopped again. Fight or flight? Which would it be? I turned around to face the boy and my past. Timmy was taken aback when he saw my face, the tears streaming with the force of a waterfall, the interpretation requiring a deftness that I did not possess.

"Thank you, Timmy. Never give up on your dreams, young man. Never! And, yes, anything is possible." They were words I now unconditionally believed in.

Timmy nodded and hesitantly confirmed his agreement, my waterworks dampening his excitement and extinguishing the fire in his eyes.

"Yes, sir," he replied quietly, his rippled forehead expressing understandable confusion.

Two minutes later, now composed, and with Timmy off in the other direction, I opened the front door at Tigers Time, my favorite restaurant, activating the familiar chimes and alerting two of my already seated friends of my arrival. Kevin and Jenny lowered their coffee cups onto the table, smiled at me, and knocked three times on the sides of their heads, followed by my reciprocation.

I first met Darlene, Jenny, and Kevin at a bereavement group that I began attending a few months after my son died.

The four of us were thrown together by our mutual grief, our friendship crafted by unconditional support.

Charlie died on October 31, 2019, one day after game seven of the 115th edition of baseball's Major League World Series. The temporal connection between those two events was not coincidental. I was devastated, the undertow of loss ripping me from the safety of my existence and pulling me out to sea, where I flailed in choppy waters. While I was comforted that my boy had managed to live a fuller life than most, even those who lived until a hundred, certain chasms are utterly unfillable. Some punctures are sure to sink even the most seaworthy vessel.

Charlie's life was remarkable. Against all odds, he was responsible for making my life extraordinary as well, dragging me from the depths to a privileged position that I did not deserve. We were co-recipients of *Time*'s Person of the Year award, the first and only time a father and son have shared the honor. Signing several autographs each day is a frequent reminder of what we accomplished.

At my request, my friends and I always meet at Tigers Time, a quaint diner located on Broadway Street, sandwiched between Stop-and-Shop Variety and Motor City Magazines. My pals never ask me why; they don't need to. I suppose that's what makes them good friends, evidence of the unspoken bond between us. My fondness for Tigers Time has nothing to do with the free lifetime bottomless cup of coffee that the owner, Micky, graciously provided me—his way of saying thank you.

Nondescript on the outside, with many meandering cracks traversing the masonry, it had become a favorite spot for both locals and visitors to the city. The inside, a shrine to the grand old game, was adorned with Tigers history and memorabilia—photos, jerseys, posters, bats, and autographs. All the greats are featured—Cobb, Greenberg, Cabrera, Kaline, Gibson, and Trammell. A friendly spirit patrols my favorite haunt, a smile across his face, soaking in the folklore and triumphant memories. I feel Charlie.

Vivid images remain of Micky and Charlie talking for hours about baseball, arguing about who was the greatest of all time. On and on they would go, yelling, laughing, smacking the table, and throwing their hands up in the air. Ten cups of coffee later, and hours after the restaurant closed, I would drag my boy away from Micky. The two would agree to disagree, knock on their heads three times, and then embrace before heading home.

After taking my seat beside Darlene and Kevin, I looked up at the chalkboard behind the counter, where Micky posts his daily specials. The same special has been there since Charlie's death. The Mr. Hustle Hamburger comes with fried onions, hot peppers, and sauteed mushrooms served on a Pepperidge Farms sesame seed bun.

Initially debuted by Micky as a tribute to my son the day after he died, the Mr. Hustle Hamburger remained as the sole special for days, then months, and then years. Micky can't bring himself to rub off the chalk. Besides, it's his bestseller, fans traveling from all over the country to sink their teeth into that delicious eight-ounce patty.

Jenny Smith, with her fair and exquisite features, arrived last. Appearing refreshed, the tanned widow removed her sunglasses to reveal the whiteness around her eyes. "I know, I look like a bloody raccoon. Don't say a bleeping word!" she ordered, showing us a soft smile and raising a clenched fist that had surely never touched another soul. She sat down and ordered lunch—vegetable soup and the Mr. Hustle Hamburger. "No onions, please."

Jenny proceeded to excitedly discuss her Caribbean beach vacation—swimming, boating, and the exotic cocktails consumed each evening, the brilliant sun serving as an all-day audience to her wonderful experience. "Every night, I left my bedroom window open and listened to the rhythmic sound of waves crashing onto the beach, gently rocking me to sleep after a long day in the sun. It's my favorite sound, I swear!"

"Oh, my favorite sound is a purring kitten soothing my senses while it cuddles deep into my lap," replied Darlene, pushing her dark hair away from her eyes and tucking it behind her ears.

"And mine is the hypnotic chirping of a bird, piercing the quiet air on a lazy afternoon, daring you to dream of better things to come. A yellow warbler will do," explained Kevin, winking at the world.

It was true, I thought, observing the excitement in my friends' eyes. Each of us has that favorite sound that comforts us—that immediately shoots a feeling of goodness throughout our body when it reaches our ear. Often, we understand the reason why it satisfies our being, and other times the explanation is destined to remain a mystery.

"David! Earth to David," laughed Kevin, waving his hand in front of my face. "You are daydreaming, my man."

"What's your favorite sound, David?" asked Darlene, the intensity in her eyes confirming her legitimate desire for an answer.

The answer was easy, albeit peculiar, requiring no reflection. "Percolating coffee," I replied casually, a response that immediately raised three sets of eyebrows.

My wife was an early riser, her beautiful blue eyes opening well ahead of the day's first rays, the brightness of her soul lighting our home hours before the sun was given an opportunity. It was a habitual morning race, the inevitable winner, clad in a nightgown, flicking on the kitchen light to commence her day, victorious again over that great ball of fire.

After a long week at my law office on Saturdays, I tried to sleep in but was routinely and prematurely awoken by her screechy, off-key singing a floor below our bedroom.

Making no attempt to remain quiet while patrolling our kitchen at those ungodly hours, she would belt out the words to Johnny Cash, Aretha Franklin, or any number of tunes that suited her eclectic musical tastes.

"And Iiiiiiieeeeeeiiiii will always love you!" she would yell out with half the power and a quarter of the skill of Whitney Houston. Or, with her wild and disheveled hair flipping back and forth quicker than an excited cat's tail, she would sing her woefully inadequate rendition of Will Smith's "Gettin' Jiggy Wit It."

Regrettably, I constantly complained to her that she should remain in bed, relax, and let me sleep in, never concealing my annoyance. Admittedly, I was an ass, firmly entrenched in a prolonged jerk stage.

Between verses, I listened to her feet rhythmically prance on the kitchen's white tiled floor on those early mornings, the only other sound that of percolating coffee. My annoyance with the lost sleep was replaced long ago with profound penitence; how I miss my wife's positive and wonderful energy. It's a peculiar feature of perspective: if you are fortunate enough to obtain it, it often comes too late.

What I wouldn't give to hear the sticky bottoms of her slippers squeak against the floor again, the sound of percolating coffee filling the background.

Every once in a while, if you peer through my back window, you will find me sitting alone at the kitchen table, sipping her favorite cup of joe—French vanilla—despite its despicable taste.

My mind drifted again to my son. The Houston Astros and Washington Nationals pushed the World Series to game seven on October 30, 2019. The Nationals prevailed 6–2 in that final game and secured their first championship in franchise history. Four of us watched every game of the series with my boy in his hospital room. When the last out of game seven was recorded in the bottom of the ninth inning, I knew it wouldn't be long until my boy took his last breath. He had been hanging on for one final "Fall Classic." He referred to autumn as the perfect season, not because of the vibrant changing colors of leaves, but because champions and legends were made during those Major League Baseball playoff games.

I feared a series sweep and was relieved when that World Series kept moving deeper and deeper, knowing that Mr. Hustle wanted to hang on to see every last out.

"My son's sound was the crack of the bat," I blurted out to my friends. The trio slowly put their drinks down and gave me their attention. "Or, as Charlie described it, the magical sound when that five-ounce sphere meets the bat." More specifically, it was the sound produced by a Louisville birch bat that sent a feeling of goodness throughout his body when it hit his ear. The reasons were not a mystery; no detective work was required. The crack of the bat was his cup of joe.

In Charlie's final few days, when he could barely keep his eyes open, the medication dulling both his pain and faculties, we turned the television up to its loudest volume. We took turns narrating every last detail of those World Series games. Although the nurses gave us disapproving looks because of the blaring play-by-play, they never made us turn the sound down, to their credit. They could also see that it was the only stimulus that perked up the patient in room 346. Even with his eyes closed, we knew he was listening and fixated on the game because a slight smile came across his face every time a crack of the bat blared from the television. Then, he would softly speak out, barely audible through his dry and cracked lips.

"Louisville. Maple," he said, even before the roar of the crowd erupted. Or, "Rawlings. Ash."

Although I should have ceased being amazed long ago, I remained so. He knew the bat's make and wood type based solely on the sound of the crack.

"Maple is the densest, Dad, and ash the most porous; can't you tell the difference?"

Each bat maker used their own brand of finish, varnishes, and laminates, affecting the sound; no, I couldn't tell the difference.

Those cracks of the bat were music to his ears—comforting sounds in those final days. It was the last sound that he wanted to hear before saying goodbye forever.

As he approached his last breath, I wondered what my boy was thinking. I smiled when I put my ear to his mouth for his final words.

My son was a science guy—a fact guy. He liked predictability—formulas and exact answers. Occasionally, we watched the game Plinko on *The Price Is Right* television show made famous by Bob Barker. The contestant drops a disc from the top of a vertical board, which then meanders its way down, unpredictably bouncing off protruding pegs until it finally comes to rest in one of several prize slots at the bottom. My son used his computer-like brain to attempt to predict where the disc would end up as it left the contestant's hand.

Ironically, both of our lives behaved like that disc in a game of Plinko—unpredictable—and one of those pegs was located across the globe. Let's start at the beginning, in Cameroon.

CHAPTER TWO

Fear Makes the Wolf Bigger

than It Is

Fear makes the wolf bigger than it is, Sophie. The words whirled within her head quicker than an African dust storm while she prepared her daughters' beds. Her father's gravelly voice, an echo from the past so clear, the decade-old advice could have been spoken yesterday. *Fear makes the wolf bigger than it is.* She couldn't expel the words from her thoughts lately; it wasn't even evident that she wanted them gone.

While the busyness of life allowed her to catapult her father's expectations away over the years, like a boomerang, they returned and buried themselves deep within her psyche, a constant reminder of what John Moussa expected of her—of what he thought was important. While the words exemplified what he stood for, the strength of her convictions had never been put to the test since he died. Until now.

What kind of man would have a rat tattooed on his forearm? John Moussa proudly wore a detailed image, permanently etched into his skin with black ink.

"A cornered rat, when faced with the choice of fighting or dying, will fight to the death," he explained to his daughter: That was John Moussa's way—an uncompromising fight for justice. He abhorred the rabbit, the cute and passive animal that froze at first sight of danger.

"Girls, come say your prayers!" bellowed Sophie, summoning her daughters after pulling back the top sheet on each of their beds. She placed her hands on her wide hips, scanned the room, and shook her head in disbelief at the countless trophies that congested the tiny room. The shiny awards filled the entirety of the house, including the bathroom, each room utilized as overflow for the spoils of her girls' accomplishments. Dusting had become the bane of her existence as the tally mounted within the family's seven hundred-square-foot house over the years.

With a smirk belying his serious tone, Joseph Bouba constantly threatened to move the family to more spacious accommodations. "Sophie, there isn't one more available inch in this house for one more trophy!"

But Sophie never regretted remaining in the home that she grew up in, despite the cramped quarters, appreciative of being surrounded by a lifetime of memories. She could think of nothing more valuable.

"Fear makes the wolf bigger than it is, Sophie." They were the final words spoken from her father's lips as he lay in a hospital bed ten years earlier, thirty-three minutes before taking his last breath. The usual erosion of time lacked any deteriorating effect on the weight of his advice.

Using his last ounce of strength, the sickly seventy-two-year-old man pulled his daughter in close and whispered into her ear. The unmistakable smell of looming death wafted up and smacked her with a backhand of reality. The reminder was stark and cruelly excessive, but there was no mistake—time was running out.

She despised, admired, and missed her father since he had died, her conflicting emotions tied in a complicated knot that was impossible to untangle. Missed birthday parties because he was at rallies, and scores of forgotten football games because he was occupied with changing the world, muddied his parental legacy. John failed to arrive at Sophie's high school graduation because he was in jail for civil disobedience, the consequence of chaining himself to the courtroom door. After his release, he looked at her, wide-eyed, to emphasize the importance of his actions. "I had to, Sophie. It was an unjust law!"

When John pulled her in for those final words from his hospital bed, Sophie was confident that his faint voice was about to express his immense love for her, or sweetly declare his only offspring as the best daughter a father could have. However, he managed to disappoint her one final time, carving no place for tenderness in his warrior mind, even at the precipice of death. Soft-heartedness made him weak, or at least he thought so. Maybe Sophie shouldn't have been surprised that the fiery activist and freedom fighter wanted his last message to be one that epitomized his life. But her understanding afforded no shield against the attack on her self-worth.

When John missed the birth of his two grandchildren by a week, he provided a qualified apology. "I'm a soldier of social change, Sophie," he explained, grabbing her shoulders and squeezing them with love or passion; she wasn't sure which. "Sophie, being a soldier requires sacrifice, both yours and mine." Her father meant it, hoping the authenticity and altruism of his message somehow camouflaged the choices that he made over family. She and her mother had indeed sacrificed. Her father lost more jobs than she could recall, preferring to quit or be fired rather than submit to unprincipled direction from a boss.

A few days after Sophie's twelfth birthday, while working for a local newspaper as an investigative reporter, an important advertiser disapproved of John's stance taken in an article and demanded a retraction. Otherwise, the client was pulling all of his advertising. John refused, despite the ultimatum and his boss's unequivocal direction to do so.

"John, you understand how significant this advertiser is to the paper!"

"We can't give in to blackmail!" replied John, raising both his hands and tone to ensure he did not mask his displeasure.

"You're doing it, John, or else!" yelled his boss.

John's face turned red, and out the door he went, refusing to bend one iota when every last fact in the article was true.

"In for a pound, in for a penny," explained John to his family that evening when he sat down at the dinner table and announced his new unemployed status.

"But, Papa, again?" replied Sophie, her shoulders slumping and hands on her face, knowing that they barely got by.

"If it were easy standing up for your principles, everyone would do it, Sophie," explained John, slightly raising his voice, frustrated that his daughter did not understand. "Sacrificing for what is right takes real courage."

John looked at the disappointment in his family's eyes, wishing he could fully explain himself. "I couldn't look in a mirror if I stayed." Why didn't they understand?

Her father was a soldier. Sophie begrudgingly respected the man who would have preferred dying with his boots on, defending his principles. She was jealous of his ability to view life with a black-and-white lens, right or wrong. But indeed, life was more contextual, with many layers of gray in the middle, she reasoned.

It was heartbreaking to see the once strong and vibrant man reduced to a shell, cancer stripping him of everything physical. Two hundred pounds became one hundred and eighty, then one hundred and fifty-five. Finally, at one hundred and twenty, his gaunt face was unrecognizable. His ability to muster that one final message meant that John Moussa was leaving this life with his spirit intact, and Sophie found solace in that.

"God is with you, Papa," responded Sophie just as softly, a response that did not directly acknowledge his final words. She spent the last ten years hoping that her father hadn't thought she was ignoring his message. His daughter ignored his last thoughts? God, she hoped he hadn't felt so. All she had to do was nod and confirm that she understood. How difficult would it have been to answer him? "Yes, Papa." That's all she'd had to say. But she had always been second best to his causes, and that resentment prevented her from acknowledging his last words, afraid to tacitly agree that she was okay with his choices.

Even so, her late father's final words inspired her. They also scared her as they circled her mind because there was no denying it—sometimes the wolf was huge, vicious, and ready to tear its prey apart with its long, dangerous fangs. And, there was no doubt, the wolf that might come knocking at her door was the strongest of all.

The loving mother pulled open the curtains and looked out onto the ten-by-ten-foot front lawn and her tiny but well-manicured garden. The daylilies and lavender bordering the walkway brought a half smile to her face. The ratty and worn curtains needed replacement, but she couldn't bring herself to change them, the softness of the cotton energizing her hands. Sewing them with her mother was the last activity they'd done together before losing her to a heart attack.

Sophie watched as three vehicles traveling north from Buea passed in front of their house at high speeds along the main roadway, linking the English-speaking south with the French-speaking north. It constituted heavy traffic for that time of night, and she chuckled at the irony. The sun was about to disappear, but the last rays of the day managed to pierce through the dirt and dust that was left swirling in the cars' wakes. It wasn't terribly different than the concerns circulating within her head. She had a lot on her mind.

Always do what's right, dear—another often-repeated message of her father's. "But what is right, Papa?" she asked firmly, tilting her head up, speaking to Heaven through the bedroom ceiling. "What is the right thing to do, Papa?" She knew John Moussa's answer; everything reduced to black and white for the soldier of justice.

Sophie missed his hugs and the feel of his bald head against hers, his touch making her feel a thousand times stronger. Oh, how she missed him, how she always felt safe in his presence, the memory prying at one end of that complicated knot.

Sophie was about to call for her daughters a second time, when the twins excitedly bound into the bedroom they had shared for the entirety of their young lives. It was once Sophie's room, her amateurishly carved initials in the corner floorboard from well over two decades earlier proof of it. She smiled every time she stared at them, musing about the self-imposed promise never to replace the floor.

"We're here, Mama," the girls exclaimed in unison with their usual youthful exuberance, their galloping footsteps on the century-old wooden floors and clacking hair braids providing advanced warning of their arrival. Sophie smiled softly when she felt Jasmine's arms tightly wrap around her from behind.

"I love you, Mama!" exclaimed Jasmine, bending down and pressing her cheek into the middle of her mother's back. Despite her young age, her long and slender legs already had her looking squarely into her mother's eyes. Sasha proceeded to hug her sister from behind, resting her cheek on her twin's shoulder.

"We created a hug chain," declared Sasha, laughing at the sight of the three females linked together, the loving version of a conga line.

Sophie closed the floral-patterned curtains, clutching them for a second longer than was necessary, turned around, and smiled. "Recite your prayers, girls, and then quickly to bed. Saturday is coming, and you both need your rest."

After quickly changing into their nightgowns, the young teenagers knelt down at the sides of their beds, clasped their hands, and silently said their prayers, a nightly ritual that had occurred ever since they could talk.

Despite the girls' advancing ages, Sophie continued to tuck her daughters into bed, regretting that the bedtime ritual was nearing an end. As Sophie pulled the sheet up to each of her daughter's chins, she knew the linens would be pushed away within minutes on account of the searing heat. Sitting precariously on the windowsill, the antiquated air conditioner struggled to control the Cameroon heat, the beads of sweat rolling down her forehead evidence that the growling machine needed replacing.

"What are you thankful for, Jasmine?" asked Sophie. It was neither a frivolous question nor one that had been asked for the first time.

Jasmine looked up at her mother, giving her both the attention and reverence she had earned. "I'm thankful that Jesus loves me and protects me. I'm thankful for you, Papa and Sasha." She sat up and blew her sister a kiss, which was quickly caught out of midair across the room.

"And you, Sasha?" asked Sophie, making her way over to her other precious girl, sitting on the end of the bed, fixing her eyes onto her daughter's and making it clear that the question was important.

"I'm thankful for God and my family, and for football," the last word said through a muffled giggle as she cupped her mouth. Sasha's face turned red, embarrassed by her slightly disrespectful comment in a home where religion, manners, and justice were no trivial matters.

"I'm very thankful for football too!" exclaimed Jasmine, pushing her face into the bedsheet to conceal her laughter.

"It's the best sport in the world, after all!" declared Sasha.

"Football is important, girls," agreed Sophie, smiling. And she meant it. Sophie Bouba was a serious woman, but she acknowledged her girls were good—extremely skilled at playing the "beautiful game." They had a future in the sport. Everyone said so. As much as she considered herself an intellectual, she adored football almost as much as her girls.

"Are you both excited about Saturday? Only three days away!"

"Yes!" the girls squealed, thinking of their championship game. Nothing excited them more than football, not even God, although the admission was never spoken.

"And where do you propose we put the trophies?" asked the proud mother, raising her eyebrows and feigning dire concern, knowing there would likely be three more that needed to find a spot in the already-crowded home.

"We will find room. We always do," offered Jasmine, knowing that she and her sister would each receive one for winning the league championship, and one of them would receive the Most Valuable Player award. It wasn't arrogance as much as a feeling of inevitability, the usual result at the end of a tournament.

For the millionth time, Jasmine looked up at the autographed photo of Alaine Ekwe, the treasured memento hanging two feet over her bed, beside a few other of her favorite footballers. *To Jasmine, the next great footballer!* Her father framed it the day she met the famous Cameroon athlete before a semifinal match versus Malawi in Cameroon's capital, Yaoundé. The exciting game, etched in her mind, kicked off a love of the game that had only strengthened since the special day.

Ekwe received a corner kick and headed in the winner, sending the home crowd into a thunderous frenzy, fifty thousand voices melding into one divine scream from the seats. The twins jumped to their feet and hugged each other in ecstasy, neither of them ever feeling such head-to-toe exhilaration.

Occasionally at bedtime, Jasmine grabbed the photo off the wall and placed it upright on her chest, staring at it, listening to the echoes of the excited fans until she finally drifted off to sleep.

"Remember, girls, nothing is more important than God and family. Both of them will get you through the toughest of times." Sophie grabbed at the cross hanging around her neck and squeezed it tightly, knowing that one of the times was rapidly approaching. She kissed each of the girls on the forehead, turned off the light, and left the room.

Sophie joined her husband for a late-night coffee, sitting herself down at the kitchen table across from Joseph, sighing as she pulled the chair in. She admired his trim figure, maintaining the same athletic build he carried in high school when they first became sweethearts. Two children had added thirty pounds to her frame, invaluable "love weight" according to Joseph.

Sophie accepted a steaming cup from her husband, forgetting that the caffeine would rob her of desperately needed sleep.

"How can you be as handsome as the day I met you?" asked Sophie. "Although, that beard of yours needs a trimming."

Joseph laughed. "You always complain about the gray clippings in the sink, so I wait as long as possible."

Never one to care about material possessions, Sophie was nevertheless looking forward to the new oven they were to pick up next week, replacing the broken fifteen-year-old one that she was now staring at across the room. She hadn't been able to fill their house with the wonderful smell of fresh bread for almost three weeks now.

"Are you worried, dear?" asked Joseph, slightly frowning, knowing full well that she was, the strain evident in her eyes.

Her nod came as no surprise.

"What are you going to do, Soph?" the softness in his voice reassuring his wife.

"I don't know, Jojo." She handed him two pages. "Please read my draft."

His wife had been stressed for months over the increasing tensions in their country and the role she was contemplating in its escalation. Joseph grabbed the papers, leaned over, and tenderly caressed his wife's shoulder, the heat of her skin warming his. She placed her hand on his and grabbed it tightly.

"I'll get the air conditioner replaced," said Joseph, a promise that he had been making for months. He pressed his hairy face up against the soft skin of her cheek. "Sunburned again, Soph?"

"Black people can't get sunburned, Jojo," she replied, both of them half laughing at their inside joke, both of them appreciating the ridiculousness of her quip. Neither of them had the heart to release their usual full-belly laughs.

"I'm sure I'm on the list," lamented Sophie, Cameroon's unrest beginning to consume her.

"If you're not, you will be if you send this," replied Joseph, glimpsing down at the papers in his hand.

"I have to speak out, Joseph. What kind of person would I be if I didn't? What kind of professor would I be? What kind of mother would I be?"

"I know, Soph," agreed Joseph, nodding his head. "It's becoming dangerous though."

"How dare the university muzzle me, Jojo!" She raised her hands in disgust, becoming excited at the thought of her employer forbidding her to discuss the "English problem" in her classroom. "It's a loss of academic freedom. It violates the core of my beliefs." Sophie shook her head, attempting to reconcile the impossible.

Joseph raised himself from his chair and put his wife's head into his chest, hugging her with all his might. She reciprocated, silent verification of the agreement they had made long ago; each of them would remain by the other's side regardless of what obstacle they faced.

"I will always support you, Soph," a sincere response laced with anxious reservations about the uncharted path ahead.

"I know you will, Jojo. I can't tell you how much you mean to me. You. The girls. All of you."

"Make this your decision, not your father's," suggested Joseph.

Sophie gently pushed him back and shot him a disapproving look. "What?" she asked with peevish displeasure. Was it an accusation that she was not independent in her decision-making?

Wisely, Joseph didn't respond, remaining silent the preferred tactic in such matters. Sophie allowed five seconds to tick by, filling the silence with a stare from her chocolate-brown eyes and an exaggerated huff before gathering herself and deciding to let it go. Now was not the time for conflict between them. Besides, her husband knew her well, and it was a reminder that she needed. The expectations of a dead man should play no role in how she proceeded, but separating the two was as complicated as splitting an atom.

"Fear makes the wolf bigger than it is, Joseph."

Joseph unconvincingly nodded his head in agreement. "Doing what is right is not always what is the most dangerous, dear."

Sophie slowly nodded her head in agreement, unconvincingly. "I have to follow my conscience. The oppression against the English is out of control."

Sophie sensed a collision of seismic consequences approaching—the desire to protect her family, job, and economic means, against the need to speak out against an accumulating injustice. The conviction to her principles was being tested, an examination forcing her to peel away the fluff and define herself. Who is Sophie Bouba? She accepted that dilemmas were not meant to be reconciled, but that provided no relief from her trepidation.

"I will not be a second-class citizen in my own country, Jojo. I'm just not! And I won't let you or the girls!"

Joseph sighed. "It's complicated, my love. I wish I knew the right answer."

Sophie pushed the day's newspaper across the table and pointed to the front story. "Look, another French-speaking judge appointed to an English court. Inch by inch, they are removing our culture."

Joseph read the first paragraph and agreed, "The government is dismantling the English common law legal system. I have no doubt, Soph."

"Jojo, history is rife with examples of men and women seeking independence from their oppressors. Call it what you want—separatism, autonomism, or secessionism, but the idea is always the same, self-determination," she explained, finally taking the first sip of her coffee.

"Maybe it's embedded in our DNA? Maybe it's human nature?" replied Joseph.

"It could have been the Protestants and Catholics in Ireland, the Scots and the English, the Hindus and Muslims in the Indian subcontinent in the year 711, or any number of conflicts that would take pages upon pages to list," explained Sophie.

Joseph nodded his head, knowing the weight of the world was falling on his wife's shoulders, or at least the weight of Cameroon's English-speaking consciousness.

"Joseph, in 1968, the Malcolm X Society was a proponent of claiming five southern states in the United States to form the Republic of New Afrika. African Americans wanted their own home. Why shouldn't we?"

"Yes, it's trite. Of course, history repeats itself," replied Joseph. It was a conversation that had occurred many times in the Bouba household.

The two were discussing Cameroon's "English problem," or more precisely, the Anglophone problem. It was a topic that Dr. Sophie Bouba had discussed extensively in her political science classes at the University of Buea. She was the first woman promoted to a department head in the university's history, quite an accomplishment for a country where women generally remained in a position of servitude to their male counterparts. When she graduated with her PhD in political science and women's studies twelve years earlier, she was the only female graduate.

The "English problem" was the unofficial moniker given by Cameroon's French-speaking majority to a problem far more complex and deadly than two words can adequately describe. The label, while pithy, was demonstrably misleading in Sophie's opinion. While she agreed it was a problem, she wholeheartedly considered it a human problem rather than an anglophone problem. That is, humans are inherently flawed, a conclusion she espoused in her classroom.

The prior week, when the substance of Sophie Bouba's last political science lecture was printed in a local newspaper, leaked by a student who had recorded it, a bull's-eye was drawn on her back by the dominant French-speaking government.

The article's title, "Professor Lectures Students— Government Systematically Destroying English Culture," grabbed significant attention in the country. The journalistic piece summarized Dr. Sophie Bouba's opinion, that the Republic of Cameroon was not the first country to be thrown into strife when the minority finally decided that the majority wasn't giving them a fair shake, and that change was needed. The government took notice. A French–English divide had been bubbling for some time, and the government was not about to let that fissure break wide open.

After its publication, the dean of her university immediately met with her and forbade her to discuss the political hot potato in the classroom. The emphatic order was given after the French-speaking minister of education contacted the dean directly. When she began to object, the dean's terse response made it clear there would be no negotiation.

"No, Sophie! I'm sorry, but both our jobs depend on it."

After receiving the unwelcome direction, Sophie had been unable to sleep for days, her academic freedom squelched by the very problem she had been discussing with her students.

The question was easy—what should she do in response? But the answer wasn't black and white, having more shades of gray than she knew existed. If only she were John Moussa, no equivocation would exist in her tormented conscience.

When the editor of the Journal du Cameroun, a nationally-read newspaper, contacted her a day later and invited her to write an op-ed piece for the paper, she told him that she would consider it.

Cameroon had a complicated history. In 1916, Britain and France seized the nation from Germany and divided the country between them. When French-speaking Cameroon won independence from France in 1960, the 20 percent of English, who were under the control of Britain, opted to join the new French-speaking country, creating a bilingual country. While the French and English lived well together for decades, that harmony disintegrated over several years. Pro-French legislation and a systematic reduction of English-speaking officials in important government roles topped the Englishes' list of grievances. Almost every government ministry became dominated by French-speaking citizens, reducing the relevance of the English.

An hour later, Joseph lay in bed with his wife at his side and read her draft. He read the last few sentences twice, knowing that her concluding remarks would create a firestorm if printed. They were downright provocative.

> What do all these conflicts have in common? Differences—skin colors, gods, faiths—and sometimes the differences are so subtle it's difficult for an outsider to see them, but they are there if you look closely.

Does it come down to the simplistic conclusion that, for the most part, we can't live with people that are different than us? The evidence mounts in favor of this awkward and pathetic proposition.

In Canada, that glorious multicultural country, where even the small-c conservatives are liberal, the minority French often elect a separatist party—it's raison d'etre to ditch their English oppressors and set off on their own utopian accord.

Therefore, the 20 percent English-speaking citizens from the African nation of Cameroon who desire independence and to create their own nation of Ambazonia is not unlike other countless separatist dramas that have played out over the centuries. It just happens to be one of the most recent.

Joseph removed his reading glasses and laid them on the nightstand. He sighed, turned to his wife, and hugged her. "It's good, Soph. Perfect. It's your decision."

Sophie slid out from underneath the covers, knelt at the foot of the queen-sized bed, and closed her eyes. She prayed for guidance and strength, asking God to help her make the correct decision. She called upon the strong hand of her unshakeable faith to shore up the mighty wobble of her convictions.

The following morning, Thursday, after a restless sleep, the professor rose before the sun and pressed Send. A ghost wrapped his arms around her and whispered into her ear, "Fear makes the wolf bigger than it is, Sophie." Silent applause from the hands of a dead man reverberated deep within her, but she was in no mood to take a bow. The Rubicon of defiance had been crossed, and consequences would follow. How big was the wolf? was the only question that remained.

CHAPTER THREE

The Beautiful Game

Sophie shifted in her chair, fidgeting, staring down at the tightly rolled newspaper lying on the kitchen table, wondering why her common sense had rebelled. Like a snowball rolling downhill, her trepidation had exponentially grown since she had clicked Send two days earlier. Perhaps she should prepare herself a coffee first, before reading? Ridiculous, she concluded, scoffing out loud at her delay tactics. Why would a woman of principles and conviction delay? Would John Moussa sit here, equivocating and vacillating, letting his unease get the upper hand and reducing himself to the constitution of a burrowing, plant-eating mammal with long ears?

The self-directed chiding worked, bullying her hands onto the Saturday edition of the *Journal du Cameroun*. She pulled the elastic band off the broadsheet and laid the conduit for freedom of speech flat on the table.

Sophie didn't need to open the newspaper; her article was posted on the front page, the title in huge bold font, screaming for attention. She knew it was coming, but her eyes bulged anyway, her preparation for the shock an utter failure. The op-ed piece took up the entirety of the front page, but it was the dagger of a headline that perforated her composure— "Professor Muzzled by Government."

Oh my God, she thought, the blood draining from her face. What have I done? The dean had already telephoned her twice, calls that she ignored, his messages suggesting the obvious. Her strong conviction did not prevent her hands from trembling. The arms of post-purchase dissonance wrapped themselves around her chest and squeezed, leaving her gasping for air. Even if she wanted to, it was too late; there was a no-return policy on her defiance.

Joseph and the twins joined her in the kitchen, forcing Sophie to gather herself before peeking up at her husband. As he pulled out a chair, their eyes met, Joseph cutting her off before she had a chance to address it.

"I've already read it," he said matter-of-factly, sparing her from having to raise it. The worry in his eyes was understandable. She knew exactly what he was thinking because she was thinking it herself. What would she do if she was fired? It was the most likely outcome. What if her husband was fired because his bank wanted no connection to Sophie Bouba and the divisive issue to which she had attached herself? Controversy was rarely good for business.

"Girls, eat quickly so we won't be late for your game," directed Sophie, hopeful that a game of football might distract her. However, her dean's tone in his early morning messages and his demand for a Monday morning meeting were difficult to push aside. "As soon as you come through the doors at eight a.m.!" he barked, fully animated with no attempt to disguise his anger.

After a breakfast of freshly squeezed orange juice paired with a banana and pineapple salad, the four Boubas rushed out of their modest residence.

When the foursome reached the dusty road at the end of the driveway, Joseph turned to his wife, ending the silence between them, "You boiled the fruit in coconut milk. It was delicious, dear."

After sixteen years of marriage, Sophie knew her husband well, the benign comment affirming his support and love for her. It was exactly what she needed as the waves of doubt crashed over her, intent on toppling her confidence. She felt like crying, but now was not the time. Instead, she dammed up her tear ducts with fortitude and kept walking, squeezing her husband's arm. Joseph knew his wife well. It was her way of saying, "Thank you and I love you."

The family commenced their usual two-kilometer walk from their house in the village of Ekona, located in the English-speaking southwest region of the country.

Joseph pointed to the cloudless blue sky. "Girls, I'm not sure which is brighter, that sun or your future in football," attracting smiles from the twins, their dreams frolicking in their forefronts.

"Papa, you say that every Saturday," replied Sasha, rolling her eyes but appreciating the compliment. She effortlessly kicked her ball up from the ground, bounced it high off of her knee into the air, and then headed it into her father's backside. The maestro, her impeccable control of the ball well beyond her years, was impossibly graceful for someone her age.

"Hey, save it for the game, Sasha!" pleaded Joseph through the laughter of the other three.

"It shouldn't be this hot for September," complained Jasmine, beads already forming on her oval-shaped face, her cocoa complexion glistening under the morning light.

"Hottest year on record, 2018," replied Sophie.

Sophie never tired of the habitual Saturday pilgrimage, enjoying the beautiful countryside and the company of her family. She had always been proud of Cameroon, an African country extending from the Sanaga River to the southern border and eastward from the Atlantic Ocean to the Central African Republic to the east. Its mixture of coastal plains, dense forest, and mountains was breathtaking and tranquil, which belied the rising tumult in the country.

Sophie stepped to the side of the road, bent down, and placed her nose into a cluster of wild red stinkwood, Cameroon's national flower. She took in a deep breath of the pink flower, closed her eyes, and exhaled.

"They're early this year," explained Joseph, looking out over the field coated with his wife's favorite flower. "They usually bloom in October." Joseph took two steps and joined his wife, pinching the base of a stinkwood with his thumb and index finger, severing the flower from the stem. "For you, my love," he offered, opening her hand and placing the spontaneous gift into her soft hand.

"Thank you, Jojo," replied Sophie, her heart becoming a tad lighter because of the kind gesture. Still, she wanted to cry, but it was not the time.

"Who would name a flower stinkwood? Really, *stinkwood*?" exclaimed Jasmine, observing her parents' tender moment against a backdrop of the wildflowers blanketing the countryside.

Each of the Boubas wore chains around their necks with crosses dangling at the end. As was usual during their walks, Joseph and Sophie peppered their two children with questions about religion, politics, and history. The girls cheerfully answered, excited about education and pleasing their parents. They passionately debated the principles of democracy and what it meant to be an equal citizen. Despite their sometimes-frank conversations with their children, any discussion about the country's English problem was done exclusively between the elder Boubas, a decision meant to protect the twins' innocence from the vulgarities of humankind.

Trekking to the football pitch was a routine they had repeated hundreds of times, their feet kicking up the dust on the roads, bouncing around their dreams with as much precision as the footballs that moved foot to foot between the twins without ever touching the ground.

During the last hundred yards before they reached the field, the lively discourse transitioned to the French language. All four were committed to learning the language out of respect for their fellow compatriots. They were proud to call a bilingual-speaking country home, although the tether to that commitment had become severely frayed, the linguistic assaults chipping away at their belief that they were welcome in their own country.

"Je suis libre comme un oiseau," announced the two girls together, flapping their arms, mimicking a flying bird. Their mother routinely told them that humans were meant to be free—"free as a bird"; it had become the family's anthem.

"If you don't have justice, you don't have anything!" preached Sophie to her students and her family. These were not whimsical pronouncements.

"Democracy and the rule of law are the foundation of any developing nation," explained Sophie, remembering her father's arrest in pursuit of justice. She understood him better now, wishing her newfound perspective had come sooner, wishing she had conveyed to him at least once that she was proud of his commitment to right over wrong. She accepted that doing the right thing at personal sacrifice was courageous, a strength that very few people carried within.

"Mom, why don't they like us?" asked Jasmine, a question that caught her parents off guard.

"Who are *they*?" asked Sophie quizzically, her feet coming to an immediate standstill, the implication of the question raising her motherly hackles.

"The French, of course!" she replied. "We know, Mother. We know they don't like us," explained Jasmine. "You didn't think we knew?"

Sophie took a few seconds to absorb her daughter's question, the answer to which was as complicated as it was simple, and certainly not capable of full discussion before they reached the pitch.

"Do you have any idea the names we are called, Mama?" asked Sasha.

Sophie did have an idea. She absolutely had an idea because she had been called them all herself, some in French, some in English, and some in pidgin English, Cameroon's native blend of the two languages. "Les Anglais, casse-toi pauvre con!" translated as, "Go away, English numskull. Or the pidgin English slang, "Mouf me dè"—"Go away, filthy man."

The insults, sometimes masked as friendly bantering, had increased over the years as the strife mounted in the country. Suddenly, Sophie realized that she had been naïve to think that her daughters would be spared the harshness of oppression from their French-speaking compatriots. A pang of shame shot through her, understanding that she had failed to raise the issue of the English problem with her children but spent hours in her classroom discussing it.

"We look the same as them, Mama, but they hate us because we speak English," explained Jasmine.

Sophie looked at her husband. Their eyes met, and Joseph slightly shook his head from side to side. Accepting the hint, she looked back at her children. "We will talk about it tonight, girls. Focus on your game!" directed Sophie, exchanging her solemness with a burst of enthusiasm. "I know exactly where those trophies are going!"

"Jasmine was in a fight yesterday defending you, Mama," offered Sasha, keeping the topic alive to Sophie's chagrin, her tolerance level for lousy news nearing its upper limits.

"What? When did this occur, Jasmine?" asked Sophie, horrified, before taking two steps toward her daughter and grabbing her arms. "Are you okay?"

"It's nothing, Mama," replied Jasmine, shooting her sister a disapproving glance for revealing her secret.

"No, it is something, Jasmine." Sophie felt like crying again and wasn't sure that she had enough strength to dam up the tear ducts this time. A ghost bent over and whispered in her ear, *Sophie, being a soldier requires sacrifice, both yours and mine.*

"I wasn't afraid at all," boasted Jasmine, puffing out her chest and scrunching her right hand into a ball.

"It's not that, Jas." Sophie stopped midsentence, not knowing what to say. She had planned and crafted many other life-lesson stories for her children, but not this one.

Jasmine looked directly at her mother, "Fear makes the wolf bigger than it is, Mama!"

Sophie's mouth dropped. Joseph swung around and stared at his daughters, his eyes leaping from their sockets. Sasha looked at her sister, realizing that their eavesdropping from three nights past was no longer a secret. Seeing the worried look on her sister's face, Jasmine now understood her misstep, their treachery revealed from her own mouth, an unforced error. The girls knew a verbal lambasting was on its way for listening in on their parents' private conversation. Maybe they would be forbidden to play in their championship game? But the admonishment never came.

"Did the two of you listen to everything your father and I spoke of in the kitchen?" asked Sophie, her head down, the tone comprised of regret and somberness.

Jasmine nodded slowly, nervous about the consequences, understanding that lying to her mother would be a far graver offense.

"I see," replied Sophie, not knowing how to handle the surprising admission, her fortitude absorbing another direct blow. "We'll talk about it tonight, girls," directed Sophie, her calm reply over a deserving terse response assuaging a measure of her guilt. "Right now, there is a championship game to play!" It was a discussion that never took place.

The foursome continued onward, everyone content to debate a lighter topic; who was the greatest footballer ever?

"Pele, without a doubt," announced Joseph. "Six goals in the World Cup when he was seventeen. Are you kidding me?" he asked rhetorically. "One thousand, two hundred and twenty-eight goals in his career. Let me repeat that figure for you ladies, one thousand, two hundred and twenty-eight goals in his career!"

The three Bouba women secretly agreed with Joseph but enjoyed disagreeing, his sour face their reward for their false opposition.

Jasmine responded first, "No, Papa, Maradona. Speed. Amazing precision. He ran circles around his opponents. Nobody could touch him at his best."

Sasha chimed in, "No way, it's Messi, the Mozart of Football, the best technical player ever. Sorry, Papa."

Joseph shook his head in disbelief. "Haven't I taught you girls anything?"

Sophie winked at her girls, loving every minute of it.

Arriving at the field, the four Boubas huddled while Joseph recited a brief prayer before the girls joined their teammates. Each of them always took a turn saying a prayer of their choice, whether before a meal, before bed, or on any other appropriate occasion.

The locals took immense pride in their pitch, football being the nation's favorite sport—the strong national teams bringing passion and pride to the masses. The feverish swinging of the linear red, green, and yellow Cameroon flag by all citizens, French- and English-speaking alike, reached torrent levels leading up to each match. A cooperative maintained the field meticulously, confirming its importance to the locals, who devoted their lives to God and football.

What local talent would rise to the top and one day find themselves playing in a World Cup or the Olympics? Such conjecture dominated the conversation in Ekona whenever an exciting young player took the field and showed tantalizing promise. This year, two names danced on the excited tongues of the locals, both players invited to the junior national team tryouts the following season. Despite their young age and the stiff competition from girls several years their senior, the head coach, Francis Adamou, visited the Bouba home a month earlier to personally extend the invitation. When the coach stepped through the front door, he burst out laughing at the sight of hundreds of trophies. "This is why I am here, because of all of these," he exclaimed, scanning his index finger around the room. "I've never seen anything like it."

Sophie and Joseph smiled under the Saturday morning sun, admiring their daughters' impeccable control of the ball in the championship game, dribbling it as though it was attached to their feet by a string. Their cross passes to each other were advanced beyond their years, such mastery presumably impossible for thirteen-year-old girls, drawing oohs and aahs from the knowledgeable crowd.

Internally, the loving parents took delight in the frequent clapping and occasional shrill brought on by their daughters' play. They thoroughly understood that nearly all of the observers, about four hundred, discussed the twins that day. Outwardly, the elder Boubas pretended to be indifferent about all of the fuss. Still, they were as excited as the fans who planned on bragging that they knew the Bouba girls long before they became famous footballers, just as they had with Joseph Bouba so many years ago.

After young children began seeking their autographs months earlier, the twins devoted hours and hours to practicing their signatures. The girls relied on more than their natural talent to become great, supplementing their genetic prowess with daily three-hour practices under their father's strict and expert tutelage, a former member of the men's national football team. The twins were inseparable, joined at the hip, whispering about their aspirations until they drifted off to sleep, exhausted, in their shared bedroom.

Despite inclusion in the 50 percent of the twenty-three million citizens who lived above the poverty level, the

Boubas remained in their tiny village rather than relocate to Buea, a city of three hundred thousand inhabitants situated at the foot of Mount Cameroon. The combined salaries of a professor and bank manager were enough to afford more luxurious accommodations, but calling themselves one of the 235 families in the tight-knit village was special. Each resident knew every other resident in the town. Besides, Sophie and Joseph enjoyed the twenty-minute drive to their workplaces.

In the *Journal du Cameroun*, Sophie's piece ignited a fire under the already-simmering collective conscience of the minority English, who perceived that they had been marginalized for years. The rulers' slow, incremental destruction was a death-by-a-thousand-cuts approach—the cumulative effect only appreciated after full reflection. English-speaking separatists, seeking independence, were tired of hiding in the bushes and were ready for aggressive action. The linguist battle lines had been drawn.

The reverberations of Sophie's defiance were swift, the government livid that Dr. Bouba, an employee on the government payroll, had used her position to embarrass the government publicly. Outrage in the halls of power was an understatement.

Sophie had difficulty focusing on the championship game, ruminating about her upcoming Monday-morning meeting with the dean, confident that she would be fired. A dead man whispered in her ear, *Sophie, being a soldier requires sacrifice*, a reminder that momentarily pushed back against her doubts. The university's faculty had been sternly warned not to comment on the English problem publicly, and Dr. Sophie Bouba purposefully violated the directive. What did she expect? Of course there would be consequences. But she was a soldier, armed with the most powerful weapons of all, conviction and a pen, shaky as they were.

Sophie took a tinderbox of discord and threw a match on it. Like most English citizens, she was frustrated with the government, the English boycott of the previous national election having had little effect. As dissidents were being rounded up and arrested, pro separatists became restless, the strife at a tipping point. She didn't appreciate that her op-ed piece would collectively push the angry English-speaking Cameroonians to finally revolt in earnest. The embers of dissidence became flames, becoming a raging inferno within twelve hours of the Saturday edition hitting the newsstands.

The government, dominated by francophones, denied a problem even existed in a way that only politicians can do, but when the shooting started that night—and when the deaths began—that untenable position could no longer be maintained.

Sophie Bouba's name was added to "the list" one hour after the newspaper hit the streets on Saturday morning. Ironically, her brazen opposition garnered her a spot in the top ten, an undesirable position that now included four intellectuals. Many considered the list an unsubstantiated rumor, its existence nothing more than speculative folklore and wild conjecture flourishing from the mouths of conspiracy theorists. But there was fear and indignation within the government cabinet meetings, genuine concern that unconstrained civil disobedience could transition to civil war. Crushing it at its infancy was the preferred course. The list was real, domestic enemies of the Republic identified, the most dangerous and persuasive antigovernment individuals ranked by their threat. Being a member became significantly more dangerous that Saturday.

As Joseph and Sophie watched the match, pro-independence fighters blocked the highway that linked the English-speaking municipalities of Buea to the south and Kumba, forty-five miles to their north. The exhibition of civil disobedience took form only a few miles from the pitch, whispers spreading the news of the blockade like wildfire through the spectators, the lighthearted chatter turning darker.

"It's starting, Jojo," muttered Sophie, staring down at the grass and closing her eyes. For months, they wondered when the escalation of the linguistic conflict would transition from loud threats and rhetoric to physical action that the government couldn't ignore. Was it today? Was it foreshadowing civil war?

Sophie Bouba played only a partial role in causing the blockade, but her timing was impeccable. On Friday, the previous day, an English-speaking driver identified by a provocative bumper sticker, *Protect the English!*, plastered on the rear, was randomly pulled over by members of the national police service as he approached Ekona.

The driver rolled down his window, puzzlement blanketing the face of a man who had broken no law, and was quickly met with a snarl and insult from the officer, "Gotam*a*!" The pejorative slur for the English was propelled with spittle and an equal dose of vitriol.

"Sortez de la voiture," came the stern request, an unambiguous order for the driver to exit his vehicle.

The driver, not even a staunch separatist, complied and exited his vehicle, knowing full well that his language, rather than a driving infraction, had him standing on the side of the road and now late for dinner with his wife and two boys. Sensibly, he initially answered the aggressive questions without any attitude, and truthfully had no knowledge of any separatist activity. But as the interrogation continued, the driver lost his composure and swore at the two officers, two men who were in no mood for backtalk. The beatdown that followed was brutal, the police eventually claiming that they were attacked with a metal pipe. Only a quick-thinking doctor at a nearby hospital kept the man from visiting the afterlife.

A farmer, an active separatist enjoying his lunch on a nearby hillside, witnessed the entirety of the unprovoked clash. Reports of the violent incident quickly spread through the south and to the anglophone militia leaders, whose call to action was catapulted to high alert. Spoiling for a fight, an article in the *Journal du Cameroun* created the final push to action, a provocative blockade that the government could not ignore.

Shortly after 7:00 p.m. that Saturday, a Cameroonian Elite Rapid Intervention Battalion made up of French soldiers entered the outskirts of Ekona after efficiently removing the blockade set up a few miles from the village. The Boubas had just sat down for dinner, three trophies resting on the kitchen table, when the rumbling of the advancing tanks could be felt throughout the village.

Sophie was about to dip a ladle into her egusi soup, chock-full of cabbage from their backyard garden, when a far-off scream froze her and her husband. It was unmistakably desperate, its pitch thrusting all calmness from their bodies, replaced with a sickening discomfort. Joseph lowered his papaya juice, sprang from the table, and sprinted outside to investigate. With the sun setting directly into his eyes, he could barely view the advancing military, unaware of the government's intention to send a message and root out those with a vocal desire to divorce the French. The rattling of machine guns from foot soldiers sent inhabitants scrambling back into their homes behind locked doors, their curiosity substituted with horror.

Commander Lafontaine of the 12th Battalion, riding shotgun in the army jeep, followed the line of tanks into Ekona. He had been given strict instructions. After scanning the list in his hand, he barked out an order, "Trois, rue Deschambault. Allons-y!" As directed, the dutiful driver set his path toward the Bouba residence.

CHAPTER FOUR

The King

"This is KRBA 690 Detroit, your favorite stop for everything sports!" announced Nelson Green enthusiastically into the microphone, the now-retired Tigers player sending his message across the Detroit airwaves. The bombastic and outgoing "Green Machine" hung up his cleats a year ago in 2017, the popular ex-Tigers player becoming the host of Detroit's most-followed talk show, listened to by millions of sports fans in Michigan. The announcer did not hold back his criticisms of the Tigers and their poor start to the 2018 season.

"What the heck is going on with our Tigers?" asked Green, referring to his former team and its subpar performance, a group that appeared destined to troll the bottom of the standings. "What are the solutions? Maybe a rebuild? Maybe the front office needs to be cleaned out? What about trading some of these overpriced stars that aren't producing? I want to hear your suggestions!"

Green took several calls until the conversation finally turned to left fielder Donald "King" Fisher. The King was hitting okay, a 0.240 average, but he had so much more promise. The Tigers' first-round draft pick was a star in college, leading the Division 1 Georgia Bulldogs to a national title with a sizzling 0.422 batting average. His speed, muscular six-foot-three frame, and Popeye-like forearms combined for an intimidating package, but the rookie couldn't put it together in his first year. It was early in the season, only a month in, but the alarm bells had been sounded, both by the Tigers front office and the fans. Maybe that multimillion long-term deal was going to be a bust? Fisher's confidence was tumbling, the constant negative chatter about his play accelerating its free fall.

"Who do I have on the line?" asked Green, the dynamic host leaning forward in his chair, his elbows resting on the desk in front of the soundboard.

"Charlie Unger, sir," replied the caller with a voice cracking through puberty.

"Welcome, Charlie Unger!" replied the Green Machine excitedly. "What are your thoughts on King Fisher?"

Green had been around the game of baseball his entire life, from little league to professional ball, and now as an on-air personality. He knew that 99 percent of fan observations were bunk, uniformed baloney, boring platitudes repeated far too many times. However, his current employment of entertaining the masses required that he placate many callers and their questionable insight. They did pay the bills, after all.

"Well, in spring training, King Fisher switched bats," started Charlie. "He changed from his Louisville X22 Slugger, a 34-inch, drop-2 bat used in college, to the Mizuno PLP 34-inch, drop-2 bat." Charlie knew the transition was prompted when Fisher accepted a huge endorsement deal from Mizuno.

"How old are you, Charlie?" asked the Machine, appreciating that an adult was not on the other end of the line. Otherwise, he might have scoffed at the caller, laying into an adult for wasting the airwaves with such uninformed drivel.

"Thirteen, sir."

"Okay, Charlie, how do you know about his college bat?"

"It was difficult to find," replied Charlie, "but I discovered a team photo of the Georgia Bulldogs, and the King was holding a Louisville Mizuno bat. I zoomed in by a factor of 8. There it was, Louisville Mizuno, 34 inches, drop-2."

"Fantastic detective work, Charlie! But here is the important question: who cares? Same length! Same weight!"

"That's the thing. They're not the same weight, Mr. Green Machine," replied Charlie politely. "Louisville uses an aerosol lacquer on their bats; it dries superfast, the moisture evaporates quickly, therefore less weight. Mizuno uses a double-lacquer process, tough but old-fashioned, a longer drying period with less evaporation, so more water is trapped in the bat. I've tested them both; there is a quarter ounce difference in the weights."

Green laughed but was surprised. Despite the theory being far-fetched, the kid sounded knowledgeable, and he wasn't sure how to respond.

Charlie continued, "That quarter ounce makes a world of difference to a professional swinging at one hundred-mile pitches," explained the young caller. "He needs to start swinging earlier, when the ball is 2.1 inches farther back from the plate, according to my calculations, but he doesn't know it."

"What are you, Charlie, a genius?" asked Green, now cackling.

"Well, yes. Yes, I am. I can send you my formula, if you want, but it's accurate. The King is swinging a heavier bat, and his timing is off."

Green released a hearty laugh. "Thanks for the insight, Charlie, or is it Mr. Genius? Do you hear that, Rodney Kilmer? Do you hear that, Timothy Earley? Get those bats weighed!" announced the host dismissively, directing instructions to both the current Tigers general manager and president with a double dose of mockery.

"I can send you my calculations, Mr. Green Machine," offered Charlie again. "Fisher has to swing a tenth of a second sooner. It's a huge difference."

"No thank you, Charlie, but thanks for calling. Let's hear from a few of our sponsors," and with a click, Green ended the call. He turned to his producer and chuckled. "A thirteen-year-old kid figured this out but the Tigers haven't? I don't think so."

***

Three miles away at Comerica Park, Rodney Kilmer sat in his office stewing over the Tigers' listless play, his job security waning with each passing day. He had just finished a telephone call with Bill Peterson, the Toronto Blue Jays GM. It was the last of twelve frustrating calls he had placed that morning to other ball clubs, desperate to trade the Tigers' underperforming high-priced assets. But there was no interest from any of the teams, unless Detroit paid for a significant part of their future salaries going forward. Rodney was in a funk, a foul mood that he shared with the country. With the civil unrest in the country, especially Detroit, everyone was on edge, and the poorly performing Tigers were contributing to the poor morale in the city.

Timothy Earley, his boss and friend, was also feeling the pressure, the team owner castigating him weekly for putting together an inept team, despite the highest payroll in franchise history. Kilmer understood that Earley's loyalty could only save his job for so long, the demands for his termination rapidly accumulating as the days marched by with no evidence that the team was improving. Even his former player, Nelson Green, was railing against him lately, using his bully-pulpit radio station to blast his frustrations across the state.

***

As Kilmer listened to the radio, his arms crossed while brainstorming over his next move, Charlie Unger provoked a smile across the GM's face, the first in weeks. Cute, he thought, but Derek Fisher wasn't the first rookie to experience growing pains making the transition to the pros. The King simply needed more time to adjust. Kilmer was hopeful, even if not confident.

Rodney removed his glasses and placed them on the desk, desperation punching at his sensibilities. He sighed, picking up the phone and pushing extension 223 for the equipment manager. "Don, it's Rod. I know this is crazy, but humor me. Weigh Fisher's Mizuno bat and his old Louisville model. Let me know if there's a difference."

Charlie put the receiver down at home. Was the Green Machine making fun of me, he wondered? Why doesn't anyone listen to me? It was frustrating. He was about to recheck his calculations, when the doorbell rang. Making his way over to the foyer, Charlie opened the front door and was greeted by Janice Hamilton, his next-door neighbor. She didn't offer him her usual smile, no evidence of the bubbly personality that she normally carried around. Rather, Janice was mighty serious.

Janice bent over, stooping to eye level, "Charlie, honey. Your dad's been in a car accident. Come with me."

CHAPTER FIVE

Twinkle, Twinkle

Mired in an existential crisis several decades earlier than most, thirteen-year-old Charlie Unger put his eye to the telescope, stared millions of miles into the night sky, and easily found the Canis Major constellation system. Thankful for the clear night, he quickly found his favorite star, Sirius, twenty-five times more luminous than the sun. Colloquially referred to as the Dog Star, it was the brightest star seen from planet Earth. The young boy never tired of staring at the cosmic diamond twinkling in the night sky, both a glittering reminder of the unimaginable vastness of the universe and the minuscule significance of the third planet from the sun. The knuckles on his right hand rapped against the side of his skull, brought on by his intense introspection.

Charlie felt incredibly small, sitting on a wooden stool in his backyard, the coolness of the Kentucky bluegrass pressing up against his warm sockless feet, pink from the earlier afternoon sun. His father would not be pleased that he forgot to apply his sunscreen after repeatedly promising that he would never forget.

"Charlie, you know how important this is. Please, Son!" his father implored him, begging him with kindness and compassion, not the qualities Charlie always associated with David Unger.

"I won't forget, Dad. I swear," responded Charlie, looking directly into his father's eyes, absorbing the concern with the efficiency of a sea sponge.

His dad had been behaving mighty strangely since his release from St. Joseph's Hospital two weeks ago, a three-day stay courtesy of an automobile accident. Although a welcome development, the peculiar and drastic personality transformation had Charlie scratching his head. Charlie might have chalked it up to the seriousness of his accident, but his father looked relatively fine when he came home, explaining that he only remained in the hospital for precautionary observation. The young boy enjoyed solving puzzles, but satisfactory answers had proved elusive so far.

Soon after his discharge, David began exercising daily, eating healthier, and sleeping at least seven hours a night. The Red Bulls, extended workdays, and fast food vanished, a disappearing act that ended his reliance on caffeine, long days, and quick meals that previously had enabled his ascension to the coveted position as a top biller. Each year, his fancy law firm, situated on the top floor of a shiny glass building in downtown Detroit, presented him with a gift, a personalized thank-you for elevating the partners' bank accounts.

It was strange observing his father cut up vegetables, tossing them in a blender with a scoop of protein powder, and then gulping down the concoction with a smile on his face.

"Got to get my eight ounces of vegetables a day, my boy," yelled David, standing over a blaring blender, giving two thumbs up. Charlie had never seen his dad eat a vegetable in years, unless the tomato juice in his Bloody Mary counted. He didn't even munch on the celery stick that he plopped into the drink after using it to mix his two ounces of Grey Goose vodka.

Charlie Unger was too young to be questioning his existence, even if that is not exactly how he described the internal conflict. Who was he? Where did he fit in? He had as much difficulty figuring others out as they did him. Why was he compelled to knock three times on his head when he was excited or in deep thought? What kind of loving God would thrust such an affliction on him, to subject him to ridicule and scorn every time he raised his hand to begin the involuntary movement? Damn that God, that glorious omniscient being who had a cruel streak running through the greatness. Charlie questioned the supreme being's existence and kept score, his autism deserving of a checkmark in the no column.

"Charlie, yes, you are different, but beautifully different!" his mother emphasized every time he was feeling down. It was difficult being a square peg trying to fit into the round hole of life. Charlie hung on to Heather's words, but he understood that *different* meant "strange," or worse, "weirdo." Different was code, called upon by mothers when they didn't want to hurt their child's feelings, a way to place a rosy spin on their child's oddity. At least that was Charlie's conclusion. He couldn't call anyone a friend, except maybe Polaris, a notion that undoubtedly added to the heap of his father's unspoken scorn for him. Overweight and a social misfit, Charlie knew he was a disappointment to his father.

"Charlie, get outside, meet some friends, and get some exercise," pleaded David. "You can't read every day, all day!" his frustration clearer than Polaris on a cloudless night.

Charlie preferred his mother's advice, "Be yourself, Charlie. Follow your own path, honey. All of the great ones do."

"Yes, the great ones, Mom. The great ones. But I'm not great."

"Yes you are!" she responded, grabbing his cheeks and gently pinching them with love. "What if Galileo just accepted that the earth was flat? Everyone would stay put for fear of walking off of the face of the earth." She laughed each time she used the example, which was often.

Charlie appreciated her support, joining in her laughter, agreeing with her suggestion, but he was an outsider in life, and it wouldn't change. Thinking outside the box wouldn't change the bullying. "Fatso." "Egghead." "Blimp." "Lard ass." "Hey, freak, why do you keep smacking the side of your head? Trying to knock some sense into yourself?" Those jabs were downright hurtful and made him question what was in the hearts of those boys who hurtled those insults at him faster than a ninety-mile-an-hour fastball. Walking through the cafeteria was a nightmare, shuffling from one end to the other, no less dangerous than running the gauntlet, the verbal volleys injuring far worse than the punishment any medieval warrior experienced.

Charlie didn't mind that his mom got the Galileo story wrong, as did most adults. Galileo found himself in difficulty with the Roman Catholic Church when he proposed that the earth revolved around the sun, not that it was flat. But her point was a fine one.

"We've got to move him up at least a couple of grades, Mr. and Ms. Unger," urged Principal Wellington at the end of grade three. "He will never be challenged otherwise." Charlie was described as precocious a thousand times since then, a word he had come to despise. Now in grade twelve, the thirteen-year-old boy had nothing in common with his fellow students.

"You're a bit of a freak, aren't you, Unger?" mocked Kevin Teele on his first day of school in grade twelve. Kevin's assertion wasn't entirely incorrect, reasoned Charlie, proud to maintain his intellectual honesty, even if it was hurtful.

Was his mother misguided with her devotion to God? She told her son that he would never feel alone if he had God by his side, but he was as lonely as a boy could be. He once read that sea turtles were the most self-isolating species in the world, masters of social distancing, but that was their preference.

While he was thankful for his father's renewed disposition, even if leery, he was skeptical as to its durability. David Unger was still a stranger to him in many ways, but Charlie knew of his father's commitment to his law office. His doctors had cleared David to return to work in two weeks, those welcoming brass doors surely as inviting as a Venus flytrap. The irrationality stumped him, one-hundred-hour-plus workweeks at an office, resulting in misery. But that bizarreness was widespread determined Charlie, adults gravitating to this puzzling behavior.

Staring up, Charlie considered his relevance, looking out into the Milky Way, a galaxy with four hundred billion stars within its confines. He knocked three times on his head as he considered the number. "Four hundred billion," announced Charlie to an empty yard, attempting to wrap his head around that mind-boggling figure without success. The galaxy was thirteen billion years old, a figure touted by most astrophysicists that was wildly inconsistent with the age of the earth claimed by the Bible thumpers. It resulted in another checkmark in the "no" column. *Bible thumpers*—the pejorative term learned from his father.

"Here come the Bible thumpers. Lock the doors and close the curtains!" yelled David, catching sight of the evangelists strolling down the street, knocking on doors and spreading the word of God. "You understand it's all BS, right, Charlie?" The words stung, not because Charlie was God-fearing, but because his father knew how important God was to his mother.

Yesterday, Charlie watched Ervin Myers, a well-known physicist, explain on a YouTube video that if the earth's oceans represented the universe, even one drop of water was too large to represent the earth. Still, despite the incomprehensible size of the universe, Charlie was fully aware that Earth was the only known cosmic object to harbor life. That had to be special, even if unexplainable. He had read everything on the subject, and admittedly, other than theories, there were no concrete answers as to how life commenced on Earth. How did the first unicellular organism originate on the planet? It was a mystery that merited a plus one in the Bible thumper column for the existence of God.

Charlie moved away from Sirius and found Alpha Centauri, followed by Vega and then Orion. Those stars were beautiful and mesmerizing, but they looked lonely, too, thought Charlie. Finally, Charlie moved the lens one and a half degrees northwest past the Little Dipper and found the most famous star of all, Polaris, situated within the Ursa Minor constellation. A staring contest commenced, Charlie intent on imposing his will and finally winning one of these contests after having lost every other one.

He and Polaris gazed back at each other so often over the last two years that he felt as though they were friends. It was an intimate relationship, Charlie feeling free to think about his inner demons, Polaris never failing to maintain his attention on the young boy. Better known as the North Star, when he looked at it, his thoughts always moved to his mother, a religious woman, who had repeated the Biblical story of the three wise men to him many times when she was alive. The star sat close to Earth's northern celestial pole, so at least the adults got that right, mused Charlie, thinking of all the times they got it wrong.

He pulled his head away from the charcoal-gray colored telescope, closed his eyes, and envisioned his mother sitting in the living room during their last Christmas together, cracking open her worn Bible, and excitedly finding Matthew 2, verse 1. The passion in her weak and hoarse voice commanded his attention. It was an hour before he opened his one Christmas Eve gift—the Celestron Delux ST100 advanced telescope that he was now peering through in the backyard.

"After they had heard the king, they went on their way, and the star they had seen when it rose went ahead of them until it stopped over the place where the child was. When they saw the star, they were overjoyed." She said it with conviction. She said it with love. Charlie knew she relied on her faith to get her through those final months. The twinkle in her eye when she discussed God reminded him of Polaris.

Even with the chemotherapy and radiation robbing her of both her strength and hair, and the acceptance that the cancer ravaging her was not slowing, she read those Biblical words with strength. Charlie didn't know how she did it, hanging on so long with the unbearable pain.

"I may not have my body, Charlie, but I have my spirit, and I have my relationship with God. And that's all I need to keep me going."

Charlie asked God for one big favor, over and over, during those last months of her life. He prayed immediately when he rose from bed each morning, and every night before sleep, but he never heard back. God was probably pretty busy— providing guidance to kings and presidents—but Charlie took the silence personally. Plus three in his father's column for no God, he reasoned.

Charlie opened his eyes and regained his focus, fixing his sights on Polaris again. Polaris winked at him, reminding him not to be a fool, not to believe in fairy tales. His mother would not have appreciated the message from her favorite star. Charlie was reluctant to accept it as well, but the evidence didn't allow for any other conclusion. And he had endlessly searched for any evidence of God, something to bring clarity to the issue, but he always came up empty.

Polaris looked down upon him again and whispered without saying a word, "You are a scientist, Charlie Unger. What kind of scientist would believe in all that mumbo jumbo? God. Miracles. The parting of the Red Sea. God is for fools. God is for people who won't accept reality."

They were strong words, but Polaris had a point. Charlie wanted to believe the Bible thumpers, yet his skepticism overruled his desire. The Bible spoke of numerous instances where the physical laws of science were broken. Polaris had been around for millions of years, long enough to have seen it all, long before Adam and Eve supposedly took up in that garden.

Charlie looked one last time through his telescope. Polaris had one last message, "And, Charlie, you know as well as I do that I couldn't have stopped over anything." It was true. A star can't stop, so the Bible had to be wrong, concluded

Charlie. How would the Bible thumpers answer that one, he thought, reminding himself that he should engage in a debate with a thumper at some point. Oh, how he would enjoy stumping a thumper. A checkmark in the "no" column.

Polaris reminded him that the story of the three wise men was pure hogwash, pure fantasy, and pure nonsense. Charlie pulled his head away and looked up without the benefit of the high-powered telescope. Was he looking at heaven or the remnants of the Big Bang?

This whole God thing appeared to be a sham, he reasoned. Would a real God allow his mother to die? Wouldn't a loving God have allowed him to prevent his mother's illness before it was too late? He could have, too, if he was just given a message, some kind of sign. Would a loving God have allowed his father to have a psychological breakdown after his mother's death? No, sir. Charlie Unger was done with God, done with fairy tales, and done with denying the truth. His capacity was now restricted to one religion going forward—the amazing game of baseball.

CHAPTER SIX

Rev Your Engines

"What are your views on the whole God thing, mister?" asked Charlie from the front seat of the bus. While he was no longer a believer, he reasoned no harm could come of hearing others' views. It was sound logic from every angle he assessed his conclusion. The question was prompted when Charlie caught sight of a billboard on Interstate 67, coming into Detroit: "To all our atheist friends, thank God you're wrong." Clever, thought Charlie. But someone went to considerable expense and time getting that message out.

"That's quite a personal question, young man," replied Sam, the affable and middle-aged bus driver looking back at him through the rear-view mirror.

Money, politics, and religion. Charlie noticed that people tended to clam up at the three subjects. "I'm not a believer, Sam. I can't uncover any objective evidence of God's existence."

Sam peeked in his mirror, smiled at his young rider, and replied, "Maybe the first question you need to ask yourself is why you're trying to prove or disprove. Why is it important to you whether God exists or not?"

Charlie deposited the answer into his repository for further assessment, Sam's answer giving him pause. Who cares if God exists? It was a good question.

Charlie used the rest of the half-hour-long bus trip wisely, analyzing the bus schedule from Plymouth to Detroit. Even without using any software, he found apparent efficiencies overlooked by the transit authority. After jotting a few notes, the boy promised himself to get a letter off to the president next week.

Sam's final comment was on his mind as he thanked the driver for the chat and stepped off the bus at the corner of Washington and Lafayette in downtown Detroit.

The death of long-time Detroit Tigers manager Skip Munchin was a big deal in Detroit. Skip was a beloved Detroit Tiger who had frequently contributed to his community, building homeless shelters and filling foodbanks to the brim with healthy choices.

The manager was a legend to Charlie, his 0.620 lifetime winning average, pulling the magical strings during a game, and making those in-game adjustments to bring the victory home. His players loved him. When he managed his last game, the crowd roared, providing a ten-minute standing ovation, a thank-you for a fantastic career. Charlie mainly had ruled out a big-league baseball career as a player, his intellectual honesty forcing him to admit that he likely did not have the genetic building blocks for the profession. However, becoming a Tigers coach was his dream, and within his grasp. He knew it. If he could attain half the career as Skip, he would reach the pinnacle of life's success—he could think of nothing grander. And if he ever had his own standing ovation…well, it was too exciting to consider.

When it was announced that a public funeral would be held for the legendary manager, Charlie attended. It was a must. He ditched school, but it wasn't a concern, never learning anything in class—always knowing more than his teachers. Charlie had stopped pointing out his teacher's errors, after his mother long ago explained to him that he was embarrassing them. However, if a teacher called upon him, he was pleased to answer and participate. He also acted as the substitute teacher if his teacher was ill, but controlling the students usually didn't work out to his satisfaction.

Charlie thought he looked good, his navy-blue suit, tie, and shiny black shoes an upgrade from his regular attire. Always critical of his appearance, Charlie felt he didn't look quite as rotund in the suit, hiding some of his imperfections, although it was becoming snug. It was the same one he wore at his mother's funeral, and he had grown since then. He ironed for the first time, requiring a crisp white dress shirt for Skip's funeral. After watching a few YouTube videos, tying a necktie was a snap. He could have asked his father for help, but this excursion was secret. Not only would his father frown upon him missing school, but also there was not a chance he would have allowed him to travel to Detroit by himself. Parental oversight had not been a strength of his dad, a man who was never really around much, preferring the confines of that corner office that he had worked so hard to obtain. It was a job he was to return to soon.

David's strange behavior continued since his discharge, quiet but friendly. Charlie wondered if his father had been abducted by aliens, a gentler version beamed down into the Unger house. It was the best theory so far, but he had not completed his analysis.

As Charlie's feet approached Sacred Heart Presbyterian Church on Shelby St., he could see the many well-wishers and reporters milling out front. At least three television cameras had their lenses pointed at the front steps of the 150-year-old landmark.

Butterflies set in, prompting Charlie to question his decision to make the trip. His social skills never topped his competencies. There were hundreds of people wishing to pay their final respects; he hadn't considered that the church might be packed with no available seats. A line to get in had already formed.

Charlie wandered to the front, the overcast sky now spitting out drizzle, reminding him that he did not bring an umbrella. His timidity transitioned to excitement when he almost bumped into legends Alan Trammell and Sweet Lou Whitaker, who were having a conversation. Both men flashed him a quick smile and a nod, the looks disappearing when Charlie knocked three times on his noggin, the legends confused by the odd gesture.

Charlie couldn't believe he was rubbing so close to such greatness, the two men having patrolled the middle infield for most of the '80s. Man, he wished he was around to see Trammel play, a Hall of Famer who spent all twenty of his MLB seasons in a Tigers uniform. He was the anchor, playing shortstop and leading the Tigers, his four Gold Glove Awards, six All-Star appearances, and three Silver Slugger Awards, deserving of legendary status.

Charlie sat down on the curb, put his elbows on his knees, and contemplated his next move, the line at a standstill, his chances of gaining entry to the church sitting at zero, he figured. He observed Don Muhovey, a first base coach from the '70s, light up a cigarette across the street.

"What are you doing here, kid?"

Charlie looked up to his left to see Marty Hoover looking down on him. Charlie didn't answer initially, the awe, rather than the cat, grabbing at his tongue.

"Are you here with anyone? asked Howitzer Hoover, stroking his bushy goatee. The Howitzer played one season in the MLB. He could throw smoke, but he couldn't master the control necessary to keep himself in the bigs—too many walks. You don't last in the MLB when you walk 1.2 batters an inning. After a demotion and seven years riding buses in the minors, he became a pitching coach for the MLB team, a position he still held.

Charlie introduced himself and politely explained that he was there alone, his father was working, and he had come to pay his last respects. Howitzer raised his eyebrows and scratched his follicle-challenged melon, wondering how safe it could be for a boy his age to be traveling alone from Plymouth to downtown Detroit.

The two began chatting about the Tigers' early season woes and what was needed to yank them out of their slump. Their pitching and defense were pretty good, but they were second to last in the entire MLB in team batting practice. The two agreed.

"Maybe they've all switched to Mizuno bats by mistake," joked Hoover, who had heard Nelson Green's on-air discussion with a young fan, not making the connection with the kid sitting on the curb. "Whoever got the King to switch back to his old bat is a genius," said Howitzer, laughing. "He's tearing it up since he switched back."

Charlie nodded his head in agreement. "He certainly is, Mr. Hoover."

"Call me Howitzer, young man."

Charlie went on in extensive detail to explain what was bothering him about left fielder Chet Field's swing. After a few minutes, Hoover looked at Charlie with a perplexed expression. He couldn't believe the analysis he had just heard from this young kid.

"What's your name again?"

"Charlie Unger."

Howitzer motioned Charlie to follow him into the church, leading him past the extended line, through the front doors to a reserved section at the front. Charlie sat down beside Hoover, looked to his left down the row, and observed dozens of former Tiger greats in attendance. He tried to control it; he wanted to stop it, but it was useless, the same result as every other attempt. He hit his head three times, attracting a few strange looks, including from Hoover.

A man named reverend William Baptiste led the ceremony, reading scripture and discussing Skip's contribution to the City of Detroit. Charlie wondered if Skip was a saint after Baptiste listed the numerous good deeds he had completed over his life. The reverend was animated and loud and exhibited one of those fire-brand personalities that never went unnoticed. Charlie found him interesting, even if intimidating, his tall powerful-looking body under a head full of graying hair, mustache, and beard. Based on some old television reruns he had watched, if the man had time warped in from the '70s, it wouldn't have surprised him.

When the service was over, Charlie remained in the church, hoping for an opportunity to speak to Baptiste, but his popularity surprised Charlie, person after person approaching him with either a handshake or a hug. Finally, after a half-hour, the reverend noticed the boy sitting alone in a pew and walked over for an introduction.

"Charlie Unger, sir," the boy responded, shaking the man's hand, expecting his large paw to be soft, but it had the roughness of hard labor.

"I get the feeling you have a question for me, Charlie."

"Well, sir. I suppose I have a few questions about God."

"You're in luck. That's my specialty," he replied, laughing, followed by a wry smile. "What's your question?"

"I mean no disrespect, but I don't believe in God."

Baptiste nodded his head, "I see. What do you believe in?"

"Science, sir. I believe in science, stuff that can be proven."

The reverend warmly put his arm around Charlie, walking with him out of the church and onto the front steps, where he extended an offer, which was quickly accepted.

"I look forward to seeing you Wednesday then, Charlie," the reverend said, shaking his hand and patting him on the shoulder.

When Charlie's father saw a television clip later that evening, he looked twice for confirmation, but there was no doubt: his son was somehow in Detroit, alone, without permission on a school day. David didn't go ballistic as Charlie had expected. Instead, they had a long conversation, David hugging him at the end and promising that they would spend more time together. The alien angle was in Charlie's consideration when he headed up to bed.

***

As soon as Howitzer Hoover left the church after the service, he immediately got on the phone with Tigers GM, Rodney Kilmer, "Hey, I've got a couple of ideas about Chet Field's hitting issues." Within two weeks, Fields batting average shot from 0.230 to .290. It was extremely embarrassing a month later when Hoover had to admit to Kilmer that the recommendations were not his own.

CHAPTER SEVEN

Layla

"Is it really you, Layla?"

"It is, my love."

He recognized her smile, her shape, but it had to be a mistake. "I don't believe it. No, I don't believe it. It can't be you."

"I'm right here, darling," she said, moving closer and extending her arms toward him.

He scanned her up and down, inspecting every last inch of her body. His favorite, a silky beige top and a tight black skirt, made up her attire. The diamond earrings he gave her for Christmas dangled from her ears.

"I wore them for you, Coco. I know how much you love these clothes."

"You are gorgeous, Layla," he stated, reaching out and running his fingers through her long hair. "Thanks for keeping it that length; it looks the best on you."

"I knew you would say that," she replied, laughing. "I thought about cutting it, but I wanted to keep it the way you like it."

"It's so soft," he whispered, moving in closer, placing his face into her hair and taking a deep breath. He breathed in every last inch of her, the intoxication of her scent setting in. Finally, he wrapped his arms around her and squeezed, her reciprocation making them one.

"God, you're beautiful, Layla. I'm never letting go."

"Oh, Coco, it's so good to see you, but you can't stay."

"Why? Why? I don't want to go!"

"I can't stay, Coco, and neither can you. I'm sorry."

The tears streamed down his face. "Please, Layla. I don't want to go."

She gently pushed him back and wiped away a tear slowly running down his cheek. "We will see each other again. I promise, okay? But for now, I have to say goodbye."

CHAPTER EIGHT

Tiger Blood

Charlie turned the key to the off position, threw his head back, and closed his eyes, allowing the warm sunshine to soak into his cherubic face. The pleasing purr of the motor choked to a halt, leaving only the occasional bird chirp to pierce the quiet afternoon air in his leafy Plymouth neighborhood.

He slapped the top of his Tiger Striper. "Well done, boy!" The clang of the metal rang out. A wild mop of red curly hair peeked out from underneath Charlie's Detroit Tigers helmet, those locks desperately attempting to escape its confines and reach for the sky, much like a plant bends toward the strongest light.

Charlie looked up to see Mr. Cooper from across the street staring out at him through his huge bay window, his nosy neighbor wearing his usual curmudgeon-laced face. The old man's head shook in disapproval a few times, loosening his comb-over, followed by the indignant closing of the curtains.

The young Tigers fan was satisfied with the decision which he had made three nights ago, guided by the sage advice of Polaris. With the heavy weight of having faith lifted off of him, he could focus on more important business and be guided by cold, hard science. Algebra, quantum physics, and the fundamental laws of nature would suffice. Relying on sound scientific principles was the way to go. It felt correct to his very core.

Novertdortis, he thought, taking in a deep breath through his nose. Oh, how he loved it. "Novertdortis!" he yelled, extending his arms out to his side, his voice bellowing out with as much force and passion as Pavarotti. His right fist rapped three times on the side of his helmet.

Ms. Jenkins, two houses down, looked up from the thistle that she was about to pull from her garden, her attention drawn by her neighbor's outburst. She fixed her stare upon Charlie, unimpressed that her quiet enjoyment had been interrupted. She shook her head, similar to Mr. Cooper. Then she looked at her husband, standing a few feet away. "Crazy kid!" she exclaimed, shaking her head again. "A psychiatrist needs to check that boy out."

Charlie looked back at his neighbor and mockingly shook his head in response, complete with a crinkled face and crossed eyes, feigning insanity. The irreverent side of his personality snuck out occasionally. Besides, what did Ms. Jenkins know? Or, Mr. Cooper, mused Charlie. Why couldn't they simply be nice like his mother? Why were there so many Ms. Jenkins and Mr. Coopers in the world?

"Novertdoris!" he yelled again, twice as loud, followed by another deep breath through his nose. That smell—that fragrance of goodness—permeated both the air and his mind. There was nothing like it.

After his neighbor turned away, Charlie pulled his cell phone from his back pocket, purchased by his father for emergencies only, and peered down in excited anticipation. It was a thrill to be communicating with the Detroit Tigers #11, even if #11 had no idea who he was—who he was texting with. In a way, this was an emergency, rationalized Charlie. The Detroit Tigers were bouncing around the bottom of the division, which was unacceptable. It was unfathomable, insufferable, unconscionable, undesirable, unthinkable, unreasonable, objectionable, and offensive. However he labeled the team's woes, the situation called for emergency action. Charlie had one dream, to watch the Tigers win the World Series, and he was prepared to do everything he could to make it happen.

As expected, there was a text message from #11.

"How did I look today?"

Charlie knew the question was coming, so he typed a reply with his pudgy right index finger without any hesitation, having thoughtfully considered his answer for the last two hours. Not only had he watched the game on television, but also he had reviewed each of the second baseman's four at-bats, in glorious frame-by-frame slow-motion detail, so many times that he had lost count.

"Better, but you are still rolling over a bit. Your hands were in a much better position today, at least in your third and fourth at-bats. Keep doing the exercises I gave you."

A smile came over Charlie's face ten seconds later when he read the reply, "Thanks, man. I owe you. BIG TIME!"

For the last year and a half, Detroit Tigers player Marshal Slinger, #11, had been driving Charlie crazy with his plate appearances, his sloppy mechanics and inconsistent swing planes. Charlie paced around the living room, throwing his Nerf ball at the television and ruminating on the former all-star's deficiencies. Slinger's batting woes were obvious; the fix was straightforward—so why were no corrections being made?

Three weeks ago, when Slinger's cell phone number was accidentally printed in the *Detroit Free Press* newspaper, Charlie texted #11 with an analysis of his swing flaws along with some suggested fixes. He did it mostly on a lark, knowing a response was unlikely, but Detroit was dead last in their division, starting the season with a terrible 5–12 record. Charlie had to act fast to try to save the season. The team had too much talent to be in the cellar.

No response arrived as a result of the initial text, not surprisingly. Charlie texted him again the following day with the same results. *Why won't anyone listen to me?* Charlie lamented that he could fix the swing of every Tigers batter, but he had no way of conveying his fixes to the players, no way to be taken seriously.

He knew that the Tigers' second baseman was likely receiving a million texts and phone calls from fans on account of that inadvertent release of his phone number. Slingers had probably switched phone numbers already.

As Charlie observed #11 at the plate during the next Tigers game, Charlie jumped off the couch after Slingers stroked a hard opposite-field single. "He just went oppo!" yelled Charlie. "He just went oppo!" Slingers pulled every pitch, rolled over more often than a gymnast, and just hit to the opposite field. "He listened to me!" hollered Charlie with all his might. Obviously, Slingers had read his texts; it couldn't be a coincidence. It was amazing how a slight and simple grip change on the bat could have such a significant effect. When Charlie saw those hands in his recommended position, he smiled ear to ear, knowing that the sophomore's fortunes at the plate were about to change. And he was correct; over the next five games, Slingers went fourteen for twenty-two at the plate, coming out of his slump in fantastic fashion. Charlie was over the moon, knowing that he could help any player.

A few days later, after the grip change, Charlie finished cutting the grass when he received an unexpected text. He read the message. *Who is this?* "Oh my God," whispered

Charlie slowly, with amazement, his eyes wider than they had ever been. Tiger #11 finally responded. Charlie couldn't believe it, dancing around the front lawn, screaming like a wild animal. "He texted me! He texted me! I can't believe it! I can't believe it!" He shouted it with all his might, loud enough that his good friend, Polaris, heard it.

Mr. Cooper opened his curtains, snarled at him through his bay window, and then quickly closed his curtains, but Charlie didn't care. He didn't care one iota, not even a little. No, sir. Marshal Slingers had accepted his advice and was now texting him. He promised to celebrate with a hamburger topped with fried onions, hot peppers, and sauteed mushrooms in between a Pepperidge Farms sesame bun.

Charlie considered his response carefully at the time; a misstep was unacceptable. Charlie sat on his Tiger Striper and attempted to settle himself down, stewing for a half hour before responding. Would the Tigers' all-star second baseman appreciate taking advice from a thirteen-year-old boy? The answer was clearly no.

Simple and adult-like—that was the best approach, no doubt about it, he decided, slowly typing his message back to Slingers. Exhilaration blanketed him as he typed the message, "Charles T. Unger—at your service."

And that exchange had kicked off a texting relationship with Marshall Slingers, #11, the two of them connecting after each game, Marshall never considering that he was communicating with a kid.

Charlie was pleased that at least one player was following his advice, that he was helping his beloved Tigers. But one player couldn't change the fortune of a team, although King Fisher's and Chet Field's fortunes had been turned around, so he had three of them turned in the right direction. He was certain that he could help the other struggling players, but how would he get anyone else to listen? He couldn't count on the *Free Press* accidentally printing all their phone numbers in the paper. Charlie knocked three times on the side of his head, the deep concentration bringing it on.

Charlie put the phone back in his pocket, taking in another extended breath. Novertdortis, always the relaxing antidote. It was strange for a boy his age to think of that moment as a slice of heaven, but he was not ordinary. Extraordinary was a more apt descriptor. Or, marvelous, fantastic, incredible, excellent—any superlatives would suffice. Not that Charlie was perfect, by any reasonable description.

Perhaps that heavenly state of tranquility was explained by the Tiger blood that coursed through his veins. Although that would be a simplistic answer, trying to describe someone with just a word or two usually is.

Charlie took in the beautiful afternoon sunlight, bathing in it, basking in it, but also begging it to somehow find its way into the dark crater that developed in his soul after his unimaginable loss. It was a warmth that he indeed needed, despite the already present and intense midsummer heat; however, he knew that it was a formidable task, even for that great ball of fire in the sky, to reach that crater. Those were the odds he faced, but he refused to surrender his hope and optimism, because without both of them, he was forced to look into an emotional abyss, and that was no way to live. And, more importantly, letting pessimism get the upper hand would betray everything his mother had taught him.

The rays that were now warming Charlie's pasty white skin—the considerably freckled kind that redheads have—

took only eight minutes and twenty seconds to travel ninety-four million miles, a miraculous mind-bending fact if you gave any thought to it at all, and the young boy was doing just that. He felt the heat on his skin, reminding him that he had forgotten to put on his sunscreen.

The juxtaposition of that wonderment against the cruel irony that those same rays took his mother's life always lingered in his mind, a contradiction that no child should have to reconcile.

The last gift he received from his mother before she died was a book of Confucius's sayings, a parting gift that she hoped would help his emotional IQ catch up with that other, more notorious intellectual kind.

He who knows all the answers has not been asked all the questions. Charlie thought of Confucius's saying 12, located on page 23, often.

Sitting on his Tiger Striper, Charlie twisted his torso and looked back over his left shoulder and through a few hawthorn branches to admire his handiwork. He furrowed his brow and stared.

Even though the Ungers' neighbors were accustomed to seeing Charlie riding that oversized deluxe grass cutting machine on their upper-middle-class street in Plymouth, Michigan, they thought it the oddest sight—a Skag Tiger Striper on a residential lawn rather than on a college or professional baseball diamond where it truly belonged. The advanced cutting machine was precisely the same one used by the Tigers to cut their field at Comerica Park.

Most of the neighbors concluded that the peculiar boy was plain crazy, which was absolutely correct if the definition was confined to the slang of "nonconforming" or "oddball." But if the accusation was that he was insane, or acted without logic or reason, then those conclusions were misguided, very misguided.

"Never make assumptions," Charlie heard someone say in passing when he was five years old, not realizing the profoundness of the statement at that tender age. With the benefit of hindsight, he now knew that assumptions were the first cousins of intellectual laziness. And there was an epidemic of laziness in the world, he concluded.

Closing his eyes again, Charlie pondered whether anyone else was like him, a question that occupied his thoughts constantly, almost incessantly. Was he blessed or cursed? Two sides of the same coin, perhaps, he lamented.

Whatever the answer, it was the consequence of having an IQ of 170 and being gifted intellectually. A genius. Yes, Charlie Unger was a genius—within the top two percent of the highest IQs in the general population—and he had the Mensa International membership card in his wallet to prove it. And, of course, there was that high-functioning autism the doctors said he was afflicted with. "Afflicted." That was the exact word used by the doctor in front of him.

"Mom, what does *affliction* mean?" asked Charlie on the ride home from the doctor's office.

"It means you have special qualities," replied Heather, slightly pinching his cheek.

But when Charlie looked it up for himself, he realized his mother didn't know what the word meant: "bothersome, burden, distress, trouble." As his eyes moved down the list of synonyms, not one neared something positive. It was the first time he realized that his mother couldn't always protect him.

Try as she might, her motherly love could never cast a wide enough net.

When he was honest with himself, he knew it was guilt that burdened him. There was a weight that he could not push away—even if he had the strength of a thousand men. Carrying the responsibility for someone's death is difficult to describe. He could have saved her. How was he to carry that failure for the entirety of his life? A real God would have prevented it—another checkmark in the "no" column.

Charlie flung his safety glasses to the ground, hopped off his Tiger Striper in youthful style, and landed with his two Nike-clad feet onto the freshly cut Kentucky bluegrass. He twisted his size sixes into his front lawn, letting those cleats take hold in the firm earth, even though there was no reason to do so. There was no reason to be wearing cleats, but that did not matter to the avid baseball fan because those cleats felt perfect on his feet, as comfortable as ten-year-old slippers.

He wore the same brand as Miggy, Miguel Cabrera, a Detroit Tigers legend, a certain Hall of Famer, and the best hitter in baseball, in Charlie Unger's opinion. It was not a conclusion based on whimsical idealization either. Rather, it was based on an informed analysis by a student of the game—perhaps a master—but Charlie decided that he would leave it to others to describe his prowess. His mother taught him to be modest—not an easy disposition to maintain when you're always the smartest person in the room.

"Bragging is almost as ugly as swearing, Charlie," she explained to him, adjusting her handkerchief that was hiding her bald head.

A few days after he turned seven, Charlie set up a large easel in the living room, grabbed a black marker, and began reproducing complex math equations on the paper to explain the different arcs a baseball would take, depending on the speed and spin coming out of a pitcher's hand. His eyes lit up, grinning at his parents while pointing at the equation that was more appropriate for a university math student:

$$(x + a)^n = \sum_{k=0}^{n} \binom{n}{k} x^k a^{n-k}$$

Charlie pushed his messy hair away from his eyes and added both an integer and a fraction to the equation, perhaps as Einstein did at the same age. His parents, sitting on the couch, looked on, amused.

"And if one accounts for the mass of the pitcher as he propels down the mound, here is the equation," explained Charlie while frantically scribbling the numbers onto the page. Pitching was the one baseball position where a more rotund shape could be quite beneficial—that mathematical equation did not lie and was the sole reason he was not wholly ruling out a career in the big leagues.

His mom and dad looked away from Charlie. They stared at each other in disbelief, just as shocked as if an alien had dropped into their house unannounced, amazed that their son's brilliance far exceeded their understanding.

"He's definitely not an extraterrestrial, but he is out of this world," whispered Heather into her husband's ear.

"He lost me at trinomial," said David, shaking his head in amazement, wondering which lineage line was responsible for that high-functioning computer in his cranium.

Heather Unger had a remarkable quality; whether it was a stranger or her best friend, that person left the room feeling better about themselves, a recipient of the redhead's wonderful disposition. Even a nearly empty glass of water looked half full to the loving mother, who found her strength through positivity and devotion to God. Her son missed that trait the most when she was gone, because Charlie had never tired of feeling better about himself when he left his mother's presence.

He knew his father loved him, but the man was always preoccupied with something else, making money, talking about their next house, or planning the next island vacation. His father certainly didn't have time for baseball. In fact, he detested the game.

Charlie continued to admire his lawn and the perfect pattern that no ordinary lawnmower could have accomplished, patting his Tiger Striper one more time. "Good job, fella." He wiped his brow, grabbed at his waist, and pulled a water bottle from the spandex holster that was tightly fitted around his rather large waist. He took a swig of his favorite drink, orange Gatorade, and savored the citrus flavor that never failed to please his taste buds. He envisioned himself in a Gatorade commercial someday, although he now kept that to himself after the mocking received from fellow students when he raised the possibility.

CHAPTER NINE

Fifteen Years

Trent Higgins lay on the upper bunk after the lights went out, preparing himself for another sleepless night in his uncomfortable state-funded accommodation, the 11,314th time that he had performed the mind-numbing routine. The lack of stimulus was cruel to his synapses, craving any reason to fire, the repetition reminiscent of a hamster wheel rotating in slow motion.

Jealousy raced through him, his snoring cell mate grabbing sleep and ephemeral relief from his wretched existence, the only available defense against an institutional charlatan with specious claims of rehabilitation. There was no whimpering in Block B tonight, no muffled sobs of a newbie after hearing the clank of his cell at night for the first time, a merciless taunt before the silence pushed the walls in so tight that it crushed your dignity. Trent's ability to feel had long ago been stunted, the capacity to care exorcised from his repertoire, shoving Trent into purgatory where zombie-like, he shuffled half alive, half dead. The inmate knew the system had won when he began rooting for death.

Ten years into a fifteen-year sentence for manslaughter, Trent had ample time to consider what might have been. If only he had maintained his composure, the regret eating him slowly from his insides, an insidious, incurable necrosis. It was a question that he asked himself every minute of every day while rotting in the penitentiary, the slow decay of his spirit filling his days. Would he have played professional baseball rather than patrolling center field for the prison team? God, he was fast—faster than anyone that he had ever run against, faster than any eastward wind off Lake Michigan.

Inmate No. 2314555 closed his eyes and thought of that tantalizing, agonizing decision he would have had to make in his last year of high school. Would he have accepted a full track scholarship at the University of Michigan, or would he have pursued his passion for baseball and reported to minor league spring training in Kalamazoo after being drafted by the Detroit Tigers out of high school? Would he have ensured a quality education or that the gave his dream every opportunity to become a reality? Oh, how he wished he could have made that decision, either choice, an exquisite delicacy of freedom. Of course, he would have found himself in Kalamazoo. Why have dreams if you don't follow them?

But Trent never had to make a final decision, a run-in with two Metro Detroit police officers two weeks before training camp irrevocably altering his path, the stubbornness of fate interloping on which fork in the road he would travel.

After a late night of celebrating his best friend's birthday, a completely sober Trent was pulled over by two police officers on Motor City Dr. in Detroit while driving home. While bopping his head to Olivia Newton-John's 1982 hit "Physical," which recently had reached number one on the charts, he saw the lights activated on top of the police car. His shoulders slumped, knowing he was traveling five miles below the speed limit and had made no traffic violations. Not again, he thought, the frequency of these stops violating statistical probability.

"Be polite, no matter what," he said to himself, pulling the car to the shoulder and placing his hands on the steering wheel in plain sight.

"License and registration," came the terse command after Trent brought down his driver's-side window.

"What did I do, officer?" asked Trent respectfully, a hint of annoyance creeping its way in despite his self-imposed promise.

"Give me your damn license and registration!" growled back Officer Burns, expressing his annoyance, determined to flex the power of his badge over the young black man who he had pulled over for no reason other than he looked suspicious driving home at 2:00 a.m. in a clunker of an automobile. Even Burn's partner, who remained in the police car, testified a year later at Trent's trial that there was no sufficient reason to pull Trent Higgins over.

"He said, 'Let's see what we have here,' then activated the sirens and proceeded to stop Mr. Higgins," he testified, looking directly at the jury.

"I will provide my license and registration, but I want to know why I've been pulled over," asked Trent, more animated now, his irritation rising.

Burns was nearing the end of a twelve-hour shift, a long day with three arrests, an overdose death, and a drive-by shooting in which a wayward bullet had ricocheted into a ten-year-old girl's chest. Tanya Mason, innocently standing on a street corner when that bullet ripped into her, looked into Burns's eyes as she took her last breath. He could still smell the burning of her skin where the bullet entered, her pink dress resembling a tie-dye pattern comprised of red blood and brown mud. Before her brown eyes shut, they silently asked him, "What's happening?" It was a look that would be seared into his mind for his remaining years.

Burns was exhausted, hungry and irritable when he pulled over Trent Higgins, a visible bloodstain on his collar. The accumulated stress of twenty years dealing with inner-city crime and violence had taken its toll, the once-friendly officer becoming jaded. While he was once prone to giving a guy a break, that attitude had long ago been replaced with a no-nonsense, no-second-chance approach, a slow transition that had been completed ten years after his rookie year.

"Get the hell out of the car," ordered Burns.

Rather than complying, Trent pushed the up button on the door and watched as his window closed. Burns grabbed the door handle, snarling when he discovered that it was locked. Trent smirked, both amused and satisfied that he temporarily had gotten the best of the officer. After Trent ignored several further demands, maintaining his grin, Burn's face reddened, and may have popped off his large frame had Trent not relented.

When Burns raised his baton and was at the threshold of smashing the window in, the lock clicked open. The officer, forty pounds heavier, opened the door and pulled Trent out, slamming him against the side of the car and cursing like a rabid dog. The overhead streetlight illuminated the spittle that flew out of his mouth as it landed on Trent's face.

"Get your damn hands off me," yelled Trent, who attempted to remove himself from Burns's grip. The adrenaline now coursing through both their bodies corrupted their sensibilities. Burns tightened his grip, those two huge paws of his clenching with all his might, his anger fueled by the senseless and tragic death of a ten-year-old girl earlier that day.

"You are under arrest," yelled Burns, who took one of his hands off Trent's arms to grab for his handcuffs. Having seen the burgeoning scuffle, Burns's partner, Gregory Handcock, had jumped from the squad car and was now a few feet away.

Trent took his free hand and pushed Burns away with all his might when that hand came off, sending the heavyset man backward. The officer's right heel caught the raised edge of a cracked piece of asphalt, causing him to tumble back. The thud of Burns's head against the asphalt was sickening to both Higgins and Handcock, each of them rushing over to the fallen man.

Eighteen hours later, while sitting in a jail cell, Trent had difficulty comprehending the update he received. He began sobbing when told that Burns had not woken up yet, that the internal hemorrhaging caused an irreversible swelling in his brain that kept him in a coma. Emergency surgery was too late.

Three days later, when Burns's family removed him from life support, the charges of resisting arrest and assaulting a police officer were upgraded to voluntary manslaughter in accordance with Michigan Penal Code 750.321, a felony conviction that carried a maximum sentence of fifteen years in prison.

The district attorney's office used all its might to obtain the maximum sentence, displaying the usual prosecutorial vigor for when a police officer dies in the line of duty. One of the men in blue was dead, and Trent Higgins would pay.

At his trial, Handcock testified that Higgins had initiated the physical contact with his partner and then became belligerent. Burns tried to grab for his handcuffs to arrest the young black man. According to Handcock, it was at that time that Higgins violently pushed Higgins backward, with deadly consequences, an inaccurate description of the events that the jury had no problem believing. Curiously, the cruiser's dashcam had not been activated.

CHAPTER TEN

Long Way from Home

"Hi, Charlie!" came the greeting from his new neighbor, who now lived directly across from the Ungers. Jasmine had hopped out of the family car and was making her way across the street to visit, seemingly reaching the Unger front yard in only two strides. Jasmine Bouba crouched down, pretended to hold a plumb bob in her right hand, closed one eye, and scanned the perfectly manicured lawn with the other.

Jasmine's long colorful braids swayed slowly, side to side, rhythmically keeping time with the hawthorn branches that were being muscled around by a southeast breeze.

"That line is straight as an arrow, Mr. Hustle!" she said emphatically. "Every time, it's perfect. I don't know how you do it!"

Charlie knocked three times on the side of his head.

She looked at him with a hint of peculiarity, raised an eyebrow, and permitted the slightest scrunch to form across her face. Jasmine had ignored his gesture their first two visits, but her curiosity now demanded answers.

"Why do you do that, Charlie? The knocking thing."

Charlie could have engaged in a long discussion about obsessive-compulsive behaviors, perfectionist behavior, and where he landed on the Autism spectrum. He settled for an answer that was slightly less involved, "I do it when I'm very pleased, or when I'm thinking extra hard." It was the truth.

Charlie set his gaze upon her and waited for a response, anticipating the mockery or incredulity, or perhaps one of those shakes of the heads that Mr. Cooper or Ms. Jenkins were so fond of dishing out. It was what he was used to, what he expected from others. In preparation, he quickly erected a wall between the two of them, ready to repel the disheartening comment that was about to be tossed.

Instead, Jasmine nodded her approval, smiled, and proceeded to gently knock three times on the side of her head. "Cool," she said, mimicking a hollow sound with her mouth as she completed her last rap. "Maybe I knocked some sense into me, Mr. Hustle," she suggested, dropping her head and laughing.

Charlie quickly pushed the wall over so he could see her clearly again, each protective brick crashing around his feet.

Charlie then received some advice from Jasmine that sounded familiar, "Who wants to be the same as someone else? I sure don't. My mom used to say that it's easy to be like everyone else. Anyone can be average, but being different takes courage. Being yourself is a blessing from God."

Charlie had limited information about his new neighbor, who had arrived a month earlier with her father. They moved in with her uncle, who had lived across the street from the Ungers for several years. Charlie's father mentioned that the Boubas left Africa after some nasty conflict between the French and the English. He didn't know much more, but it was clear the Boubas had traveled a long way to escape their home. Charlie inquired about the circumstances that had brought her to America during their last visit, but Jasmine changed the subject. He figured she knew how to build a wall too.

"Thanks, Jasmine. I mean about the grass, but you say that every time," replied Charlie, appreciating that she spoke to him without any infiltration of sarcasm or insult.

"Only because it's true, Mr. Hustle," she replied, flashing him her beautiful smile while pretending to analyze his cut lines one more time. Then, she took two steps and pressed her body against the Tiger Striper. She patted the deluxe riding lawnmower with as much affection as a pet dog and then wrapped her long exotic arms around the nozzle and hugged it. Charlie watched as she gently put her lips on the machine and gave it a quick peck.

The act was corny, it was childish, and it was so, so beautiful. Charlie nodded, approving the affection afforded to his Striper. He looked over at Mr. Cooper's big bay window, followed by a glance toward Ms. Jenkins's house, disappointed that neither of the crotchety busybodies was observing.

"She's a beauty!" exclaimed Jasmine, patting the Striper. And then she was gone as quickly as she had come, her long slender legs gracefully returning her torso home after being summoned back with a wave from her father. She was a testament to athleticism, her feet not even touching the ground as she bounded across the street, her red-and-white braids lagging well behind her head. She might as well have been a gazelle racing across the Sahara Desert, the way she effortlessly covered the ground as though it wasn't even there. Or perhaps a cheetah was a better descriptor, her strength and power just as evident as that magnificent predator.

Her dark hair and skin effortlessly soaked up the afternoon sun as she jumped into her father's arms as only a child can do. Joseph Bouba could barely manage her five-foot, five-inch frame, his legs stiffening underneath him as he braced. The man barely reacted, except for a quick shake of his head and the pure white hair that covered it, signaling his displeasure. He was annoyed, but it was hard to blame the fellow for being serious, mused Charlie, thinking of all that unpleasant business he'd left behind. Charlie would discover later that Jasmine's father had aged fifty years overnight in Cameroon, his black hair streaked with distinguished gray becoming snow white seemingly overnight.

Jasmine smiled incessantly when she was with Charlie, her personality shining light onto some of the darkness that followed him around. Admittedly, Charlie was confused; he'd caught her a few times when she was off on her own, unguarded—the girl was carrying something mighty heavy around with her. He just knew it. Charlie recognized the slumped shoulders and forward-leaning posture when the weight of the world became too much to bear.

"You can't fake a twinkle in the eye, Charlie," his mother repeatedly told him. He wasn't sure what was held in Jasmine's eye; he wasn't sure about his own either.

Jasmine and her father were almost through their front door when she suddenly turned around, looked back at Charlie with those big brown eyes, and hollered at him, "God bless you, Charlie Unger!" She waved at him, her hand still moving side to side as it disappeared into the house.

Charlie wasn't fond of all the God talk. "God bless you." "God loves you." "God will watch over you." "Trust in God." Blah, blah, blah. He was in no mood for God or fairy tales, but he appreciated that wave, a simple gesture of warmth and friendship.

He wondered if Jasmine ever played baseball? She would be great—that speed and athleticism. There was never a female player in the MLB, but there is a first for everything.

She and Charlie had kept to themselves initially, both of them content to stare from across the street, sizing up each other like boxers, neither having the courage to throw the first punch and cross the street. Neither of them knew what to make of each other. Charlie wondered where the girl with a Lamborghini engine under the hood had come from, what had brought her to a foreign land. And Jasmine did not know what to make of the crazy pale kid with a grass-cutting obsession and a Chevrolet Chevette engine under his hood. Witnessing the boy hugging that monstrosity of a machine added to the confusion. Her father had told her to stay away, but her curiosity had a different agenda. Besides, even if it was strange, someone who cared for a lawn with that kind of detail and love couldn't be dangerous.

The girl from Cameroon, transplanted to a world that might as well have been Mars, was feeling around in the dark, looking for the light switch, anything to help her navigate these new, unfamiliar waters called the United States of America.

Jasmine's introduction to America had not been smooth. She was just hanging on, drowning, the anchor of grief dragging her under, her new classmates stepping down on her head, intent on keeping her underwater.

"Look how dark she is!" remarked one of her classmates on the first day of school, mocking her for her skin color. Jasmine was perplexed, the comment coming from an African American. Not once in Cameroon had the color or shade of her skin been commented on. Her English, yes, but never her color. The land of the free—she wasn't convinced.

Finally, Jasmine had made the first move to connect with her odd neighbor, desperation for a connection pushing her across the asphalt street toward Charlie—those fifteen steps taking more courage to take than traveling those 6,275 miles from Cameroon to Detroit. Charlie was sitting on his Striper and looked up when he heard a voice.

"You have the best lawn on the street," she said tentatively, unknowingly putting Charlie at ease by raising one of his favorite subjects. Grass and baseball were two subjects Charlie could discuss for hours.

Charlie raised his hand and knocked three times on the side of his Tigers helmet, immediately bringing a puzzled look to Jasmine's face. She cocked her head to the side and raised her right eyebrow, confused. She doubted that it was an American cultural norm that she was unaware of, but she couldn't be sure.

Only 24 percent of people have the ability to raise just one eyebrow, a trivial fact that intruded on Charlie's thoughts. Could she wiggle her ears, too, he wondered? Only 10 percent of the population could accomplish that act.

"Thank you," replied Charlie tentatively, barely looking up from the ground.

"Why do you spend so much time making it so perfect?" she asked politely.

Jasmine had asked him gently, softly, absent of any judgment, just like his mother used to. Given that the Ungers' lawn looked ready to host a Detroit Tigers baseball game, it was a reasonable question. Charlie put his geriatric neighbors to shame with his weed-free, perfect lawn and expertly shaved edges at the street curb.

But the question was as simple as it was complicated, and Charlie did not answer Jasmine, at least not that day. But he did respond by describing the different varieties of grass and how he created the Old English *D* in the center of the lawn by using his whipper snipper to remove all of the grass. That visit kicked off the first of many, and with each one, they were both able to turn on the faucets of their souls just enough to let their vulnerabilities slowly drip out.

On their second visit, Jasmine bestowed him the nickname Mr. Hustle. Charlie had talked and talked about baseball, intermixed with numerous scientific facts. He explained Pete Rose's accomplishments and those fantastic 4,256 hits.

"His nickname was Charlie Hustle," explained Charlie.

"Why did they call him that?" asked Jasmine.

"Because he ran hard to first base every time, no matter what. Every time, Jasmine. If he popped up the ball in the infield, he would run hard, even if there was only one in a thousand chance it would get dropped. He never assumed it would be caught. Pete Rose was the opposite of lazy, never taking a play off." Charlie's eyes lit up as he discussed Pete.

"Kind of like you and that brilliant brain of yours," replied Jasmine. "If you don't know something, you find the answer. You never let it pass. Your brain always hustles to get the answer. Your brain never takes a play off."

And from that day on, she referred to him as Charlie Hustle, a tribute to his intellectual prowess and insatiable appetite for knowledge. And Charlie loved it. It didn't matter to Jasmine that he lumbered and lacked coordination, or that his orthotics barely gave him any relief from those flat feet he was born with.

Despite the uniqueness of that high-powered brain of his, Charlie shared one incredible love with millions of his fellow Americans—the love of baseball. Like Ms. Jenkins and Mr. Cooper, some considered Charlie's intense passion for

America's favorite pastime as extraordinary, over the top, and maybe even unhealthy. It was not an unreasonable assessment, but Mr. Hustle saw absolutely nothing wrong with devoting his life to the greatest sport on Earth and his beloved Detroit Tigers.

"Charlie, I'm sure you have Tiger blood coursing through your veins?" said Heather, laughing, when her son listed sixteen Tiger stats in a row without taking a breath during dinner at Tigers Time while celebrating Detroit's Central Division title. His parents had nearly finished their meals, but nothing had moved from their son's plate as he listed off his favorite players' accomplishments.

"Ty Cobb—0.368 lifetime batting average; Al Kaline—2,384 games played; Miguel Cabrera—138 intentional walks," and on and on he went. He'd been called a walking encyclopedia of baseball, which was the ultimate compliment, in Charlie's careful consideration.

According to Charles T. Unger, there was nothing finer than that magical game played between those white lines, especially on a hot afternoon with those amazing smells wafting through the stands. Could you love something too much?

It was a beautiful warm July day for southern Michigan and Plymouth, a city of ten thousand people situated a half hour northwest of Detroit. Charlie wiped the sweat on his brow, thinking of his quick visit with Jasmine from a few minutes ago, chuckling at her plumbing of his cut lines.

Charlie loved the heat, but he could do without the incessant application of sunscreen on his pale skin, but his father insisted, and for good reason. Tanning was forbidden because of his mother's death from melanoma, the treacherous cells hiding, scheming, and then multiplying under the skin until it spread to her brain. His father was not about to let his son suffer the same fate.

The fear on his father's face sprang to attention whenever the sun baked his skin the slightest shade of pink, knowing Charlie's 50 percent chance of inheriting the CDKN2A gene from his mother would significantly increase his risk of developing melanoma himself. It was a heck of a thing for Charlie to consider each time he looked up into the sky at that raging celestial orb, so massive it would take another seven billion years to burn out.

But Charlie knew that he had a 50 percent chance of not inheriting the gene, which sounded a whole lot better than the way his father explained it to him, a view that did not require an IQ of 170. Rather, he only needed an old-fashioned positive outlook, not dependent on his oversized brain. It was advice that his mother gave him often, and no matter how many times he considered it, he found no flaw in her logic.

"Charlie. You're so smart in here," she said, pointing at his head and then gently knocking on his noggin, "but happiness lies in here," she explained, always becoming serious as she pulled up his pajama top, putting her hand over his heart and rubbing it gently.

And Mr. Hustle was very positive—positive he could turn around his Tigers fortunes if given the opportunity. After meticulous analysis, Charlie had carefully drafted and sent twelve letters over the last few months to Tigers general manager Rodney Kilmer. But there were no replies, not any evidence that his letters had been received, much less considered. After watching successive Tigers games, Charlie became further dejected when it was clear that not one of his recommendations had been followed, despite his rock-solid analysis. What was up with the Tigers' management? wondered Charlie.

For example, left-handed pitcher Dwight Stone gave a subtle tell every time he threw his curveball, a slight twitch in his left elbow just before he commenced his windup. Hitters knew when he was throwing it, and hitting it hard almost every time. Stone continued to repeat that tell, and batters were crushing him all over the park. Charlie couldn't sleep the night before he pitched, knowing that Dwight could be performing better.

Then there was Big Bobbie Branson, the Tigers' occasional designated hitter, who was mired in such a slump that he had been riding the pines for a month. When Charlie compared his swing to 2012, when he hit .280 with thirty-five home runs, it became obvious that Big Bobbie was opening those hips early and flying open. As a result, he could not hit the outside pitch; every pitcher was nibbling on the outer corner with their pitches, and Branson felt hopeless at the plate.

"Why is nobody listening to me!" Charlie yelled at the television when Branson struck out again on an outside change-up.

Charlie closed his eyes again, straddling the Striper like a horse, taking in a huge breath, and knocking three times on the side of his head.

"Novertdortis," he said out loud. It was the word for freshly cut grass, coming from the Latin term *nova odor mortis*, meaning "the fresh smell of death." He couldn't get enough of that smell, although he wasn't particularly enthusiastic about the name, which did not appropriately reflect the marvel of the fragrance.

Charlie visualized the release of those green leafy volatiles that emitted that pleasing smell into the air, a biological process that began the healing process for those blades of grass that had just been sliced by the Tiger Striper. Charlie wondered if anyone else gave a darn about novertdortis, but he knew that he wasn't the only one that loved the smell. He and novertdortis fell in love during his first visit to Comerica Park when the smell of freshly cut grass permeated the air. It was the first and only time his father had brought him to a game.

The Unger men sat in section 204, row 3, seats 5 and 6, the stubs eventually framed and placed on Charlie's bedroom wall, where he could look at them every night before dozing off. That first visit to Comerica was "PMD," pre-Mom's death, an outing pushed by Heather when she gave Charlie two tickets for his eighth birthday, but David was reluctant. Based on all those calls his father took during the game, his dad must have been too busy, his shiny glittering glass office demanding his devotion.

It was unfathomable that his father was reluctant to spend a glorious afternoon taking in hours of America's favorite pastime, a resistance that had Charlie questioning his paternity; however, they shared a peculiar middle toe, a quarter-inch longer than their big toe, and that settled the issue to Mr. Hustle's satisfaction. The only occasions he heard words of blasphemy project off his mother's tongue occurred in shoe stores, attempting to fit shoes on those misshapen feet of his. It wasn't surprising that Charlie and

David had a wide assortment of sandals and flip flops, which were hardly ideal for the harsh Michigan winters.

Charlie was in awe of his experience at Comerica, the smells and sounds exhilarating beyond his wildest dreams, stimulating all five of his senses. He had difficulty explaining it, but Charlie believed he was meant to be there; it was his Shangri-la, his utopia, his earthly paradise. There was no other place on planet Earth as comfortable as sitting in the stands watching those extraordinary athletes run out onto the field.

"Dad, why does grass smell the way it does?" asked Charlie while scribbling his observations into a notepad.

"I have no idea. Because that's how it smells," replied his father, both an unenthusiastic and unsatisfactory response in Charlie's consideration. Unsatisfactory answers had become commonplace to the sharp-minded kid, perhaps expected when your intelligence hovered at the 99th percentile.

"Isn't it the best smell in the world, Dad?" said Charlie, closing his eyes and taking in a prolonged breath.

"It makes my nose run, Charlie, to be honest," replied his father, who struggled with allergies each spring.

But then his father looked down at his son, seated to his left, and gave Charlie the best advice he had ever received—simple yet brilliant—advice that Charlie considered every day thereafter.

"If you don't know something, Charlie, go find the answer. It's out there, somewhere. Ignorance is not bliss. It's laziness."

It was true, thought Charlie. What kind of mind wonders something but doesn't take the time to find the answer? Later that evening, Charlie snuck onto his father's study, typed his father's password into the computer, and discovered the answer to his question: novertdortis.

The Unger boys had arrived a full ninety minutes prior to the first pitch of Charlie's first game at Comerica, allowing them to take in batting practice, one of them more enthused than the other. Mr. Hustle pulled out his pad and took meticulous notes on each of the Tigers as they warmed up their bats. They all took ten swings, Charlie examining hitting mechanics, including swing plane, weight shift, and hand position. Hitting was peculiar because mechanics were important, but hitting was also an art; what works for one batter might not work for another. If boxing hadn't already taken the "sweet science" moniker for its own, Charlie would have snatched it for hitting.

For example, Charlie read the biography of switch hitter Stephen Saxon, considered the best hitter ever, behind Ted Williams. But his mechanics were unorthodox. Instead of keeping his weight back, he was a bit of a lunger, which made him susceptible to off-speed throws because he could not wait on pitches. The phenom came out of high school hitting .670, an unheard-of average, and accepted a full-ride scholarship to UCLA. Well, the hitting coach of the Bruins immediately started changing everything about that unorthodox swing that had previously pushed Saxon to unreal hitting stats. The well-meaning coach pushed Saxon off the perch of hitting greatness into an extended slump that had him riding the pines for the last third of his rookie year.

It was not of the same caliber of downfall, but Charlie was observing Tigers' current rookie, Nelson "Rocket" Richardson, ride the pines because of his slump. Charlie knew exactly what the Rocket's problem was and had informed the

Tigers' general manager of the fix in one of those twelve letters. Still, it appeared that the message either didn't reach the Rocket or it was ignored, because the Rocket continued to step two inches to the left of the pitcher when he swung rather than directly at the pitcher. After smacking a couple of early season dingers, the player was attempting to pull every pitch to left field and had abandoned his successful all-field hitting approach. The fix was as clear as Polaris on a cloudless night.

Charlie couldn't stop thinking about his young neighbor Jasmine's graceful strides, the way she knocked on her head three times and made him smile. He patted his Tiger Striper and then began assessing his work with a more discriminatory eye than Jasmine, although he never tired of her praises. But before he could establish a formative opinion, his attention was interrupted when the Ballins' car pulled into their driveway, two houses down.

Charlie provided a brief wave to the mother and teenage girl; a polite reply did not follow. Rather, he was afforded a crusty frown from mom and two sets of eyes diverted to the ground.

It was curious how all the neighbors flocked to the Ballins' house, with warm greetings and freshly baked cookies in hand, when they moved in six months ago, the same behavior conspicuously absent when Jasmine's uncle moved in. Charlie didn't have to scratch his head hard on that one, the revelation bringing three raps to the side of his skull, courtesy of deep thought and an unfortunate conclusion.

CHAPTER ELEVEN

Wake-Up Call

"It's time for your medication. Wake up, Mr. Unger." Nurse Laura Smith gently shook her patient's right shoulder. When that failed to stir him, she raised her voice and shook with more force.

"Time to get up, Mr. Unger!" After a minute of stirring, David raised himself to a sitting position in his bed, squinting as he adjusted to the harsh overhead lights. He held out his hand, accepted the pills, and then swallowed them down with a gulp of water.

"Thank you," he replied groggily, the roughness of his voice evident after a sixteen-hour sleep.

After gaining equilibrium, he focused on the tall nurse and her crisp white uniform, a woman he had never seen before. With the aid of her name tag, he addressed her, "Good morning, Laura."

"Good morning, Mr. Unger. How are you feeling?"

"I'm not quite sure; different, I guess. Almost too good."

She smiled. "You're lucky to be alive."

His mind quickly scanned through the past forty-eight hours. "Yes, I am."

Melissa Thomas, the hospital social worker, pushed open the door and entered the hospital room, nodded at her colleague, and then set her eyes on the patient in room 611.

"I'll be going, Mr. Unger. You have a visitor," explained Laura. "I'll leave you two," she said, stepping through the door and out into the hallway.

Melissa pulled up a chair beside the bed, sat down, and introduced herself. "I'm the hospital's social worker. It's a pleasure to meet you, David."

"Likewise, Melissa."

"I understand you're lucky to be alive," she said, her compassionate eyes suiting her profession while they patiently waited for an answer.

"That's what everyone keeps telling me, Melissa," replied David sheepishly, the antiseptic smell of the hospital lingering in his nostrils, the stark white walls cold to the senses.

"What happened last night, David?"

David shrugged his shoulders and remained quiet, confident he was not up for this conversation, ambitious to exclude introspection on today's agenda.

"The police reported that you hit a tree traveling at about one hundred and twenty miles per hour. Is that true?"

"I'm not sure," replied David, offering the bare minimum. "I'm really not sure."

"You sheared a forty-foot Juniper in half," explained Melissa.

"I don't recall a lot, to be honest," replied David, a bald-faced lie necessary to fulfill his ambition.

"The strange part, David, is that there was no evidence that you braked. No skid marks. No evidence at all that you attempted to slow down or stop."

David shrugged again, knowing that Melissa's temperament prevented her from pushing too hard.

"Did you try to slow down?"

"I don't remember," replied David, the falsehoods accumulating. It was a conversation he was not prepared to have, at least that day, and after ten seconds of silence, Melissa raised the white flag and changed subjects.

"You're a single dad?"

"Yes, my wife died a couple of months ago. Cancer. It was terrible."

Melissa nodded, compassion in her gaze. "I understand your neighbor is watching over your son."

"Yes, I'm thankful for that," said David, the guilt washing over him, appreciating that his son needed him more now than ever after losing his mother.

"Maybe we can have a conversation another time? It's important that we talk," urged the social worker.

"Yes, maybe." David looked up and nodded.

Melissa stood and headed for the door. With a hand on the doorknob, David surprised her with a question, "Melissa, do you believe in God?"

"I usually keep my beliefs private, David, but, yes. Yes, I do."

David nodded his head.

"Why do you ask?"

"No reason. I was just wondering," replied the patient.

And with that final exchange, Melissa left David with his thoughts. David put his head back on the pillow and stared up at the ceiling, his blank face concealing a mind in turmoil, trying to make sense of what had happened. Would he ever be the same?

David ignored the successive pings from his cell phone, urgent inquiries from his office regarding client matters, carefully disguised as get-well messages. He had a son at home that needed him, and here he was flat on his back, helpless. What had brought him to this point? Shame and regret joined hands and arrived for a visit, his tears cleansing the dirty film that had obscured his vision for so long. Suddenly, a clarity came upon him, one that had been absent for as long as he could remember. He couldn't wait to get home.

CHAPTER TWELVE

He Don't Wanna Walk You!

Jasmine came bounding out her front door, flying over the three steps of her entrance without touching a step, the sound of her clacking braids heard across the street. Charlie performed a mental calculation, estimating her sixty-yard dash time, reminding himself to ready his stopwatch next time.

"Good morning, Charlie Hustle!" she exclaimed, grinning ear to ear as though she didn't have a care in the world, which was untrue. She knocked three times on her head and made the hollow sound that she had become accustomed to making. Their visits had become a daily ritual, now numbering double digits. Jasmine taught him everything about Cameroon, but she put that wall up when he poked around for the reasons that brought her to the USA.

"Hi, Jasmine," he replied, pleased to have the visit and interruption.

"What are you doing, Mr. Hustle?" she asked quizzically, looking down at him on his knees with a pair of tweezers in his hand.

Charlie explained that he was plucking weeds out of the lawn, a twice-a-week ritual, ensuring that the lawn was as perfect as Comerica Park. It was a tedious process, but necessary. As a consequence of his affliction, he couldn't sleep at night unless he was positive there were no weeds in the lawn, a number that had to be zero. He tried using one of those stand-up weed-removal tools, but some very healthy grass always came out with the intruder, leaving unacceptable holes in the lawn. So tweezers became the go-to tool.

Jasmine sat down beside him, grabbed the tweezers out of his hands, and started plucking away. The two of them couldn't have been any more different physically, sitting there. Charlie watched her hawk-like, but was pleased with her deliberate and careful attention to detail. Not one blade of grass was removed, exactly as he liked it.

The comfortable shade they shared disappeared as the sun showed itself from behind the hawthorn tree that anchored the front lawn.

"Do you have your sunscreen on, Mr. Hustle?"

Charlie nodded yes. She asked every day now, even when the sky was

overcast.

"You can still get a sunburn when it's cloudy, Charlie!"

After a half hour of watching Jasmine remove weeds, his neighbor asked him a question, "Why do you love baseball so much, Mr. Hustle?" She stopped plucking and looked up at him with her big brown, doe-shaped eyes. She always asked reasonable questions, even if they were difficult to answer.

He had always loved the game; he couldn't explain it, but it was as though the passion was part of his DNA, passed down to him as part of his genetic code. If you asked someone why they ate, you would be told because of hunger. His desire was similar.

After his mother died, the game became more important. His dad died in a way too. First came the depression—and then his father's inability to get himself out of bed, except to add a shiny toy to his collection.

Charlie had lost both of them, and the game was all he had left.

Since his mother's death, he read twenty-two books on baseball strategy and thirteen on hitting mechanics and studied one hundred hours of videotape on certain Tigers players, all of which played a role in his recommendations to the ball club. He still had not received a reply. The season couldn't be saved if the team waited too long to implement his suggestions.

He recently took all of his Tigers Topps baseball cards and meticulously placed them in the folder of a collector's album, placing his top three of all time on the first page. Since being introduced, he had every Tigers player baseball card inserted by rank of greatest moments. Kirk Gibson's card was at the top; when he put his head on the pillow each night, he thought of the most significant moment in Tigers history—Kirk's second home run in game five of the 1984 World Series.

"He don't wanna walk you!" said manager Sparky Anderson to player Kirk Gibson.

"He don't wanna walk you!" Charlie must have repeated those words a thousand times in his head. No, it was closer to a million, thought Charlie. Sparky was calling it like it was— this was a showdown "mano a mano."

While Goose's manager spoke to him on the mound, Sparky pretended to swing with an imaginary bat in his hands, instructing Kirk to swing away. The excited buzz filled the stadium.

Of course, pitcher Goose Gossage should have walked him. As that ball headed over the right-field fence, Sparky yelled, "Get outta here! Get outta here! You don't wanna walk him! Don't walk him! Don't walk him! Ha, ha, ha."

Charlie watched that sequence a thousand times, Gibson high-fiving Parish and Walker at home plate, the crowd going wild. And the roar—the stadium screams becoming one incredible uniform sound. There was nothing like it.

Charlie looked back at Jasmine, who was still waiting for an answer. She hadn't taken her eyes off of him, watching the wheels grind in his mind, knowing he must have been thinking of something memorable. It reminded him of his mother, the way she dropped whatever she was doing and gave him her total attention. Jasmine smiled, still waiting for an answer, but ironically, he couldn't, not that day, anyway. He was sure that baseball was always there for him; the game loved him back as much as he loved the game.

Charlie looked down at the Kentucky bluegrass under his feet; he loved the way it felt on his bare legs, those blades propping him up, cushioning him from life. Fourteen Major League Baseball parks used pure Kentucky bluegrass for their fields, including his favorite team, the Detroit Tigers at Comerica Park. Although not suited to Michigan weather, his favorite grass was Bull's-Eye Bermuda, ideal for warmer climates and tolerated shade.

Charlie was livid when the Arizona Diamondbacks replaced their Bull's-Eye Bermuda at Chase Field with synthetic turf. The game was meant to be played on grass, where a fan could enjoy novertdortis. Charlie wrote six letters to the Diamondbacks president of baseball operations, Franklin McNeil, expressing his displeasure. It just wasn't right, downright heretical, thought Charlie. He only stopped writing when Mr. McNeil personally called Charlie to apologize for the turf change, explaining how the team needed the climate-controlled dome in the brutal Phoenix summer heat. It was not suitable for natural grass. A fifteen-minute philosophical debate ended when Mr. McNeil offered two courtesy front-row tickets behind home plate anytime Charlie wished. McNeil promised that they would continue their conversation when Charlie came to visit. Charlie acquiesced but made it clear that his opinion on the subject had not changed one bit, despite the very generous offer.

"Charlie, why do you love baseball so much?" asked Jasmine for a second time.

"It's difficult to explain," replied Charlie, contemplating his answer. "It's something you have to feel." Charlie's eyes lit up. "I have an idea! I'll show you."

The two hatched a plan to attend a Tigers game together, Charlie intent on showing off the game he loved to his friend. Jasmine was excited to attend a professional game and investigate all of Charlie's fuss for herself. It wasn't football, the greatest game on Earth, but she was enthusiastic about their planned outing.

"Thanks, Mr. Hustle!" Jasmine effortlessly popped up to her feet without using her hands in one graceful motion, flashed him her beautiful smile, and returned home in a manner that never failed to mesmerize him. He was confident that she could beat out any throw to first. As usual, when she arrived at her door, she stopped, turned around, and waved to Charlie. Her warmth never wore out its welcome. Only a fool would take that graciousness for granted; Mr. Hustle looked across the street knowing he would never become foolish.

Charlie pulled out his telephone and exchanged a few texts with #11. He was pleased with the second baseman's progress, but new habits don't always take hold right away.

He reminded the player to continue with the exercises he had given him.

"Thanks, buddy!"

Thanks, buddy. Thanks, buddy. Charlie stared at the text and repeated those words in his head a few times, shaking his head that he was buddies with Slingers. Before he had an opportunity to place the phone back in his pocket, it dinged again with another message from Slingers.

"Hey, Charles. I hope you don't mind me asking. One of my teammates was wondering if you could help him out? He will compensate you."

Charlie's eyes opened wide. Now we're talking, thought Charlie. Of course, he wanted to assist and bring his team back to greatness in any way possible. Compensation was not necessary. Charlie didn't need money. It had taken some time, and a dab of deceit about his age, but he had set up a Questrade account, his trading algorithm producing fantastic results. Before purchasing his Skag Tiger Striper, he had turned his $800.00, accumulated from birthday and Christmas gifts, into a sizeable $9021.33. He knew that math would be valuable, but he had no idea that it would pay dividends this early.

"Absolutely, I will assist him. No fee required. Anything for the Tigers! Charles T. Unger, at your service." Charlie was excited, wondering which player it was. What if it was Miggy?

He patted his Tiger Striper one more time and continued to admire his work, his perfectionist eye a regular source of consternation. It took eight attempts, but Charlie considered this his best work yet, nudging toward perfection, his decision to replace the straight stripe pattern with a checkerboard pattern, the coup de grâce. It took him twice as long to cut, but he didn't care. Determining the best degree of angle on the Striper was challenging. Good old-fashioned trial and error determined that a forty-two-degree angle bend in the grass created an ideal contrast, considering the sun's location in the summer.

Before having the Striper, Danny utilized a rudimentary method, which yielded marginal results; however, the physical toll of pulling a sled loaded with bricks over his lawn to create his pattern was unsustainable for the heavy-set boy standing four-foot-eleven. Hunched over and limping, Charlie knew the long-term consequences for his vertebrae were dire. Research and a sizeable reduction in his bank account allowed for a Skag Tigers Striper to be delivered at the Unger home. The looks on the neighbors' faces, some of them wandering out of their houses to investigate as that giant machine was unloaded, were priceless. Unfortunately, his parents had the same look, unaware that the Striper was being delivered.

"Where are we going to put that, Charlie?" asked David. "And where did you get the money for it?"

"I won it, Dad," explained Charlie, using a pinch of deceit.

When Charlie reviewed the American Statistics from the Pediatrician Society, he discovered that he was in the 48th percentile for height and 88th percentile for weight, technically obese.

"Get him on a diet, or he will likely have some serious health problems," the doctor told his father solemnly.

Charlie agreed that he should lose weight, especially if it stopped the constant bullying from his classmates, but shedding weight was more challenging than pushing a thousand-pound boulder uphill. He had tired of the insults, which now included "Mr. Unhustle." He could distract himself from those insults by thinking of his mother's death, the immature barbs paling in comparison.

While he understood that he likely had no future as a professional baseball player, he didn't shut the door completely. There were numerous examples of professional players who did not fit the typical stereotype athlete, such as Pewee Reese and Bartolo Colón. Charlie knew he would rely on Newton's law—mass × acceleration = force. He had mass locked up, assisted by his love for foot-long hotdogs. Yes, Charlie loved the mighty frankfurter, first made in Frankfurt, Germany, paired with an S. Rosen poppy seed hot dog bun. Charlie was grounded for two weeks when he purchased three cases of the soft and tasty buns from the Chicago company. Using his father's credit card without permission for the buying frenzy was the most egregious error of his ways, rectified when Charlie secured his own Detroit Tigers Visa Platinum Card, a dab or two of deceit required. He always made his payments on time, was proud of his superior credit rating, and now had enough points to fully purchase two Tigers tickets.

Regardless, every night, when he placed his head on his pillow, he just knew that he would wear a Tigers uniform someday. It had to happen; it was his destiny.

CHAPTER THIRTEEN

Gravity Pull

"Thanks for coming, Charlie," greeted reverend William Baptiste, extending his hand. "I expected to see your father here too." His soft-toned, gray-buttoned sweater and tan slacks seemed inconsistent with the man Charlie had seen at the funeral. Even his wild hair appeared tamer; perhaps a barber's scissors had made its way through that thick crop of locks.

"Oh, thank you, Reverend," he replied, his hand engulfed by William's. "My dad had some errands to run, so he dropped me off." The microscopic fib scratched at his conscience more than usual, given his audience was a man of the cloth.

William led him to a small but comfortable office where he sat him down in a wingback chair. "Sorry, Charlie. We'd normally meet in my library, but it's being painted."

Charlie realized he had no idea exactly what he and the reverend would discuss.

"I understand from our last conversation at the Skip's funeral that your relationship with God is in crisis."

Hmmm. The reverend put the cart before the horse, concluded Charlie. If he was a lawyer, he would have immediately jumped to his feet. "Objection, Your Honor, no such foundation exists for the statement. The statement assumes facts not in evidence. The reverend has not proven God exists; hence, it is premature to discuss a relationship with God."

It would be rude to advise the man that the essence of his existence was based upon a pile of bunk, a mountain of hooey extending higher than the Himalayas that even the most skilled Sherpas couldn't scale. Instead, the young boy sat quietly, furrowed his brow for several seconds, and carefully contemplated as benign an answer as possible.

"I haven't had much time for God, Reverend." It was a wishy-washy reply that Charlie wasn't satisfied with, but didn't puncture a hole in his intellectual honesty.

Reverend Baptiste nodded his head slowly, knowing there was more to the story.

Charlie went on, "My mom and I used to go to church all the time; she loved it. She said she never felt alone with God as her constant companion. It's just . . . It's just . . . I'm sorry, but I'm a scientist, sir. I don't believe in God." There, he said it; his intellectual integrity released, freer than the white dove released to the skies at the funeral.

"When is the last time you attended church, other than for a funeral, Charlie?"

"Shortly before she died," replied Charlie, remembering the calmness she displayed in church despite the life-and-death battle raging in her body. Nothing would keep her from attending—not her vomiting or the clumps of hair that fell into the sink.

His father never attended church, a stack of pleadings and legal briefs always pulling him to that glittering office.

William handed a glass of water to his visitor, sensing Charlie's mouth was drying.

"I'm sorry. When I look up into the sky, I don't see heaven; I see the remnants of the Big Bang—the cosmic boom that created the universe. We're all bags of particles, governed by the physical laws of the universe," stated Charlie,

115

lowering his head, realizing he was inching awfully close to referencing a pile of bunk.

William raised his body from his chair, slowly walked to the window, and stared out onto the orphanage's backyard, several children in view merrily playing on a jungle gym donated by a local organization. A crisis of faith was hardly novel. The reverend was not immune, the hands of doubt frequently grabbing his faith, shaking it around, waiting to see which tenets became dislodged. Charlie Unger was not alone, but he was on the younger side for such deep questions.

"I have questioned my faith many times, Charlie. However, in the worst of times, I've leaned on it mightily, when I'm sure nothing else could have kept me propped up, even the people I love. It's given me formidable strength." He turned around and walked back toward his young guest. "I didn't invite you to convince you of anything. However, I have invited a friend of mine to meet you; he may provide you with another perspective."

William and Charlie exited the room, climbed a set of stairs, and walked through a maze of halls until they arrived at a double door labeled Games Room. Pushing the slightly ajar door open, the sounds of a ping-pong game in process became louder. A man and a boy, aged six or seven, were laughing because of their inept play. They placed their paddles on the table when Baptiste entered the room.

"Julian, please excuse us," said William, sending the young boy scampering from the room.

As he approached for customary greetings, Charlie stopped, statue-like, immediately recognizing the spectacled man and his white chest-length beard.

"Michael Star," said the man, coupled with a warm smile.

"Yes, I know," replied Charlie. "I've read two of your books," forgetting to introduce himself. Charlie tried to stop it; he sure wanted to stop it, but there were not enough sandbags to hold back the stimuli flooding his brain, a signal that sent his right hand up, striking the side of his head three times.

Star didn't miss a beat. "Autistic compulsion. Many of us have them, Charlie. I've got one too. Sometimes comes with the territory. Get me angry, and I'll be stomping the floor with my right foot for ten minutes."

It was the first time ever that he felt so at ease with his bloody head knocking. The most intelligent man on the planet had a tic too. It was settling in that he was not alone.

Star, a famous and renowned American physicist, was a legend in the scientific community. *How Big Was the Bang?* and *Walking Back in Time* were bestsellers that Charlie had read in record time, huddling under his blankets with a flashlight when it was well past bedtime. Star espoused the theory that there was absolutely nothing prior to the Big Bang and that the concept of time only commenced after the Big Bang. Charlie was starstruck, his typically learned tongue rendered silent by the flash of greatness before him, a man with an IQ of 198, the highest of any currently living American. He was literally the smartest man in the world, who became a household name after winning sixty-two consecutive matches and $3 million on the television game show *Jeopardy*. It was an unattainable dollar figure playing Plinko.

"Michael is a well-known scientist," explained Baptiste, Charlie unable to contain a chortle and snicker due to the understatement.

The three sat down on wingbacks, Charlie now surmising that reverend William Baptiste was a fan of the comfortable armchair style. Without asking, Baptiste poured three glasses of lemonade and placed them on the glass table that separated the three of them.

"Charlie, I've brought you my new book. The release date is a month away, but I want you to have it early." Star reached into his briefcase, removed the hardcover book, and placed it in Charlie's hand.

"Thank you, sir," replied Charlie, grabbing the hardcover book and gazing down at the cover, *God and Gravity: A Scientist Who Believes in Both.*

"I understand that you're quite the scientist, like me," said Star, a grin and two quickly raised eyebrows signaling he was in his comfort zone.

Was Charlie the only one finding irony that his last name was Star? An astrophysicist with the name Star; he wanted to laugh, because it was hilarious, but that would have to wait. Charlie blushed—to be mentioned in the same breath as the most famous physicist in the world was indescribable.

"Yes, sir. Science is everything to me! Well, that and baseball."

"That's terrific, Charlie. Maybe we can work on something together someday?"

Charlie blushed again, the possibilities shooting off in his brain with fireworks intensity. "Oh, yes, I would love to work with you."

"Listen, Charlie. As you are aware, I know a few things about science and evolution, not so much ping-pong," explained Star. "I go to church every Sunday and consider myself very spiritual."

Charlie continued to nod, and nodded some more, so much that Michael finally put his hand on his head to stop him. Star could see the wheels grinding within Charlie's head, that super-powered computer calculating the point Star was making.

"As much as science can tell us, there are many, many mysteries. I don't believe that science will ever be able to explain them all, probably because science isn't searching for answers in the right spots."

"Like what? What kind of mystery?" asked Charlie.

"Consciousness, free will. Why did the Big Bang even happen? Read the book and we will meet again, and you can tell me what you think of it."

"Oh, I will," replied Charlie, tightly grasping his gift with both hands.

The three men enjoyed their lemonade and played a few games of ping-pong, Charlie finding another scientist who shared his level of coordination. He could now boast that he beat Michael Star in a game of ping-pong.

Reverend Baptiste walked Charlie down the front steps and onto the sidewalk. It was as sunny as when he arrived, but the day seemed brighter somehow. He looked down at his feet to make sure they were touching the pavement, because Charlie Unger felt like he was floating, his book clenched in his hands. He still didn't believe in God, but he would read Star's book.

Charlie shook William's hand, feeling as though he knew the man much better now, and started walking away, hoping he could snag the 2:30 bus.

"Where are you going, Charlie?"

"To catch a bus. I better hurry," replied Charlie, shuffling away quickly.

"Wait, what about your father? You said he dropped you off to run errands and would pick you up later."

Charlie put his hand to his ear, feigning that he could not hear. "Goodbye, Reverend!" he yelled, waving as he hustled away faster, feeling badly about his lying tongue but knowing he was ready to take on the world—to make his Tigers great again. Time for a new tactic, he reasoned. Yes, sir.

CHAPTER FOURTEEN

Such a Fine Chap

The door to Trent's cell slowly slid open, the grinding metal ringing through Block B as it disappeared from his view. The creaking twelve-gauge frame was a cruel daily reminder that twelve white men and women had decided that he was not safe to roam the streets of Detroit.

"Higgins, let's go," ordered Officer Siskinds, a twenty-year veteran of the Michigan State Correctional Facility, an affable family man whose work environment demanded his constitution remain a guarded secret. A growl and clenched teeth proved a better pretense for a no-nonsense SOB who would rip your head off if you failed to follow his direction.

Siskinds began escorting the inmate to his weekly half-hour visit with Thomas Gregory, the prison chaplain. It was the sole opportunity to escape the cold lunacy of the institution that Trent had called home for the entirety of his adult life. Thomas's ten-by-ten office was an oasis, using the term loosely, an island where the circling sharks couldn't snap at his heels.

His successful arrival required the passing of twelve other cells down a long, narrow corridor.

"No religion gonna help you in this hellhole," snarled Eduardo Hernandez, his face pushed up against the bars. The M19 Colombian gang member cackled, displaying his two remaining teeth. "No God gonna help you in here, son!" he yelled.

As the two men approached the last cell before they would exit the block, Trent anticipated another verbal barb. Glen Fordham, the leader of the Michigan chapter of the Aryan

Brotherhood, was standing at his cell door, waiting for Trent. Known as Patch to the lieutenants in the white supremacist gang, Fordham put his index finger to his neck and made the gesture of a knife cutting his throat, an unequivocal threat to Higgins's life. His shaved skull, head-to-toe tattooed body, and unrelenting bulging eyes were an intimidating presence. "Death to Pigs," a squiggly prison-made tattoo on his right forearm in red ink loosely resembling the same message scrawled in blood on the LaBianca fridge in 1969 during that murderous rampage.

After three minutes, and having survived the toil of the emotional gauntlet, Trent arrived at his destination.

"Go in, Higgins. Remember, I'm right outside this door," barked Siskinds, placing his hand on Trent's back, pushing on his orange jumpsuit.

Trent entered, the chaplain cheerfully greeting him, the only human being in the prison that treated him with any decency. The juxtaposition of the warm welcome against the coldness of the institution was enough to create condensation, but it was only sweat on Trent's brow.

"It's good to see you." The white button-up shirt, gray slacks, and polished black shoes could have been worn by anyone. Only the clergy collar set him apart from someone sitting in a cubicle behind a desk.

"Thank you, Chaplin. It's good to see you as well."

It was the most innocent of exchanges, but it meant everything to the prisoner, the civility of politeness and friendly tone in short supply behind the cinder block walls.

After sitting, Trent accepted a cup of coffee and pretended to be a normal human being, a risky psychological trick.

Chaplain Gregory sensed that Trent was not himself, something other than the usual uneasiness of being housed in a dangerous correctional facility. "What is it, Trent?"

Trent paused for a moment, not prepared to discuss what was on his mind, so he changed the subject. "How are the Tigers doing, Chap?" It was a nickname that Thomas did not object to, the informality facilitating a breakdown of the many communication barriers.

"Mediocre, Trent; the Toronto Blue Jays will be difficult to beat. Although Cecil Fielder and Mickey Tettleton are lighting it up for the Tigers."

"I heard Fielder is leading the league in RBIs," said Trent, dreaming of witnessing one of those hits.

"He is," came the response. "However, 1992 is the first year in league history where a player led the league in RBIs at midyear and was left off of the All-Star team. I can't believe it!"

"The Tigers will make the playoffs, Chap. Have you been to a game lately?"

"I have." The answer pleased the inmate.

"Tell me about it, please," replied Trent, who closed his eyes and listened to Thomas describe the game. It was not the first time.

"I was in section 224, three seats in from the aisle, seventy-two degrees and sunny. I arrived forty-five minutes early."

As expected, Thomas described every detail in beautiful, vivid style: the cheering, the cracks of the bat, the songs blaring over the loudspeaker, and the mouthwatering smells wafting through the ballpark.

"Did you have a beer, Chap?"

"Of course I did." Knowing the drill, Thomas described the opening of the can, the hissing sound when the inner pressure equalizes with the outer. "Ice-cold Miller Lite. I had two."

Trent could taste that icy cold beer running over his tongue and down the back of his throat, quenching his thirst.

"I'm sure you had a snack?"

"Foot-long, onions, tomatoes, and jalapenos. A streak of mustard. Sesame bun."

Trent tasted the hot dog, salivating at the illusionary experience.

"Kitsburg won it in the ninth, a stinging double into the right-field corner that sent Bishop home from first with two out. The crowd erupted; every fan was on their feet, screaming and clapping," explained Gregory.

Trent nodded but remained quiet.

"The guy seated behind me spilled half of his Cracker Jacks on me when he jumped out of his seat," said Chap, laughing and pretending to brush the sugar-coated popcorn out of his hair.

Trent joined in the laughter, jolting him out of his trance. He opened his eyes and looked at Chap; both men quietly stared at each other, both thinking the same thing—it had been well over a decade since Trent had laughed. Thomas had managed to draw a smirk or the odd smile from Trent, but never a laugh. Why today? It was a question both of them were considering.

Trent closed his eyes again. "Did they have the seventh-inning stretch, Chap?"

"They sure did."

"Did they play it?"

"Yes, sir. They did."

Sir. A word used to denote respect for someone in a position of authority. Trent appreciated the irony.

Higgins heard the song, plain as day, as if it was being broadcast through the speakers in the corner of Chap's office. *Take me out to the ball game, Take me out to the crowd, Buy me some peanuts and crackerjacks, I don't care if I ever get back.* Trent went through all four verses in his mind, humming the last two. He sighed when he was done, opened his eyes, and looked at the chaplain again.

"The crack of the bat. It's the best sound in the world, Chap. The crack, then the roar of the crowd. Nothing beats it."

Thomas nodded. He was a pleasing-looking man, resembling Mr. Rogers with his round spectacles and conservative clothing. His gentle, patient demeanor was well-suited for his profession. The man's eyes had seen it all; his ears had heard it all. Trent figured that Thomas likely had a story too. Sure, it might not be as tragic as his and the other men's who called prison home, but he had one. Everyone did. He might have asked, if he'd had more time.

"I have a lot of regrets, Chap."

Trent never discussed anything personal, so Thomas was surprised at the admission. He never pushed an inmate to share, understanding that each prisoner dealt with their incarceration in their own way. It wasn't always healthy to deal with your demons in prison; clamping off your emotions is a widely-used technique when doing hard time.

"Tell me more, Trent."

"It doesn't matter, Chap. I'm no different than any other man in this place. Who doesn't have regrets in here?"

"Why are you telling me this today?"

Trent explained that one of the black gangs had pressured him to sell drugs in his block. He had been doing it for years, believing that he had no choice. Realistically, he didn't, if he wanted to survive. But something changed inside him, and he couldn't do it anymore, his refusal bringing repercussions.

"You need the protection of a group if you want to survive in prison. Blacks with the blacks, Hispanics with Hispanics, Whites with the whites, skinheads with skinheads. Protection from your pack in this jungle. You know what I'm saying, Chap?"

Chap knew it. Race and color always determined the alliances, perhaps a microcosm of society.

"My gang pulled my protection, and now Patch Vernon is coming for me."

"You could ask the warden for protection, Trent."

Trent looked at him and flashed him a disapproving look and slight shake of the head.

"I know, Trent." Thomas knew that seeking help from the warden was also a death sentence, in a place where snitches were as reviled as child predators.

"Why did you make that choice?"

"God, Chap. As soon as I let the Lord into my heart, I could handle anything."

Thomas approved with a nod.

"Chap, I know that you probably hear this all the time. I'm innocent of the charges that landed me in this place. It's important to me that at least one person believes me."

"I believe you, Trent," replied Thomas sincerely.

A loud knock on the door advised the men that their half hour was completed. The pair stood and shook hands as usual, but longer and tighter than normal.

"You will never be alone with God at your side, Trent."

"I know, Chap. I want to thank you for all these years."

"I will see you next week," replied Chap, the last words he said to Inmate no. 2314555.

Trent Higgins did not make it to next week's meeting, his life ending the following day.

CHAPTER FIFTEEN

A Brief History in Time

Charlie invited Jasmine to his house, elevating their friendship beyond his front yard, an exciting escalation, in his view. Scheming was on the agenda, a detailed plan to attend a Tigers game without their fathers' knowledge. Charlie knew how to obtain excellent tickets; that part was easy.

Jasmine took one step into Charlie's upstairs bedroom and stopped, her feet becoming glued to the carpet. Her doe-shaped brown eyes pushed out of their sockets; she dropped her hands to her side, opened her mouth, and left it there. She was not prepared for what was before her. Was this for real? The only comparison: the old family home in Cameroon and the overflowing trophies crowding every room. But this was at another level, an unbelievable level.

She turned to Charlie in disbelief. "I knew that you loved baseball, Charlie, but this is amazing! Weird and amazing," she said slowly in a whisper. She didn't blink as she turned her body 360 degrees, at a measured pace, so that she could take it all in. It reminded Charlie of the revolving Summit Restaurant, located on the seventy-first floor of the Marriott in downtown Detroit that took an hour to rotate fully.

"Wow, Charlie. All I can say is wow!"

This was more than the love of baseball—this was something far more intense, if that was possible, thought Jasmine. She understood being in love with your favorite team and players, but words could not adequately describe his room. Not one bare inch on any of the four walls was free— Tigers memorabilia and science-related material covering it completely, so thoroughly that she didn't know the color of Charlie's walls.

Behaving as though she had a ticket to a museum, Jasmine commenced walking around the room, inspecting everything. First, she read some of the twenty framed letters he had received from past and present Tigers players. Then, she looked at the ten baseball jerseys hung from his ceiling fan with the names of his favorite players stitched on the back: Morris, Gibson, Trammell, and others, all of whom Jasmine did not recognize.

Fifteen autographed baseballs, some in cases, some on stands, dotted the room. Above his headboard, a blue-and-orange Tigers sign blinked on and off. There were too many posters to count, a celebration of unparalleled proportions.

At least a hundred books were piled in the corner. Jasmine grabbed the top book and read the title, *Living in a Godless World*. She picked up the next one, *Speaking to the Dead*.

"Charlie, you will never be able to read all of these books in your life."

"Ha, ha, ha," laughed Charlie. "I've already read those. These are the ones I still need to read." He pointed to sixty books stacked in the opposite corner. I'm going to read *God and Gravity* first.

A three-dimensional solar system replica dangled from the ceiling at the south end of the room. Behind it, on the south wall, a life-sized poster of famed astrophysicist Steven Hawking was featured prominently.

"Who's that?" asked Jasmine, pointing to the man in the wheelchair.

"Who's that? Who's that?" repeated Charlie, his voice tiptoeing toward incredulity. "Only the most famous astrophysicist in the world." He walked over and kissed the poster. "I love this man." Charlie pulled a hardcover book from his bookshelf.

"Read this," he said, handing her the book. "It will change your life."

She looked down at the book, *A Brief History in Time.* "What's this?"

"His greatest work. Brilliant. Transformational. It's the best book ever written," explained Charlie.

It was now Jasmine's turn to exhibit her incredulity. "Best book ever written! Uhhhh, sorry, Mr. Hustle. The Bible is the best book ever written!" Jasmine fixed her stare on Charlie and placed her hands on her hips, signaling the seriousness of her proclamation. "I have one that you can borrow. It's brilliant. Transformational. It will change your life."

Charlie thought about his response, knowing well that religious types, Bible thumpers, became roused when you questioned their faith. They didn't take kindly to being told they believed in a bunch of baloney. Before he could contemplate a response, Jasmine continued.

"What makes your book so much better than the Bible?" she asked genuinely.

"Well, there are a few things, but the main one is that mine is true, based on science and facts," explained Charlie, worried now how his only friend would react.

His response did not go over well. Jasmine couldn't think of a crueler statement, thinking of her mother's words, advice that she had clung to since that awful night.

"Remember, girls, nothing is more important than God and family. Both of them will get you through the toughest of times." She visualized her mother grabbing at the cross around her neck, knowing that Mama meant every word. Her father loved her, but he was a different man now, grief refusing to let him move on, stripping him of the foundation that he had built his life on. Grabbing at the cross around her neck, Jasmine fought back the tears.

Charlie recognized that tears were about to breach her bottom eyelid, a levy that was at its maximum use. Picking up on social signals was not Charlie's strongest skill, but he had no difficulty with this one. He decided to change the subject, which suited Jasmine.

"This is my autographed photo of Miguel Cabrera," motioning to his side table and the framed 8 x 11-inch photo standing upright. Sometimes, Charlie would place it on his chest, staring at it until he drifted off to sleep.

"Your bed looks comfy, Charlie." Jasmine swiped her hand across the top of the Detroit Tigers comforter, all the signatures of the 1984 World Series players imprinted.

"It's comfortable, but I have difficulty getting to sleep."

Jasmine nodded her head. "Me too. Earphones with my favorite music help."

"Hey, that's what I do!" replied Charlie. "Well, it's not exactly music."

"What do you listen to, Mr. Hustle?"

"It's a compilation," he explained, making his way over to his desk. He took the mouse and pressed Play. Immediately, the sounds of a restless baseball crowd came through the speakers, followed by a loud crack of a bat, and then the wild roar of the crowd. Charlie let it play four times.

"You said it was a compilation, but it was the same every time," said Jasmine.

"It was a different bat and different wood each time," explained Charlie.

"Mr. Hustle, I couldn't tell the difference," said Jasmine quizzically, unsure whether she could accept Charlie's explanation.

"Practice, practice, practice," replied Charlie, with some semblance of pride, knowing his compulsions were the main reason he was an oddball. He thought of those four hundred billion stars in the Milky Way. Surely there was life out there, somewhere, and surely that life was stranger than Charles T. Unger, he mused.

"Mr. Hustle, when I scored a goal playing football, I could always pick out my mom's voice. Sometimes I would stare at a photo of my favorite footballer for hours and hours, dreaming of playing for the Cameroon national team. I dreamt of scoring the winning goal, fifty thousand fans screaming, but I'd still be able to pick out my mom's voice."

Charlie looked at her, knowing something about her pain.

"I don't dream about that now, Charlie. I don't dream about anything anymore."

"I'm sorry, Jasmine. It's a heck of a thing not to have dreams."

"What's that, Charlie?" asked Jasmine, pointing to an easel placed in the middle of the room with a bunch of different-colored lines drawn on a diagram.

"It's a spray chart, Jasmine. Tracking where the Tigers hit the ball. I have it on my computer, too, but it feels better doing it on paper."

Jasmine picked up a baseball and looked at the signature. "Who is Pete Rose?"

Charlie smiled. "He's the original Mr. Hustle."

"He may be the first, but you're the best, Charlie."

"I think you're the best, Jasmine." He couldn't believe he said it, the words flying out of his mouth before he knew it.

She stopped and looked at her friend, "Thanks, Charlie. I needed that." She continued to move around the room, "Charlie, you understand that football is the greatest sport on Earth, right?"

Charlie smiled. It was a conversation for another day. Rather than responding to the outrageous assertion, he walked to his closet and pulled out a wrapped gift.

"Happy birthday, Jasmine!" She was turning fourteen the following day.

She took the sphere from him, pleased to see the colorful and cheery balloons on the wrapping paper. "Thank you, Charlie! Can I open it now?"

Charlie nodded yes.

Jasmine was confident she was about to receive her first globe of Earth. After a few rips of the wrapping paper, it became evident the gift was not a globe. As she pulled the last piece of paper off the gift and threw it to the floor, Charlie was prepared, ready for a smiley face and warm thank-you, but her excitement had turned to solemness.

She looked down at that brand-new official Major League Soccer Adidas ball. Her hands began to tremble, and the tears trickled. She just stared at it, never lifting her head.

Charlie didn't know what to say. What had he done wrong?

"I've got to go, Mr. Hustle," she said, wiping a tear off her cheek. And then she was gone, putting the ball under her left arm and exiting the room.

CHAPTER SIXTEEN

Boycott

Two days later, Charlie and Jasmine sat comfortably on the couch in his living room, Jasmine flipping channels on the television, when something caught Mr. Hustle's eye.

"Turn it back, Jasmine. Yes, there. Hey, it's Reverend Baptiste!"

Reverend William James Baptiste stood on the steps of Detroit's old City Hall, the majestic stone building behind him, a gargoyle or two peeking down on him. He was at his best, his fiery side on full display, hands waving passionately, calling upon the black citizens of Michigan to take action. Luckily, God had spoken to the reverend and provided guidance; the reverend said so. Baptiste called for a boycott of the Detroit Tigers baseball games, a plea that amounted to an unholy attack, reasoned Charlie.

"What?" hollered Charlie, the sacrilegious words bringing Charlie to his feet. Yes, like kings, queens, and heads of state worldwide, Baptiste became another influential person monopolizing God's time.

"Professional sports in America are a grotesque symbol of oppression. Football. Basketball. Baseball. All of them. I call upon all my fellow brothers and sisters to keep their feet firmly planted outside the confines of oppression." In the next ten minutes, Baptiste mentioned God fifteen times.

In Charlie's opinion, it was strange that God desired everyone to stay away from Comerica Park. Didn't God have better things to do? Furthermore, how was it that Reverend Baptiste even knew what God wanted?

"Objection, Your Honor. No foundation!" yelled Charlie at the screen.

"What?" asked Jasmine, turning to him.

"Nothing. Nothing," replied Charlie, not wishing to repeat his mistake from his bedroom when he'd questioned the veracity of the Bible. He wasn't fond of seeing those tears in her eyes.

"Is there something about the Tigers organization that is oppressive?" the reporter asked William.

"I'm sure all those who work for the Tigers are fine people. I'm talking about a much larger issue. Only one owner is black in the NFL, NBA, and MLB." He threw his hands up in the air. "It's reflective of society as a whole."

Jasmine and Charlie turned their heads and looked at each other.

"Maybe he's right," retorted Jasmine, looking at Charlie, the reverend's words stirring her, reminding her of the racial injustices she had been subjected to in America.

"I don't know," replied Charlie. William was a thoughtful man, and he sure looked convincing. "It doesn't feel right, Jasmine." Charlie knocked three times on his head. Jasmine did so as well.

Detroit and many other larger American cities were in the midst of protests, some peaceful, some violent—spotlighting racism and the poor treatment of minorities at the hands of police. Charlie hadn't paid much attention to it. His father told him it was complicated.

Many in the community disagreed with Baptiste's call to boycott, the targeting of the classy organization with a stellar history of community involvement and promoting diversity.

Tigers president Timothy Earley responded to Baptiste's call for action, confirming the Tigers' commitment to diversity and equal treatment. "I will have no further comment beyond this one."

Charlie wondered how Luis "Mad Dog" Maddison felt about Baptiste's call for a boycott. Mad Dog, an orphan who grew up under the care of the reverend in his inner-city Detroit orphanage, was an aging veteran on the team. What was his position on all of this? He had repeatedly been quoted saying how much he admired the reverend and considered him a father.

A week earlier, Charlie and his father were waiting in a line to eat at the Crab Shack on Michigan Avenue in celebration of David's birthday, when Mad Dog and his long-time girlfriend exited the restaurant, stepping out into the warm summer air. Mad Dog must have been celebrating his birthday, too, because several fans yelled, "Happy birthday," to him.

Charlie made a beeline to the center fielder to say hello and snag an autograph. Mad Dog, smiling and kibitzing with fans, was in a great mood and was pleased to oblige Charlie in a friendly chat. Mad Dog laughed, almost uncontrollably, when Charlie recommended that he pull his hands in a little tighter on his swing. Although he was hitting okay, his power numbers were down, and Charlie was sure that it was because Mad Dog wasn't keeping his hands tucked in toward his body enough during his swing. It was well known that good hitters always kept their hands "inside the ball," and Charlie felt that Mad Dog's hands were drifting toward the plate, robbing him of power. He had looked at video so often, he was confident this was the problem.

Two weeks later, after Mad Dog went on a home run tear, both Charlie's and David's mouths dropped to the floor as they watched television in their living room, listening to Mad Dog explain to a reporter to whom he credited his recent power surge.

"Well, it's the funniest of things. I met this kid coming out of the Crab Shack on my birthday, and he told me to keep my hands in tighter. It worked," he said, laughing and mimicking his new hand position. He shook his head in wonderment, laughed again, and shrugged his shoulders, bemused to what he had just admitted to every fan in Michigan.

"What was his name, Mad Dog?" asked the reporter enthusiastically while holding out the microphone.

"He introduced himself as Charlie Hustle," replied Mad Dog, who then looked directly into the camera, smiled, and pointed. "Charlie, wherever you are, thank you, my man! I owe you."

Tigers general manager Rodney Kilmer was relaxing in his plush, executive office at Comerica Park, watching the same interview on his seventy-two-inch television. He turned the volume up and listened to his star explain to everyone that a kid was responsible for his increased power numbers. Why was he paying considerable salaries to his hitting coaches on staff when he could hire Charlie Hustle?

"Charlie Hustle," he said out loud. He began racking his brain. "Charlie Hustle," he repeated. The name sounded familiar to the GM, who had occupied that office for seven years. Kilmer stood there for another minute, thinking. He rushed over to the corner of his office and grasped an unopened letter off his credenza. "Well I'll be damned," he said out loud as he looked at the return address from a Charlie

Unger in Plymouth, Michigan. He proceeded to open the letter, followed by the eleven others that he also hadn't opened. Rodney was surprised he hadn't thrown them out.

After reading every word Charlie Unger had written, an hour later Kilmer leaned back into his chair and put his arms behind his head. Although there had been improvements in the team's play, his job was not yet safe, not even close. Nelson Green called for his firing every day, Monday through Friday, between 2:00 and 4:00 p.m.

Each of Charlie Unger's suggestions made some sense, all of them backed by sound reasoning. They were more detailed than some of their internal assessments. The boy must be getting the suggestions from someone else, he determined. It had to be. The alternative was too far-fetched, too crazy. Within thirty minutes, Kilmer ensured the letters were in the hands of the appropriate coaches, with strict instructions to institute every last one of the recommendations. "No exceptions, gentlemen!" emphasized Kilmer.

Charlie no longer considered himself religious, unless one considered baseball a religion, and if so, Mr. Hustle was the most religious person on the planet. As far as he understood the dictionary definition, *religion* was "the belief in, and worship of a superhuman controlling power." There was nothing that had more of a grip on Charlie than the game of baseball, which was superhuman in Charlie's estimation.

CHAPTER SEVENTEEN

Miggy Mound Combo

A tenth birthday is a once-in-a-lifetime event. Charlie was stoked, thinking of the Miggy Mound Combo that would soon be in front of him, while he bounded up the front stairs to his house after school. Only his inclusion in the eighty-eighth weight percentile kept him from arriving home in a flash. He glanced at his stopwatch while stepping through the threshold—a new record; it took him eight minutes and fifteen seconds to run home from George Washington Secondary School, where he was a grade nine student. Impressive, he thought, pleased with the new time. If only he hadn't hit that red light on McNabb Avenue, he would have been forty seconds faster.

The stopwatch remained in his pocket on days when Ms. Hopkin's delicious cookies and chocolate chip muffins created a detour, her scrumptious treats pushing record attempts to the following day. She stood there, apron wrapped around her waist, with a plate of her goodies in one wrinkled hand, waving Charlie in from her corner-lot house with the other. David Unger was not impressed, grumbling when the lure of the white-haired grandmother's baking from three houses down sabotaged his son's diet.

However, a detour today was unthinkable, Charlie shaving twenty-three seconds off his best time, the excitement of his birthday providing his Chevrolet Chevette engine with a little extra horsepower. His mom and dad were taking him to Tigers Time Restaurant to celebrate, his menu choice firmly implanted in that brain of his. The sweat on his brow and the need for an ice-cold drink conjured up visions of The Gibson

Goblet, a twenty-ounce soda pop contained in a take-home cup adorned with Kirk Gibson and Sparky Anderson photos. In large, orange letters embossed on the cup, it stated, "1984 He don't wanna walk you!" Six of the cups sat in the Ungers' kitchen cupboard, a total that would increase by one after his birthday dinner.

Gibson's inspirational home run off of Goose Gossage in game five of the World Series was Charlie's tonic for the blues. If he felt down, he would pull up the clip and watch Gibson perform his magic, goose bumps suddenly appearing on Charlie's skin. He had now watched the sequence 1211 times. Goose's manager, Dick Williams, wanted Gossage to walk Gibson, but Gossage refused. The rest is history—the home run clinching a World Series victory.

Charlie's mouth was watering when he closed the front door behind him, anticipating the Miggy Mound Combo, a six-ounce, double-patty cheeseburger with large curly fries dusted with spicy Sparky seasoning. It was his regular order, and he loved it. If his father allowed it, he would also munch on two pieces of Corn on the Ty Cobb, followed by a piece of Georgia Peach Cobbler. The Hall of Famer spent twenty-two years with the Tigers and set almost ninety MLB records.

The restaurant walls were lined with framed newspaper articles of essential moments in Tiger history. Last year, when he and his family attended the restaurant for his birthday, Charlie walked every inch of that restaurant, almost zombie-like, reading every last one of those newspaper articles. The owner, Micky, joined Charlie, describing himself as the number one Tigers fan, to which Charlie politely objected. They enthusiastically bantered about who was the greatest

Tiger of all time; Charlie ate his cold burger when he returned to the table.

"Charlie, why do I feel I celebrate each of your birthday dinners without you?" asked Heather, smiling, always supporting her son's love for the game.

Charlie hoped Micky was at the restaurant tonight, wanting to discuss the Tigers' middle infield.

When he entered the house, curiously, nobody was on the main floor. The helium balloons and Happy Birthday sign he had expected in the foyer were nowhere to be seen. Nobody was there to greet him, his mother's usual, "Happy birthday, brainiac!" absent for the first time in years.

Charlie tiptoed upstairs, and then down the hallway, making his way to his parents' room, where Charlie could hear a muffled conversation through his parents' bedroom door. It wasn't regular chatter. It was a serious discussion, distressing conversation. Charlie placed his ear against the quarter-inch crack in the slightly ajar door and was startled to hear his father sobbing. He had never seen his father cry, the desperate sound wiping any birthday excitement clear from his body. Charlie lined up his right eye against the crack and peered through, observing his father hugging his mother, his chest heaving in and out, the despair evident on his face as the tears streamed down his face.

They didn't make it to the restaurant that night. There would be no Miggy Mound Combo, and those ten candles that his mother had lovingly placed in the triple chocolate cake, prepared for her son earlier that morning, never got lit.

His mother had received devastating news that day—incurable melanoma skin cancer had spread throughout her body, a death sentence that irrevocably changed all of their lives.

CHAPTER EIGHTEEN

Double Trouble

"Push, Arlene!" encouraged Dr. Kingston, hunched over in between the teenager's legs. It would be the 4,100th time the obstetrician had positioned himself between birthing stirrups and brought life into the world. He would mingle in the staff lounge, cut the cake, and accept congratulations for an outstanding career in two days.

His old eyes, well into their seventieth year, peered up into Arlene's young ones, a mixture of agony and excitement staring back. This would be his last birthing, one final opportunity to deliver a baby into an increasingly complicated world.

"Push, Arlene! Push! I can see his head!"

Dr. Kingston maneuvered the baby's right shoulder, and then the left, bringing him out of his cramped quarters and into roomier accommodations.

"Give me a big push! One final push!"

With a scream, Arlene pushed her son out into the world. Kingston cut the umbilical cord and put the baby into the nurse's hands, who in turn offered to put the newborn in the mother's lap.

Arlene shook her head.

"Are your sure, dear?" asked Dr. Kingston, the baby whisked to a corner for heart, hearing, and muscle tone tests, along with a drawn blood sample for a further battery of investigations, all routine.

Arlene shook her head, her eyes refusing to follow her baby carried away.

"Okay, Arlene, here comes the second. Let him join his brother!"

Ten minutes later, Dr. Kingston saw the crown of the baby's head, his expressive face giving way to raised eyebrows and puzzlement, complete with a corrugated brow. He looked at Nurse Campbell, bewildered, who shrugged her shoulders and placed her hands out in front, palms up. She was just as confused.

Dr. Kingston had reviewed Arlene's intake form hours earlier, his usual step to confirm any allergies or other conditions that could affect the delivery. The parents were two perfectly healthy African Americans.

Dr. Kingston continued, delivering a beautiful healthy boy into the bright lights, his brother having done the harder work, easing the pathway. Again, Dr. Kingston cut the umbilical cord, and again, Arlene declined the offer to hold her baby.

Dr. Kingston enjoyed his party two days later, shoving pound cake into his mouth, shaking hands, and reminiscing about the trials and tribulations of the medical field. He also had one fascinating story to share from his final delivery.

CHAPTER NINETEEN

Kicking It Around

Charlie was pleased to see Jasmine push open her front door and use those strong muscular legs of hers to propel her out onto the lawn toward him, a soccer ball tucked under her arm.

Charlie had just finished putting the final touches on the Old English *D*, now permanently etched into the lawn. He got up from his knees, not quite sure what to expect. His well-meaning gift had cost him some sleep, Jasmine's reaction both confusing and upsetting.

"Hey, Mr. Hustle," said Jasmine, her greeting paired with an awesome smile that always brightened his day. Relief took over.

"Hey, Jasmine. Thanks for coming over."

"Listen, Charlie, I never thanked you for the gift, softly tossing the ball to him. He raised his hands to catch it, a severe case of fumbles intervening, causing the ball to drop onto the Kentucky bluegrass. They both laughed when the ball hit the ground, his athletic limitations well known to both of them.

"If you and I are going to remain friends, you will no longer refer to the beautiful game as soccer, Mr. Hustle. You will no longer refer to this as a soccer ball. Football. Football. Football. The greatest game on Earth is called football. What is it with Americans changing the name?"

Charlie knew she was wrong. The name soccer originated in England in 1863 when the Football Association commenced, a name that morphed into the short form

Assoccer, and then eventually soccer. But perhaps now was not the time to point this out, he demurred.

"Charlie, I haven't kicked a football since my mother and sister died. I couldn't. I just couldn't."

Charlie hadn't considered the painful memories the game would bring up. What a shmuck, he thought.

"But I've done a lot of thinking." She walked over to the Adidas ball and looked down at it. "Back up a bit, Charlie." Once he complied, she kicked the ball to him, which rested at his feet. "Now, your turn."

He stepped back and smiled, following through with his right foot, kicking the ball with all his might. Shockingly, Charlie made strong contact. He looked up in horror as he sent the ball directly toward Jasmine's face, a screaming torpedo that was going to smash those magnificent features. The one time he'd managed something athletic, it would require facial reconstruction surgery. A broken nose and gushing blood would follow. A call to 911—ambulances and paramedics rushing to the scene, onlookers wondering what the heck Charlie Unger had done this time. It was going to happen; he knew it.

But Charlie was wrong, his assumptions mercifully incorrect. In an instant, he appreciated why Jasmine called soccer the beautiful game, a revelation that warmed him to the core. Suddenly, he understood the girl from Cameroon a million times better.

Rather than ducking for cover, or instinctively throwing her hands up for protection, Jasmine casually tilted her head down and took the missile off her forehead, sending it eight feet straight up in the air. On its way down, she positioned her body under the ball, letting it skim off her chest, slowing it down so she could easily kick it back up with her right foot. Jasmine proceeded to keep the ball up in the air with successive kicks back and forth from each foot, then took it back to the top of her head, where it came to a stop momentarily. She let it slide off the back of her head, down her back, and off her rear end and then kicked the ball back up with the heel of her left foot, the ball sailing softly over her head and landing into her outstretched hands out front.

Charlie was stunned. What words in his extensive vocabulary did he possess to describe the graceful exhibition that played out in front of him? None of them seemed adequate. A symphony—an elaborate composition where every musician contributes to creating a precise harmonic blend of separate sounds. Yes, it was similar, her feet, legs, head, and body acting as the harmonic elements, all of them working in perfect tandem.

He was speechless, but he forced something out of his gaping mouth, "That was incredible, Jasmine. I mean it. Incredible."

"Thanks, Mr. Hustle. I wanted my first kick since leaving Cameroon to be with you."

He could have been mistaken, but he didn't believe so. He hadn't seen it before in Jasmine, something that was impossible to fake. His mother told him so, and he believed it—believed it with every fiber in his flawed body. Yes, when Jasmine began manipulating that ball, making it one with her, he saw a twinkle in her eye. It was magical, a twinkle twice as bright as Polaris. He had given her more than a football for her birthday, and he could not have been more pleased.

"Tell me we will always be friends, Mr. Hustle." Her eyes welled. She didn't blink or try to wipe the tears away. Jasmine wanted him to see that she was vulnerable, trusting that he would not hurt her, trusting that he would take her fragile shell and gently hold it in his hands, protecting it by any means.

Charlie took three steps toward her, momentarily forgetting every hang-up that weighed him down, stepping out of his comfort zone and moving in close. "I promise," he whispered. "I promise." It was the answer she needed.

"Now move back, Mr. Hustle. Let me teach you how to kick a football. You don't kick it with your toe; you kick with the inside of your foot."

A fierce debate raged, neither of them giving an inch, each of them remaining resolute in their convictions as the ball passed between their feet.

"Football is the best sport on Earth, Charlie. I have so much to teach you!"

"You're crazy, Jasmine Bouba. Baseball is by far the best," but Charlie reckoned he would check out the game of football, because what he witnessed merited a thorough investigation.

CHAPTER TWENTY

That's a Fair Question

Charlie loved the fair. Sure, the food formed part of the allure, vendors offering creations found nowhere else on Earth. Fried Coca-Cola, or better yet, batter drenched in Coca-Cola, deep-fried, and then drizzled with sugar and topped with whipped cream. Or, triple cheese donuts—three all-beef patties, six slices of cheese, all wedged between a tasty Krispy Kreme donut. Deep-fried Oreos rounded out Charlie's top three fair foods. Honorable mentions included corn dogs, pickle dogs, chili dogs, frozen cheesecake on a stick, and deep-fried butter.

David Unger was not pleased with Charlie's nutritional choices, but leafy greens, vegetables, and meatless meat were nowhere near as appetizing. Meatless meat, for goodness' sake, was the best example of bafflegab that Charlie had ever seen, surely a gimmick by a marketing genius who did not know a thing about taste.

Charlie and Jasmine moved their friendship to level three, leaving the confines of the Unger family lawn at level one and the interior of his house at level two. Jasmine argued with her father for hours before he finally agreed that she could attend the fair with the strange kid from across the street.

Charlie was accustomed to attending the local fair with his mother, but stepping through the gates with Jasmine felt different, grownup, almost as if he was on a date.

"Do you have your sunscreen on, Charlie?" asked Jasmine.

Charlie nodded while heading to the ticket line.

Charlie couldn't get enough of the stimulating atmosphere—children laughing and screaming, lights blinking on and off in rapid succession, and carnies beckoning in potential customers. And of course, with the wonderful smells wafting through the air, all of his senses were on high alert.

Jasmine was wide-eyed as the two strolled through the throngs of daytime revelers, amazed at the excesses on full display. She had never seen anything quite like it, the festivals back home limited to wonderful local foods and an abundance of singing and dancing. After riding the Ferris wheel and then the Tilt-A-Whirl rides, the duo looked at each other and started laughing, the combination of the exhilaration and dizziness bringing on lightheadedness.

"Jasmine, let's play my favorite game?" asked Charlie, his equilibrium returning.

"Of course, Mr. Hustle!" She had no idea what he was referring to. She would have agreed to almost anything, the delightful sights and sounds raising her spirits.

Charlie motioned, and the two leisurely strolled toward the games area, the jocular calls from the carnies becoming louder as they approached. After passing the Whack-a-Mole and ring toss games, Charlie set his sights on the baseball toss. After handing the grizzled carny a five-dollar bill, Charlie stepped up to the line, the goal to knock down six milk bottles stacked in a pyramid. Charlie grabbed one of the three very used baseballs and eyed the milk bottles situated ten feet away. Charlie looked up at the wall of stuffed animals and picked out the one he wanted to win for her, Yosemite Sam with a baseball bat in his hand.

"Okay, son, knock 'em all down and win an extra-large prize of your choice!" yelled the carny, a rough-looking man with an eye patch over his left eye and a maze of tattoos covering both arms. One of them, with a serpent winding his way around a dagger, was impressive, but the one above spurred Charlie's interest. "Bless you, Boys 1984" was inked on the left bicep, the most beautiful tattoo Charlie Hustle had ever seen.

"Hey, mister, where did you get the baseball tattoo?" asked Charlie.

The man looked down at his beefy arm. "I got it in 1984 after the Tigers won the World Series. You weren't even born yet."

Charlie knew all about that magical season and kept nodding while listening to the explanation. Unless you were a faux fan, you knew everything about that season when the Tigers left their cross-border foes, the Toronto Blue Jays, in the dust on their way to 104 wins and a World Series championship. Starting the season with nine straight wins and then thirty-five of their first forty games, the team excited Tigers fans like no other. What a fantastic time it must have been to be a fan, thought Charlie.

"I guess you're a Tigers fan?" asked the man, who scanned Charlie and the authentic Cabrera jersey he wore on his back.

"The biggest fan alive!" exclaimed Charlie, his eyes still fixed on that amazing tattoo.

"My buddy owns a tattoo parlor on Gratiot Avenue. He inked it for me. He's still there."

Charlie stepped up and let the first ball fly but watched it embarrassingly sail two feet wide. He furrowed his brown in disappointment and then listened to a smattering of snickering from behind him.

"You throw like a girl, lard ass!" came a voice from behind, followed by more snickering.

Jasmine turned around and scowled at a group of boys from her high school that she recognized.

"Ignore them, Charlie," said Jasmine, irritated—shooting an icy stare at the boys, who laughed some more.

Charlie picked up his second ball, determined to do better; however, the round projectile suffered a similar fate, sailing well wide to the other side. More snickering and laughter slumped his shoulders.

Another pejorative landed on his ears. "Wow, still a girl, blimp!" came the yell, followed by more guffaws.

Indeed, Charlie's throwing form was poor, barely getting that ball back behind his head during his windup and not taking much of a step toward his target—ironic, given he could perfectly assess others' mechanics.

"Wow, close, kid," said the carny, a blatant lie. "I think the wind caught that one. "What's your name?"

"Charlie Unger," replied Charlie, quietly, embarrassed to announce it too loudly after his first two pathetic attempts.

"Mine's Rudy. This one will be the magic ball, Charlie Unger! Knock them all down, and in addition to the large prize, I will get my buddy to give you a free baseball tattoo, if your parents approve, of course."

Rudy must have been confident to make such an offer, probably putting his young customer's chances near zero at knocking all of the milk bottles down. Charlie grabbed the third ball and closed his eyes, visualizing his next throw, getting into a trance, and rehearsing the path of the flight.

"Can I throw it, Charlie?" asked Jasmine, suddenly.

Charlie opened his eyes, turned around, and looked at Jasmine and her beautiful smile. He turned back to Rudy. "Is the offer still good if she throws?"

"Absolutely!" he replied, laughing.

Having never thrown a baseball before, Jasmine grabbed the ball and moved her hand over the ball until it felt right.

"Look, Aunt Jemima is going to throw!" came the comment from someone in the same group of boys.

Charlie's face turned red with anger. He turned around, rage quickly fueling his two steps forward toward the jackasses, not caring about the insurmountable odds, intent on inflicting some sort of pain. He had never raised a fist in his life—today would be the first.

But Jasmine put her hand out and grabbed his shirt tightly, preventing him from proceeding further. "No, Charlie. That's not the way. That's not how we win."

"I can't let them get away with that," he replied, the red remaining on his face.

"I've been letting those types get away with it ever since I arrived in America," she said, incredulity forming in her stare, the sting of racism never abating.

Charlie uncontrollably knocked three times on his head, bringing further ridicule from the group of teenagers.

"Let it go. I've got a ball to throw," implored Jasmine, the face in front of her losing some of its rouge.

The surge of adrenaline began to dissipate, Charlie's breath and equilibrium returning to normal on the back of Jasmine's steady eyes.

She tapped twice on the Old English-style *D* on the front of Charlie's cap, took a deep breath, and readied herself. She reared back, extending her right arm as far back as possible, and took a giant step forward.

Charlie closed his eyes on the ball's release, opening them when he heard the contact with the bottles, pushing them even wider at the sight of all six glass containers gloriously hurtling through the air. Cheers from onlookers commenced as the bottles completed their descent to the ground, followed by a triumphant cacophony as they bounced around before coming to a rest. Raucous applause continued, sending one undesirable group slinking away.

Rudy's eyebrows turned up, the shock turning to laughter. "I've never seen anyone throw the ball that hard." He stared at Jasmine. "You must play ball!"

Charlie let out a whoop that could be heard clear across to the other side of the fair, commenced a little jig, and then laughed hysterically. Without thinking, instinct taking over, Charlie took two steps and hugged Jasmine, the excitement tearing down his inhibitions. Jasmine returned the affection by putting her arms around her friend. She grabbed him tightly, tighter than knocking down six bottles warranted.

"Pick a prize off the wall, darling," directed Rudy.

It was an easy choice. "That one," said Jasmine, pointing.

Rudy put Yosemite Sam in her hands, which she immediately transferred into Charlie's.

"Give me a second, Charlie," said Rudy, who disappeared through some curtains and returned ten seconds later to hand Charlie a business card. Charlie took it from the carny and read it: "Glenmore's Tattoo Parlor, 12002 Gratiot Avenue, Detroit, Michigan."

"You give Glenmore a call, and I will set you up," said Rudy, still smiling and shaking his head in disbelief. He had never seen anyone, girl, boy, or adult, throw a ball that hard. Charlie was thinking the same, attributable to her flawless throwing form. It was the reason Houston Astros' second baseman, Jose Altuve, weighing only 165 pounds, could hit home runs the same distance as men twice his size.

Several children and a few adults approached Charlie and Jasmine to congratulate them, but the bullies were long gone.

Charlie and Jasmine walked away from the baseball toss game, a touch of swagger accompanying them, strutting like peacocks, Charlie holding out Yosemite Sam as if it was The Commissioner's Trophy presented each year to the World Series champion team.

A few games of ring toss and darts filled the next hour, with mixed results, but nothing could strip the glow of success that surrounded them as they basked under the afternoon sun. Charlie couldn't stop thinking about Jasmine, knocking those bottles down and sending those deplorable creeps away with one amazing throw. With all those eyes on her, she cleared them from her mind and performed like a champion with game-seven World Series pressure. It was the stuff legends were made of.

Tiring, and with no tickets remaining, the two decided to leave, both of them required to be home in an hour, at 6:00 p.m. As the two friends headed for the exit, a flashing neon sign caught Charlie's attention: Medium Marlene. The sign was placed just outside a small gray, nondescript tent. No carny was present, yelling, waving, and drumming up business. Charlie handed Yosemite Sam to Jasmine and walked the ten steps over to the tent door, which was folded open. He peaked inside and saw a woman, who looked to be 110 years old with a sizeable hunch, her advanced osteoporosis taking over. Perfectly still, seated in a wooden chair with her eyes closed, Charlie wondered if she was having an afternoon nap, but she was meditating.

As he contemplated whether he should disturb her, Jasmine joined him at his side. It was all a touch creepy. Charlie wanted to turn around and escape the tent's confines, but something he did not understand held him.

Tools of the trade, such as tarot cards, were displayed on a solid oak table that was as old as Marlene. Charlie glanced at a sign on the wall: Medium—Communicate with Your Loved Ones. Charlie was about to grab Jasmine's hand and retreat when the elderly woman's eyes popped open. Marlene's piercing green eyes looked directly at both of them, which startled the pair, because she gazed straight through both of them. Charlie's urge was to run, to have his keester back out in the sun forthwith, to break free of those eyes that had now locked on them, pulling them in with the force of a black hole.

Without saying a word, she softly waved both of them over.

"We don't have any more money," blurted Charlie, hoping a lack of commercial tender would abruptly end their interaction. Jasmine stopped blinking, her brown eyes darting back and forth between Charlie and the woman with long silver hair tightly pulled back.

"Don't worry about money, Mr. Hustle," she replied, her crooked smile not terribly reassuring.

Mr. Hustle? Did she just call him Mr. Hustle? How did she know his nickname? Charlie scanned his body to see if his name was printed on his body, knowing that it wasn't. Did Rudy make his way down here and tell her? Charlie looked back over his shoulder through the open tent door and could see Rudy at his station, waving people in. That explanation didn't make sense. He turned to Jasmine, who knew exactly what was racing through his mind.

"I didn't tell her," she said, scrunching her face.

The bizarre situation was not quickly solved by logic, the boy of science perplexed, his thinking cap pulled tightly around his head but providing no answers.

"How do you know my name?" asked Charlie, politely and pensively.

"You told me," came the reply. "You didn't use words, at least as you understand them."

Marlene's answer was as clear as a towering fly ball in the middle of a blinding midday sun without sunglasses, thought Charlie.

He looked at Jasmine again, who shrugged her shoulders.

"You are a long way from home, young lady," asserted the woman, directing her attention to Jasmine.

Jasmine's eyes stared back at the woman, her flummox keeping her speechless.

"Please come and sit—both of you," she repeated, just as softly as the first time. "Don't worry about the money, dear."

Charlie wasn't sure what to do, arriving home by 6:00 p.m. impossible if they accepted the offer. Assumptions—the first cousins of intellectual laziness—raced through his mind. He didn't want Jasmine to be tardy, Joseph Bouba already cold to Jasmine's time with him. The reasonable answer was to politely decline and skedaddle.

But Charlie couldn't leave. Jasmine didn't want to either. Marlene's presence was too strong, more powerful than a Klingon tractor beam pulling in the Enterprise.

Like his first visit to Comerica Park, Charlie felt drawn to be there, the urge permeating his entire body. "If you don't know something, Charlie, find the answer, because the answer is out there, somewhere." His father's advice, given at Comerica Park, never left him. Ignorance is not bliss. It's laziness.

"I know we'll be late, Charlie, but I want to stay," whispered Jasmine in his ear.

Charlie glanced again at the sign—Communicate with Your Loved Ones. It was crazy to consider, a man of science entertaining such nonsense. Charlie chuckled inside, being drawn into such nonsense. This was ridiculous, he concluded, finally coming to his senses.

Charlie and Jasmine took six steps and plunked themselves down into the two chairs in front of their host. Charlie scanned the room, which was rather bare, perhaps not unexpectedly. How could this woman make a living, holed up in her tent without hustling in the crowds like Rudy?

"My name is Marlene," offered the medium, who was still looking right through Charlie's soul.

"I'm Charlie," responded Mr. Hustle, "but you probably already knew that."

Marlene laughed slightly, appreciating her young guest's sense of humor.

"Why are you here, Charlie?

Charlie didn't answer immediately. Instead, he fixed his sight on the wall: Medium—Communicate with Your Loved Ones. Marlene nodded.

"May I take your hands, Charlie?" she asked as she reached out with hers.

Charlie was silent but instinctively reached out and grabbed the wrinkled hands covered in beauty marks.

Charlie nodded yes, not knowing what to expect, but mesmerized by the mysterious woman in front of him, considering she was likely a charlatan. His pounding heart suggested he was a believer in Marlene's capabilities.

Marlene's hands were soft, not at all like they looked, an indescribable sensation pulsating through his mind and body when they touched. Marlene closed her eyes and appeared to enter a trance. She remained silent for about two minutes.

"Charlie, does Goliath Slayer mean anything to you?"

"Goliath Slayer?" repeated Charlie, scrunching his face, coming up empty after scrutinizing the inventory in his brain. Charlie Unger's power of recollection was formidable, the young boy confident the strange name was not in his past. "No, that means nothing to me."

"Yes, the Goliath Slayer. He is coming through very strong," explained the woman.

"What about my mother?" asked Charlie. "Heather Unger. I need to speak to her," he begged. "Please! Please! I need to apologize."

With her eyes closed, Marlene shook her head, "Goliath Slayer is very strong. It's overwhelming everything else."

Charlie began to well up. He wanted his mother—one last opportunity to speak with her. He let go of Marlene's hands, on the verge of crying, not inclined to display his pain in front of Jasmine. "Charlatan," he screamed from within. Goliath Slayer. What a farce. With the first tear, he jumped out of his chair and rushed out of the tent into the sunlight. He tucked his face under his arm and cried, hoping that nobody paid an ounce of attention to the blubbering fool.

Jasmine appeared at his side a minute later, Charlie now having the waterworks under control, his bloodshot eyes the only corroboration of his sorrow.

She put her hands on his shoulders. "You will speak to her someday, Mr. Hustle. I know it. I know it."

Charlie nodded his head, but he was not confident. The idea was too fanciful. Instead, he erected a wall in record time, promising to remain free of the black hole enticing him with false hopes, intent on sucking him into emotional oblivion.

"Marlene asked that you come back and see her another day. She wants to speak to you again," explained Jasmine.

Charlie nodded again, but it was inconceivable that the wall could be scaled successfully; it was mighty high.

CHAPTER TWENTY-ONE

Getting Inked

A day later, Marlene safely on the other side of the wall, Charlie took a bus from Plymouth to downtown Detroit. It was his usual practice to use every minute efficiently, solving problems that he had deposited into a special folder in his mind labeled Unambiguous. Not so today. Mr. Hustle enjoyed the hour-long ride along Interstate 96, staring out the window but not focusing on anything. He remained inside his head. However, he took a brief notice of a billboard, "Searching for Answers? God has the answers (833) THE-TRUTH." Charlie had the mind to jot down the phone number and determine what answers could possibly be at the end of that number. Why bother calling a number when you could speak directly to God?

Not seeing the forest through the trees—the idiom was on his mind. Was he seeing the big picture? It was not easy to turn his high-functioning brain off, but sixty minutes passed without him coming to one conclusion, without narrowing any issues, or without making a mental to-do list.

He had asked Jasmine to join him, but she couldn't escape the clutches of her protective father, deciding that she save her best ruse to join him at the Tigers game tomorrow. He missed her company, the images of those milk bottles fresh in his mind, the reason he was on bus #62. She reciprocated his hug. What did it mean? It probably meant nothing, he concluded. Don't get ahead of yourself, Unger—the idea as fanciful as communicating with the dead.

Charlie enlisted a different strategy to ensure that he could make his treks, including the inner streets of Detroit, without parental permission interfering with his plans. It was as brilliant as it was devious; he simply did not tell his father what he was doing or where he was going. It became easy after his mother died, his dad's long working hours leaving no time for parental oversight. But since David came home from the hospital, Charlie required a new repertoire of excuses, his father taking a noticeable interest in his whereabouts. Perfect grades took most of the heat off; how much mischief could a kid with flawless grades get into? Some guilt did accompany his fibs, but they were necessary.

Once downtown, he transferred buses at Chrysler Drive, taking bus #156 eastbound, crossing Interstate 375 for another six blocks out of the downtown core and into a sketchy neighborhood.

"Are you sure this is where you want to get off, son?" queried the driver, his concern turning to alarm when Charlie nodded his head.

"Yes, sir," replied Charlie, thanking the man, taking two steps down, and hopping onto the sidewalk.

Admittedly, Gratiot Avenue, east of I-375, was questionable, an area Charlie had frequently seen on television, the three-dimensional in-person introduction more threatening than he had imagined. He passed Tony's Liquor, Big Al's Beverages, Victory Liquor, and Smoke and Toke on the first block of his travels, au pied. Charlie began running through some French translations, impressed with what he remembered from an afternoon on Babbel a couple of years ago.

A block past Danny's Discount Furniture, his destination came into view, a hundred meters past several abandoned commercial buildings.

"Sorry, I don't have any change, mister," said Charlie when the homeless man extended his hand. It was true.

Charlie thought all night about the tattoo he wanted and where he would place it, somewhere discreet, away from the prying eyes of his father. He was concerned about Rudy's words, "with your parents' approval." He put his father's chances of allowing him to get inked at something about four billion to one, the same number of stars in the Milky Way. Best not to ask permission, reasoned Charlie, ruling out all possible alternatives. He pulled a note from his pocket, written by his father, authorizing the tattoo, to be used only if Glenmore raised the issue of parental consent.

"Un document falsifié," announced Charlie to himself, continuing to work on his French.

Glenmore's Tattoo Parlor sat between an abandoned building and Larry's Liquor Mart. Charlie estimated the crumbling exterior had last been painted two decades ago. Perhaps low overhead translated into competitive pricing on Glenmore's tattoos; however, Charlie did not have to concern himself with price, thanks to Jasmine's missile of an arm and its heat-seeking precision.

Charlie stepped through the front doors, chimes announcing his arrival. The room was dim, an unintentional throwback to the '70s, with worn orange shag carpet, wood paneling, and the scent of incense wafting throughout the room. An array of tattoo choices covered all four walls, extensive eye-popping choices that could leave you circling the room for hours before you decided. If a customer desired a fiery dragon, Glenmore had it. Tweety Bird—Glenmore had it. For Bible thumpers, Jesus Christ and Moses were on the menu.

Charlie became disappointed when a quick tour around the circumference did not identify any Detroit Tigers options, worry setting in because nothing else would do.

Bob Marley's 1973 song, "I Shot the Sherriff," shot out of the surround-sound system, an apropos choice for a room stuck in the '70s. Charlie tried to relax, moving his head back and forth with the music, trying to be cool, but resembling a pecking hen.

A man with swaying dreadlocks suddenly appeared through a doorway of multi-colored beads hanging from the top of the doorframe, dancing his way into the room.

"Ya, mon. Yes, l'il mon. Welcome to Glenmore's. What brings ya here?" The man smiled genuinely, carrying a sparkle in his eyes, the variety not susceptible of forgery. "I've never seen such a youngin in here before."

"Are you Glenmore?" asked Charlie.

"Yes, l'il mon," replied Glenmore, putting out his fist and inviting a fist bump.

"Charlie Unger, sir. I'm here to get a tattoo," announced Charlie, bumping fists with the owner. "Rudy sent me. Promised me a free tattoo."

The puzzled look that formed across his new Rastafarian acquaintance's face did not bring Charlie confidence that Rudy had informed Glenmore of his promise. Charlie was relieved when Glenmore called Rudy and straightened it all out. However, Glenmore was mighty suspicious of the note Charlie placed in his hand; a ten-minute debate followed on the document's validity before Glenmore seceded his position.

After chastising his customer about visiting the area without parents, Glenmore provided Charlie with a catalog of sports tattoos, a development that lit Mr. Hustle's eyes. It didn't take him long; the choice was clear—the Old English-style *D* in navy blue on page three.

"Great choice, Chuck!" exclaimed Glenmore. "Let's get to work."

After three hours of artistic magic and surgical precision, the four-inch-by-four-inch Tigers logo was impeccably placed on his right upper arm, at the shoulder, high enough that short sleeves could remain in his wearable wardrobe. Swimming in front of his father would be problematic, a hurdle that would require some ingenuity to overcome; luckily, Charlie was not one to lounge around pools or beaches. His dad would love the artwork, but timing was everything.

As Glenmore rotated a small mirror around his shoulder so that Charlie could view it from every angle, Charlie knew those three hours of pain were necessary. He hadn't expected that the repeated jabs of the needle would bring out a tear or two, but it was worth it a hundred times over, feeling stronger than Superman when it was over.

As Charlie slipped out of his chair, readying himself to leave, he glanced to his right, double-taking. Was that who he thought it was? No, it couldn't be. Charlie stared out of the corner of his eye, calling upon his peripheral vision to confirm the man's identity. The fellow, thirty feet away, shaved head with the graying beard, was finishing up a tattoo on his back with one of Glenmore's associates—a bald eagle clasping a baseball bat in its claws. The magnificent piece of art was now almost complete; the vibrant red, white, and blue colors bursting off his back had Mr. Hustle reconsidering his choice. The tattoo must have taken days to finish, Charlie unsure if he had the pain tolerance.

The man paid and exited Glenmore's, Charlie following him out to the street, evaluating his features and waffling on whether to approach him. Athletes look quite different in their civilian clothes, without a uniform and baseball hat.

"You following me?" asked the man, somewhat sternly, maintaining his back to Charlie out on the street.

"To the end of the earth and back," replied Charlie, thinking as quickly as he could.

"Fly too close to the sun, and you'll burn your wings. That's Nicholas Casiple," explained the man, turning around to face Charlie. He was huge—probably six-feet, four-inches tall, 220 pounds of pure muscle. Charlie became thankful when the guy flashed him a quick smirk, interpreting the facial gesture as an invitation to continue.

"Wherever you go, go with all your heart. That's Confucius," explained Charlie, leaving not a split second between idioms. Charlie could have gone on with this game for an hour, the man having no idea who he was dealing with, but thought better of it.

"You're George Haverson, right?" asked Charlie.

The man was not accustomed to being noticed. He raised his eyebrows and nodded slowly, trying to figure out why a young kid, quoting Confucius, was alone in one of the worst neighborhoods in Detroit. Even George felt uncomfortable, but he had been getting inked at Glenmore's for the last three years, ever since he was traded to the Tigers from the

Dodgers. The forty-year-old journeyman ballplayer had played for eight different teams over a twenty-year career.

"What's your name, buddy?" asked George.

"Charlie Hustle," he replied, thinking it best to use a pseudonym until he further evaluated his predicament.

George's eyebrows lifted again. "Charlie Hustle," he said, laughing.

"It's a long story, Mr. Haverson."

"I got time, kid."

The two proceeded to show each other their tattoos, both proud of the artwork permanently placed on their bodies out of respect for the game they loved.

"Do your parents know you are alone in this neighborhood, Charlie Hustle?"

Charlie explained that his dad was home recovering from a car accident and that his mother died earlier in the year from cancer.

"Wow, you got the shitty end of the stick, man."

It was a thoughtful response. Charlie loved idioms, but that one grossed him out. In ancient times, before indoor plumbing, a stick was used in outhouses to knock over the cone of feces that developed before it rose up out of the hole. In the darkness, before electricity, as one felt around for the stick, one hoped to pick up the correct end.

George was never a starter, always a seldom-used utility player, plugging holes wherever his team needed him. A career .202 hitter, George was never a fan favorite and could comfortably walk the streets without being recognized. He was in his last campaign, having already announced his retirement. His deteriorating skills were no longer capable of allowing him to keep a grip on the pinnacle of baseball—the Major Leagues.

Darkness was descending fast. The couple of street lamps that still had working bulbs came one, prompting George to look down at his new acquaintance and consider his circumstances. He had a dinner meeting in twenty minutes.

"How are you getting home, Mr. Hustle?"

"Bus, sir."

"Bus! Not a chance. Let me give you a ride home, okay?"

A ride home with a Detroit Tiger. Wow. That would be incredible; he had a million and one questions to ask George.

"I live in Plymouth," replied Charlie, realizing the distance might be a dealbreaker.

"Plymouth!" exclaimed George, knowing the drive was at least thirty minutes.

Charlie's head bent down in disappointment, realizing that George must have believed that he lived nearby.

George removed Charlie's Tigers hat, rustled his red curly hair with his hand, and bent down in front of the boy. He took his finger, put it under his chin, and raised Charlie's head until they were looking directly at each other.

"Well, we better get going then," said George. In thirty feet, they arrived at George's black SUV parked at the curb; the two jumped in, and off they went.

"Charlie, how do you know all of these sayings?"

"I guess because I read a lot," replied Charlie, the mischievous smile of the Cheshire Cat on his face. Nothing could have foreshadowed a ride home with George Haverson when he rose from bed this morning.

"My father was a philosophy professor," explained George, "one of the first black professors at an Ivy League school. He meant everything to me but died when I was fourteen."

George let his admission sink in. Charlie turned his head away from the window and returned his attention to George.

"I'm sorry, George. I'm sure you miss him."

"Not a day goes by, little man. It was tough, but you know the pain of which I speak."

Charlie nodded but remained silent.

"My father told me that all of these sayings help us make sense of the crazy world we live in, a world where a lot of cruel things happen."

Charlie pulled up his sleeve to look at his tattoo.

"It is during our darkest moments that we must focus to see the light," announced George.

"What?" said Charlie.

"It is during our darkest moments that we must focus to see the light. Aristotle," explained George.

"Sometimes it's tough to see the light, George."

"I know, kid. I know. Trust me, I know all too well. But the light is always there—sometimes you just have to work extra hard to see it."

Charlie nodded again.

"My dad loved philosophy. We spent hours tossing back and forth sayings and then discussing what they meant. I know them all."

"I know them all," boasted Charlie, smiling and lightening the mood.

"Oh, do you now?" replied George, laughing.

George mulled over a thought, then offered his passenger a wager. If Charlie could identify who was responsible for five sayings, George would arrange a private box for Charlie at the next Tigers home game. Charlie's eyes lit up, thinking about a luxury box, watching the game in style, but after carefully considering it, he made a counter-proposal.

"If I get all five correct, would you ask Rodney Kilmer to read the letters I sent him? I sent twelve letters with suggestions on how to turn some underperforming Tigers around."

"Was one of the letters about me?" asked George, laughing hard. "Actually, I don't want to know. You got it, kid. I'll talk to Rod. You ready?"

"Loaded for Bear, George."

"Life is like a baseball game. When you think a fastball is coming, you have to be able to hit the curve," said George.

"Jaja Q," replied Charlie. "I hope they're all this easy," he said with a wink at his driver.

"Hitting is fifty percent above the shoulders," came the second one.

"George, is this amateur hour? Ted Williams, of course," replied Charlie, smiling, the grin of the Cheshire Cat returning.

"Excellence is the gradual result of always striving to do better."

"That's a bit of a trick, but you don't know who you are dealing with—Pat Riley," answered Charlie.

"I never said they would all be baseball sayings. Three in a row. Impressive, Mr. Hustle. Okay, here is number four, 'You wouldn't have won if we'd beaten you.'"

Charlie looked at George. "Yogi Berra. You're giving me Yogi Berra sayings, for goodness' sake."

George laughed. "Okay, I underestimated you. The fifth is difficult though. 'Hope is like a buoy. It can keep even the heaviest of hearts from sinking to the bottom of the ocean.'"

Charlie looked at George and scrunched his face, his brain quickly scanning his archives, but the answer did not come to him. He started to panic, the thought of losing George's connection to Kilmer unsettling.

"Well, Charlie? I thought you knew them all," said George, raising his eyebrows, the smile of the Cheshire Cat now across *his* face.

"You know, George, that sounds exactly like something your father would have said."

George quickly hit the brakes and pulled over to the shoulder, stopping the vehicle abruptly. "How did you know that, Charlie?"

"I've never heard that saying before. Your dad was a philosophy professor. It was an educated guess."

George looked at his passenger, astonished. He couldn't believe it.

George drove from the curb before addressing Charlie again, "My dad told me that shortly before he died. It has served me well."

"Dreams keep me going, George. Maybe they're the same thing. I'm going to coach the Tigers someday. I'm going to make the Tigers great again too."

CHAPTER TWENTY-TWO

6.45 Seconds

Charlie stood within the mecca of baseball—all five senses pushed to their limits by the overwhelming stimuli. He took it all in, aware that forgetting even one minute of the experience would constitute treason of the highest order.

David put his arm around his son. "It's pretty special, isn't it, Son?" both of them gazing around at an empty Comerica Park.

"It's more than special, Dad. It's more, much more." Although he had tossed God aside, *heaven* was the only word that fit.

Charlie looked out to the brick wall in left-center field, "June 20, 2006, first inning, history was made."

"How's that, Son?"

"Miggy hit it out of the park. Literally, out of the park." Charlie pointed. "Right there is where it flew over, between the foul pole and the fountain. He hit a Nate Karns pitch, and it landed in the concourse, a 461-foot bomb that bounced out the gates and onto Adams Street."

Charlie had forever tried to buy that ball from Corry Kinny, who picked up the ball in front of the Athletic Club, over 500 feet from home plate. Oh, how he wanted that ball, the only one that had left the park. It was not for sale; Corry had given it to his grandmother.

Charlie was walking on water, the softness of the tightly cut Kentucky bluegrass buoying each step, lifting his spirits, reminding him that there was no other place on Earth that he would rather be. It was different than being in the stands. Trotting to first base, he plopped both feet on top of the bag and slowly revolved 360 degrees until he was back facing his father. Here he was, at the epicenter of Tigers greatness, ground zero.

Rodney Kilmer appeared, stepping out of the tunnel and onto the field with a newly-acquired spring in his step, courtesy of the Tigers' improving play. He waved at Charlie and David, motioning to his visitors to join him behind home plate.

"Welcome, gents," greeted Kilmer, extending his hand with a friendly grin. "Thanks for coming."

"Oh, thank you, Mr. Kilmer. This is awesome, sir," replied Charlie, his body still buzzing with excitement.

"Please, call me Rod. Both of you. It's a pleasure to have you two here. Look, here come the boys now."

Charlie carefully watched the steady drip of greatness flow from the hollows of Comerica Park out onto the manicured field for practice. Marshall, Miggy, Walters, Sanderson, and Johnson huddled around the batting cage and began taking swings. Charlie was so close, he wanted to reach out and touch them.

Miguel Cabrera took the cage. Crack. Crack. Crack. The crack of the bat repeatedly echoed throughout the empty stadium, Miggy's successive moon shots landing in the upper deck.

"God, he's good, Dad."

"He sure is, buddy. He suuuuure is."

Charlie was in complete awe of Miggy, although he still had a couple of pointers for the best hitter in baseball. The rhythmic sounds continued: crack, crack, crack—the most beautiful sound in the world.

Kilmer smiled, pleased that his young guest was glowing.

"Charlie, I heard you call into Nelson Green's radio show to discuss your theory on the King's bat. You were correct, just shy of a quarter ounce difference."

Charlie nodded. "I knew someone figured it out when he switched to his old bat a day later."

"Yes, Charlie, and since he switched back, he's hitting."

Charlie cut him off and finished Rodney's sentence, "three-thirty-four average, an on-base percentage of four-thirty-six, and slugging percentage of eight-ninety-seven."

"Ha, ha, ha, of course you know," laughed Rodney. "Remind me never to underestimate you, Charlie Unger."

"When I heard you on the radio, I thought your name was familiar, but I couldn't figure out why. It was bugging me, driving me crazy, really. It finally came to me when I was watching *Sports Center*. The hosts discussed how well Mad Dog was hitting since he accepted some advice from a kid outside the Crab Shack. You know what he said, 'Well, it's the funniest of things. I met this little kid coming out of the Crab Shack. He introduced himself as Charlie Hustle'; it got me thinking."

Rodney put his hand on Charlie's shoulder. "Those were Mad Dog's exact words. And then I began piecing it together, the same boy that helped Mad Dog, was the same boy that helped Derek Fisher, was the same boy that sent me twelve letters. Then, George Haverson came to see me with an interesting story about a brilliant kid he had met."

"Are you the same Charlie Hustle?"

"Yes, sir, Rodney. I am, the number-one Tigers fan on the planet."

"Where did you get this kid, David?"

David shook his head. "I don't know. I don't know how I got so lucky." Pangs of shame revisited David, punched him in the stomach, and reminded him of how he had never fully appreciated his son. But those days were gone.

"When I told team president, Tim Earley, that I ordered the coaches to implement your changes, he turned white," laughed Rodney. "Then he said, 'Rod, if this works, tell me why I need you,' and I'm not sure I have an answer to that question.

"Since I asked our coaches to implement your recommendations, we've moved to sixth in team batting average. I thought I had it all figured out, but there was more. Yesterday, Tim dropped into my office and shut the door. He pulled out his phone and called his assistant, 'Michelle, I saw Billy Hamilton down the hall. Please send him up to Rod's office.'"

David and Charlie looked at their host, only one of them having an inkling where the story was headed.

"Ten seconds later, we let Billy in, and Tim told him he heard a rumor that a couple of players were receiving playing instruction from someone outside of the organization. Billy became sheepish; it was poor form to seek instruction outside of the organization, a signal that the organization's coaching staff is not competent."

"I don't see what this has to do with us, Rod," said David.

"Well, Billy admitted that he and at least another seven players were receiving instruction from someone they referred to as the guru. None of them had ever met the guy they only knew as Charles T. Unger."

David looked down at his son. "Is this true?"

Charlie nodded.

"Tim and I just about fainted, gentlemen," explained Rodney. "Tim looked at me, 'Rod, get that boy down here!' and that's when I called you."

After finishing a couple of complimentary hot dogs loaded with chili and cheese, Charlie began a critique of Kelvin Walter's swing, but was interrupted. A jocular voice bellowed from a man climbing the three steps out of the Tigers' dugout.

"Well, I knew I recognized this wonder boy. I was hoping I might get a chance to thank you one day."

Charlie turned around, instantly recognizing the Tiger. "Hey, Mad Dog!"

Luis turned around and shouted to his teammates, "Guys, this is him! Charles T. Unger."

Within thirty seconds, Charlie was engulfed by players; slaps to his backs and messages of appreciation followed, Charlie taking center stage. Laughter and ribbing ensued when the players realized that they had been receiving instruction from a young teenager. Mr. Hustle was knee-deep in his element, at home where he was 100 comfortable, in complete synchronicity with the world.

An hour later, after the last player was finished in the cage, Kilmer let Charlie take a few of his own cuts, without much success, although he did manage to foul off one pitch that was thrown underhand from six feet away.

"Well, Charlie, you are already a top-notch baseball instructor. We'll have to work on the hitting," declared Kilmer, patting his head with a bout of laughter.

Then Kilmer turned to David. "Come on. Take a few cuts. You look to be in top-notch shape."

"No, no, I'm sure you're busy," replied David, declining the invitation with a wave of his right hand.

"Not really," came the reply. "Not today, anyway. Come on," he said, handing David a bat.

Charlie looked at his father, realizing that he had never seen his father swing a baseball bat and had no idea what to expect. David considered faking an injury, before reluctantly accepting the bat. Hawk-like, Charlie watched his father step into the batter's box.

Wow, thought Charlie, recognizing his father's athletic stance and ideal bat positioning, impressive for someone who hadn't swung a bat since he was a teenager. But getting into good position was much different than hitting the ball, so Charlie tampered down his excitement as his dad readied himself at the plate.

Charlie and Rodney watched as the pitch arrived, with little expectation or anticipation. Charlie later described what happened next as reminiscent of Robert Redford in the baseball movie *The Natural*. In Mr. Hustle's favorite scene, the aging Redford hits a home run well over the outfield fence and into the lights, causing a cascade of sparks to drench the crowd. His father's sweet swing hit that ball with such a loud crack that everyone in the park turned to look, including every Tigers player who remained on the field. Louder than a thunderclap, faster than a bullet, higher than Polaris, the ball sailed to straight-away center, the deepest part of the park, and cleared the wall by twenty feet.

Time came to a standstill. Nobody moved, their eyes fixed on the ball that was now rattling around the seats. Every eye refocused back at the man in the box, mouths open. The expressions on the faces of Kilmer and Charlie were priceless, with dropped jaws and saucer-sized eyes.

"Holy crap, David! Where did you play your ball?" asked Kilmer, his mouth returning to its previous open position after completing his question.

David stepped out of the batter's box and sheepishly replied to his host, "I last played in high school, but I gave it up."

"Why, man?"

"Life got in the way, I guess," replied David.

"You have got to be kidding me! Take a few more swings," urged Kilmer excitedly.

David knocked the next six out of ten pitches into the bleachers, causing nonstop shaking from Kilmer's head, his disbelief not dissipating. When David had ripped his sixth ball over the wall, several Tigers players had returned from the clubhouse to the dugout to watch David put on a display. They all had the same question—who was this guy, and where did he come from? Was he a prospect? If so, they had never heard of him, but he looked too old to be a prospect.

Kilmer looked at the thirty-six-year-old lawyer, wondering where the hell this guy had been for the last ten years. He was still in unbelievable shape.

"How fast can you run, David?" asked Kilmer.

"No idea," responded David, although he knew he was fast as lightning in high school.

Kilmer waved over the athletic trainers and directed them to set up a sixty-yard dash, the benchmark distance for evaluating baseball players' speed.

"Oh, Mr. Kilmer, I don't think so," objected David respectfully, not interested in being put on display in front of the players, who now numbered fifteen. Additionally, several coaches were strolling out of the tunnel after being beckoned by the players.

"Please, David! Humor me. Please," begged Kilmer. David was reluctant but didn't want to be rude, given the generous hospitality he and his son had been shown.

"You have to, Dad!" exclaimed Charlie, who couldn't contain himself. "You have to!" Charlie looked over at the dugout. Cabrera stood there in the crowd of players, the icon's eyes glued on his father.

"Do it, man," yelled Miggy, followed by more encouragement from his fellow players.

"Go for it, buddy!" yelled Mad Dog Madison.

"The boys want a show, David. Come on," encouraged Kilmer. "What's it going to hurt?"

David, feeling the pressure, slowly nodded his head in agreement and commenced some stretches and sprints to warm up. He approached the line and waited for the signal, second-guessing his acquiescence. Hearing the word, "Go," David took off. A cheetah travels up to seventy-five miles per hour at top speed, a blistering pace used to bring its prey down. Charlie couldn't tell the difference, convinced he had witnessed the blazing wildcat streaking across the field, every limb working in perfect tandem, not an ounce of inefficiency in his father's stride. By thirty yards, every observer knew David's time would be fast. But how fast?

After crossing the finish line, all eyes went to the electronic board. A split second later, the time popped up on the electronic board, 6.45 seconds. Charlie knew that anything under seven seconds was elite speed. Current Tigers right fielder Russel Simmonds had a bronze medal in the one-hundred-meter dash in the 2012 summer Olympics and a best time of 6.31 seconds over sixty yards. The world record was 5.99 seconds.

Charlie immediately appreciated that his father, at age thirty-six, had just run a sixty-yard time at world-level speeds without proper shoes.

Mr. Hustle stared at his father strolling back from the finish line, the questions piling up, wooziness from the performance setting in. Who was the man walking back toward him, his chest heaving in and out? How could Charlie not be aware of his dad's speed and hitting abilities? The display was exciting, but an interloper arrived, a melancholy riding in on the back of so many questions. Did he really know his father? It was a question that brought on loneliness.

Charlie shook his head, snapped out of it, and put his arms up in the air. "I can't believe it! I can't believe it!"

Kilmer jogged over to David, despite wearing a full suit. "Who the heck are you? And where the heck have you been?"

Clapping from the players and coaches ensued, the exhibition of athleticism a great success.

At Rodney's request, David hustled to the outfield and shagged some balls, proving that he could also catch and take a proper line to catch a fly ball.

"David, some work is needed in the outfield, but when you can run like that, you can track down fly balls that most outfielders can only dream of getting to!"

Kilmer needed to digest the unexpected events. What he'd observed was exceptional, but now what? So what? The guy was thirty-six. He didn't have answers.

CHAPTER TWENTY-THREE

What Happens in Cameroon, Doesn't Stay in Cameroon

"Wow, Charlie! It's beautiful," exclaimed Jasmine, pulling her eye away from the telescope. "It's mesmerizing, absolutely mesmerizing!"

"That's Polaris, the North Star," replied Charlie. "It's the most captivating object you'll ever set your eyes on." He wished he could stare up at it for the rest of his life.

"The North Star," repeated Jasmine, smiling, pleased at the memories it conjured up. "My mother loved the Biblical story of the Three Wise Men. She told it frequently."

They both thought about their mothers, who were never far from their thoughts.

Jasmine shuffled her rear end off the stool and flopped to the ground, laying her back onto the Kentucky bluegrass. She placed her hands behind her head, clasped her hands, and looked up into the night sky.

"What are you doing?" asked Charlie. "I thought you wanted to look through the telescope?"

"I do, but let's just look up for a while without it," replied Jasmine.

Charlie plopped himself beside her, not nearly as gracefully. Oh, how he loved how that Kentucky bluegrass licked at every part of his body, reminding him of how amazing his father had performed earlier in the day in front of all those Tigers. His dad had them shaking their heads in amazement. Whoever said, "They can't take that memory from you," must have been talking about today.

Following suit, Mr. Hustle put his hands behind his head and stared up, neither of them caring that five minutes of silence followed.

"NASA recognizes eighty-eight constellations," announced Charlie. "They all have a story, mostly myths. There's Andromeda of Greek mythology, daughter of Cassiopeia, who was chained to a rock, destined to be eaten by a sea monster. And there, Hercules, son of Zeus, a Roman mythological hero. Phoenix, over there; reminds me of me, a mythical bird that can revive itself from its own ashes. At least, I hope."

"And which one reminds you of me?" asked Jasmine.

"Oh, that's easy. Pegasus. Right there. A divine winged horse that brought forth springs from the earth wherever it walked. A magnificent, strong, and beautiful creature."

Charlie put his hands palm down in the grass beside him, keeping his eyes fixed on the sky, wondering about her reaction but afraid to know. He was unaware that she had already turned her head toward him, brought on by the kindest words that had ever found her ear.

He felt Jasmine's hand slightly brush up against his, surely an accident, the alternative unfathomable. It had to have been an accident? Of course it was. But she continued, slowly sliding hers until it covered the top of his, his skepticism evolving into belief, one finger at a time.

"Thanks for protecting me at the fair," she said, her hand grabbing tighter.

"I would have been pummeled, beaten to a pulp," he replied, knowing he would never be a fighter. A lover was also questionable.

"And yet you still would have gone through with it, Charlie."

Yes, he would have, without hesitation. Charlie Unger would have done anything for the girl beside him. It was difficult to process what that meant; what was the consequence of such certitude?

"Charlie, why do you love looking out at the stars?"

"I'm hoping that answers to some of my questions are out there."

"What answers are you looking for?"

"I'm trying to make sense of the world, I guess," he responded, quietly, his voice trailing off.

"I'm looking for my mother and sister. I know they're out there," explained Jasmine. "I'm looking at heaven right now. They're so close." She stretched her free arm toward the sky as far as possible, wiggling her fingers. "A little farther and I could touch them."

Charlie tilted his head to his left—looked at Jasmine and those beautiful brown eyes of hers searching for her own answers.

"What happened in Cameroon?" he asked, Jasmine never having been willing to discuss the circumstances. She hadn't spoken about it with anyone, not even the school counselor, her wall keeping everyone back.

"My sister and I had just won the league championship football game. The four of us, my mom, dad, and Sasha, returned home to celebrate. We were all giggling as my mom put dinner on the table, because we had to find room for three more trophies in our house."

Charlie turned his hand over and grabbed Jasmine's, feeling her pain.

"We heard this blood-curdling scream, the kind of which I'd never heard before."

Jasmine explained that the army had advanced into their tiny English-speaking town and began shooting indiscriminately. Her father ran back into the house after investigating the commotion, a horrified look on his face that Jasmine had never seen before. She did not require an explanation, his eyes confirming that peril was upon them; it was all she needed to know.

He knew that his wife might be a target for speaking out against the government. Consequently, the four of them frantically grabbed what they could in thirty seconds.

"'Run, girls!' screamed my dad, the front crashing in while the four of us scrambled out the back door. We sprinted across an open field, heading for a grove. I've never run faster," explained Jasmine. "It's amazing what you can do when your life depends on it."

"Then what happened?" asked Charlie, otherwise frozen, gripped by the story.

"Two of us made it; the two fastest made it to the grove. Mama and Sasha were shot in the back, a few feet before the tree line. I tried to go back, but Papa wouldn't let me. We kept running, eventually making it to the US embassy the next day, never setting foot back in our house because of the danger. The French were turning in English separatists, even those who had been friends for decades. My uncle sponsored us, and we made our way to America."

Charlie didn't know what to say. What could he say? He racked his brain for something to soothe her pain, but it was impossible. He knew a thing or two about it.

"I'm sorry, Jasmine." It was the best he had; it would have to do. Thankfully, it was all she expected. "I'm glad you're here."

Jasmine nodded her head. "You know, Charlie. Sometimes I feel like I stepped out of one pile in Cameroon and into the exact same pile here. Je suis libre comme un oiseau," announced Jasmine, her eyes clouding over. "Free as a bird. Someday, maybe. But not today. I was never called the N-word until I came to the United States of America."

Jasmine explained how their village was burned to the ground that awful evening. There were five deaths, including two children, the massacre barely making the international news wires, such mundane events in Africa not having the necessary gravitas to claw themselves to the front of the line.

Charlie was sick to his stomach, certain there was no God. Regrettably, he placed two checkmarks in the "no" column.

CHAPTER TWENTY-FOUR

Game Day

Charlie and Jasmine arrived two hours before game time. The Tigers were hosting the Toronto Blue Jays, and Charlie wanted to be at Comerica Park the second the gates opened, not wanting to miss any batting practice. A notepad, stuffed in his back pocket, would be used to take detailed notes during batting practice and the game. Charlie figured he had Rodney Kilmer's ear now, the GM receptive to listening to his views.

Late last night, Rodney Kilmer called the house and spoke to his father, an hour-long conversation, raising Charlie's intrigue. What could they have discussed for an hour? Putting his ear to the door didn't help, nothing but incoherent muffles making their way through. And his father wasn't revealing anything; perhaps his legal training and commitment to confidentiality tightened his lips. Not knowing affected Charlie's sleep last night, ruminating on the content of their talk, or, as Charlie preferred, his commitment to focus kept him up half the night. His mind was racing.

Jasmine was nervous taking the bus from Plymouth to downtown Detroit for the game, having told her father she was spending the day at the library. She bugged Charlie the entire ride, repeatedly requesting an explanation for why they were making the trip when they did not have tickets to the game.

"Don't worry. I have it covered," he replied each time, displaying a devilish smirk and a wink.

After hopping off at the corner of Madison and Brush, Charlie directed Jasmine, "First, we need to go to Adams Avenue."

"What for?" came the reply.

"I'll show you."

Within a minute, Charlie was standing over a bronze plaque embedded in the street in front of the Detroit Athletic Club: "Miguel Cabrera * June 20, 2006 * 461 feet."

"The only home run to make it clear out of the stadium grounds." Charlie bent down and rubbed the plaque. "Do it, Jasmine. It will bring you good luck."

Jasmine followed him to the ground and did one better. She plunked her rear end on top of the plaque and shuffled her behind back and forth, bringing several looks that reminded Charlie of Ms. Jenkins and Mr. Cooper. "Hopefully, this will give me all the luck I need," she said, laughing.

The excited pair continued to the stadium, Charlie steering them away from the front gates, turning down a narrow side street. After one hundred yards, Charlie stopped in front of a black door labeled "Employees Only." Charlie knocked seven times in a rehearsed pattern that Jasmine did not recognize. The door opened halfway, allowing them to slip in and out of the sunshine.

"My man, Mr. Hustle," greeted the middle-aged man, who smiled and gave Charlie a high-five. Jasmine smiled, proud that Charlie's nickname was catching on.

"How's Lynette, Frank?" asked Charlie.

"B+ average, thanks to you!" replied the appreciative man, his weathered hand fist-bumping Charlie's. "The two of you are in section 120, row 1, seats 5 and 6," explained Frank, now lowering his voice and looking over his shoulder. "Roger and June Leitch are in Europe at some fancy symposium, so you're all clear. Right behind home plate."

Charlie and Jasmine set off for their seats.

"What the heck was that all about, Charlie?"

Charlie explained that he tutored Frank's teenage daughter in math in exchange for unutilized seats from wealthy season-ticket holders who were out of town. "They're great seats every time," explained Charlie as they descended the stadium stairs to the front row.

"They are fabulous seats, Charlie," agreed Jasmine, excited to attend her first professional baseball game. "I'm sure it won't be as exciting as football though."

With eighteen pages of notes safely in his back pocket from batting practice, Charlie readied himself for the game. The crowd clapped as the Detroit pitcher's first toss of the game, a nasty curveball, snapped down over the plate and into the catcher's mitt, creating a thud.

"Steeeeeerike one!" yelled the umpire, shoving his arm into the air, providing synchronized oral and verbal signals.

"I could listen to that sound all day," remarked Charlie. "The curve is my favorite pitch."

"Oh ya, why?" responded Jasmine, clapping with the crowd.

"Newton's law. Gravity. The Magnus effect." Charlie explained that he could see the ball's spin generating greater pressure on one side, the difference in pressure from the other side causing lift, or the Magnus effect, making the ball curve. It was the same reason airplanes flew and sailboats could travel faster than the wind. Science was the perfect lens to look out at the world with as far as Charlie Unger was concerned, and he was humbly perplexed that not everyone shared his vision.

Jasmine listened to his explanation and offered him a story, "My mother loved paintings. She loved how they made her feel, always discussing her emotions when looking at them. Not once did she talk about the technique the painter used, or how masterful the painter must have been to produce such a beautiful work of art."

"I get it, Jasmine. Kind of like knowing how a magician does his trick. It doesn't seem so magical after you know. But I love knowing. I have to know."

It was an exciting game, the contest entering extra innings with the game tied 3–3. Jasmine became engaged, the raucous crowd reminding her of home and the packed football stadiums. She introduced her stomach to the foot-long hot dog, slushie, and corn dog-stuffed egg rolls, all Comerica Park delicacies.

Charlie had taught her the words to "Take Me Out to the Ball Game" on the bus ride, which she cheerily sang during the seventh-inning stretch, prompting them to flag down a vendor and grab a couple boxes of Cracker Jacks.

The sun was shining, Charlie in a state of nirvana, surrounded by his favorite sounds and smells, and explaining the game he loved to Jasmine. The two teenagers laughed and laughed, exchanged high-fives, and sang along with each song that blared out of the stadium's system.

In between the ninth and tenth inning, Jasmine took a deep breath. "Don't you love the smell of freshly cut grass? It reminds me of home when they cut the pitch."

Charlie quickly turned his head and addressed her. "Of course, I do! Novertdortis!" exclaimed Charlie, who began explaining the scientific reasons for the smell, but was cut off.

"I just want to enjoy it, Charlie," she said, laughing and patting his knee.

In the bottom of the twelfth inning, both of them became nervous, neither of their parents knowing their actual whereabouts and neither of them having contemplated extra innings when devising their plan to return home on time.

Marshall Slingers stepped to the plate with two out and nobody on base.

"His hands are still in a great position, Jasmine," exclaimed Charlie, focusing on those huge paws wrapped around the end of a Louisville birch bat. Charlie smiled and shook his head, still in disbelief that he was responsible for sending the infielder on such a batting tear.

Ball one. Ball two. Strike one. The crowd was on its feet, everyone clapping and stomping their feet in unison.

"Let's go, Tigers, let's go!" screamed forty thousand fans, cheering on the home team. "Let's go, Tigers, let's go!" The stadium was shaking with excitement, precisely as it was at Jasmine's first football game, during Cameroon's semifinal match against Malawi in Yaoundé.

The fourth pitch was released from the pitcher's hand. The stadium briefly hushed as the ninety-six-mile fastball covered the sixty feet and six inches to home plate, anticipation clinging in the air.

"Crack!" The impact from the Louisville birch bat against the magical white sphere shot an echo throughout the stadium. The ball flew off Marshall's bat, a rocket headed to dead center, buoyed by the roar of the crowd. Charlie watched that ball sail 420, a no-doubter, easily distancing the center-field fence, the walk-off home run sending the fans into a wild frenzy.

Jasmine jumped up and down, throwing her arms in the air. Then, she did something unexpected, so memorable and extraordinary that it stuck with Charlie Unger forever. And while he always loved the sound of the crack of a bat, it became his cup of joe that day at Comerica Park.

Jasmine turned to him and threw her arms around him in jubilation. She hung on, not letting go as expected. She clung on as though her life depended on it, and maybe it did. Startled, it took a second for Charlie to react, finally wrapping his arms back around her, confused by the warm tingling in his stomach. Jasmine put her lips to his ear and whispered, "I love you, Mr. Hustle."

Was he dreaming? Had he gone to heaven? He took one hand off the girl that he loved, raised it, and knocked three times on the side of his head. Two checkmarks in the "Bible thumper" column for God. Yes, sir, thought Charlie—a no-doubter.

CHAPTER TWENTY-FIVE

Contract Dispute

Charlie was in love. The girl of his dreams loved him—a divine winged horse that brought forth springs from the earth wherever it walked. A magnificent, strong, and beautiful creature. Sometimes he called her Peg, short for Pegasus; she appreciated the flattering reference to Greek mythology.

Three days later, Jasmine's whisper was in and out of his thoughts as he and David sprawled on the couch, watching a contestant play Plinko on the *Price Is Right*. David hopped off when the doorbell rang, opening the door and accepting an envelope from FedEx. Sitting back down beside his son, he tore open the envelope and started reading aloud. David had been presented a minor-league contract for single-A baseball in the Tigers minor league system with the Lakeland Flying Tigers.

Charlie became giddy listening to his father read the contract offer. "My dad is going to be a professional baseball player!"

"Whoa, Charlie. I'm not quitting my job to play baseball for peanuts at the age of thirty-six. Besides, your school is here. It's flattering but impossible."

"Dad, I'm thirteen now and attending university in two years. I can skip a year. Let's do it. Let's go! You have to. Where's your passion?"

David angrily threw the papers to the floor, stood up, and glared at his son. "Don't talk to me about passion. I've given up every damn dream I've ever had to be responsible, to do what's right, to take care of my family. How dare you ask me where my passion is!" Then, he picked up the ten-page contract, ripped it in half, and threw it across the room, sending pieces flying in every direction.

His father's outburst sent Charlie scurrying to his room, where he jumped on his bed, his thirteen-year-old emotions overwhelming his 170 IQ. His father had shown disappointment and frustration with him before, but nothing approached the loss of control he just witnessed. What nerve had he touched? Charlie was scared. Worse, he felt alone. God, he missed his mother.

Charlie sobbed into his pillow like never before. Why did someone with such a gift for playing the game detest picking up a bat and swinging for the fences? It was incomprehensible. The game of baseball was magical; it brought tingles to the recesses of his soul, provided him unmatched peace. How could a father and son be so different?

A glass half full would have appeared empty, his father's outburst bringing him down like never before; a memory of the night those birthday candles didn't get lit punched their way in and fought for his attention.

An hour later, David knocked on his son's door, entered, and sat down on his bed, sighing with regret. Charlie's head remained slumped, his face positioned directly down at his Tigers bed comforter, not looking up at his father.

David tenderly patted his son's thigh. "I'm sorry, Son. You didn't deserve that." David wrinkled his brow, wondering if now was the time to tell his boy. "It's time we had a discussion, Charlie."

"I used to love the game of baseball, almost as fanatically as you," explained David, smiling at the memory. "I ate, slept, and breathed the game."

Charlie looked up at his father, his interest piqued. "I knew it. I knew it," he declared slowly, his voice starting hushed and ending loudly. Instantly, the admission changed everything. Who *was* his father? In part, the question disappeared in a brilliant flash, answered by his father's words. The lonely feeling inside, harbored by years of doubt, was knocked aside and replaced with an understanding that, yes, he was his father's child. Yes, they shared a love for the mighty game of baseball, a connection that he had forever yearned for.

Charlie's eyes puddled, his brilliant brain unable to outsmart his emotions.

"I was a high school baseball star." David placed three old newspaper articles into Charlie's hands: "High School Student Outshines Them All," "No Ceiling for Teenage Phenom," "Georgia Bulldogs Pursue Unger."

Charlie held them in his hands, reading every word, savoring every accolade. Despite their worn and crinkled condition, he carefully held them in his hands, protecting them, much like one might gently hold a robin's egg to protect its fragile shell.

"I had my choice of universities to attend and play on a full scholarship." David put his head back and sighed, his lungs unable to exhale a lifetime of regrets with one breath. "I was so good, Charlie."

"What happened, Dad?"

"My father was a strait-laced, no-nonsense man who considered baseball a waste of time. 'Two percent of college players get drafted, David. And how many of those players get to the pros? Only two percent of those.' That's what he said to me."

"But you were so good. You had a chance to make it!" implored Charlie.

"I did, Charlie. But my father thought baseball was a waste of time. He thought those endless hours I spent on baseball were better served to study and to prepare for my academic future."

David proceeded to explain the circumstance that ended baseball in his life. One day after school, David was practicing on his high school baseball diamond and lost track of time. His tardiness for the dinner table was not particularly significant on its own, but it was the final straw for his father, whose frustrations had been building over the years. His dad drove down to the diamond, and a screaming match ensued.

"I never felt connected to my father, questioning whether I was his son. Charlie, I became so enraged that I threw my bat away in disgust while arguing, striking him in the head and knocking him unconscious. It was beyond reckless, but I had no intention of hitting him. The horror I felt, seeing him lying in the dirt, blood oozing from his forehead, was indescribable."

Charlie listened, his ears on high alert, wondering why he had never heard the story before.

"A frail elderly woman walking by with her dog witnessed the whole ugly incident and called an ambulance and the police. I was charged criminally with assault causing bodily harm."

David explained that his father woke up while the paramedics assessed his condition. He could have immediately told the police it was an accident, but he wanted to teach his son a lesson. David sat alone in a jail cell for three nights before his father finally dropped the charges.

"He abandoned me, Charlie, forever rupturing our already difficult relationship."

"At least he finally came to his senses, Dad."

David shook his head. "Yes, I suppose, Charlie. But by the time the charges were dropped, I had already been vilified in the newspapers and media. Spoiled brat, violent criminal, anger problems, ungrateful son. You name it—I was called it. All of my scholarship offers were pulled. Even though the charges were dropped, no school wanted anything to do with me. When I walked out of jail, I never returned home. I haven't spoken to my parents since."

"What did you do with no home?

"I quickly got a job waiting tables. I worked my butt off, saved every cent. Finally, I enrolled in a community college—my first step toward law school. It's where I met your mother."

"It was an accident, Dad."

"It was. But it was a painful and shameful episode in my life. I was embarrassed and didn't want you to know about it. Your mom knew. My bitterness ate at me, Charlie."

"I know what it's like to love something so much you can't stand having anyone get in the way of that love," admitted Charlie, sitting up and hugging his father.

"It spoiled my love for the game, Charlie. I'm sorry that I haven't shared in your passion all of these years. It's my biggest failure as a father. Your excitement for the game reminded me every day of that painful chapter in my life, and I couldn't overcome it."

Charlie's eyes widened. "It's not too late. I know it sounds crazy, but you are meant to play baseball again. I know it deep in my heart."

David looked at his son, comforted by his hug, appreciating his son's presence. It was a moment long overdue.

"There's a lot to consider, Charlie. Baseball careers end at my age; they don't begin."

Charlie shook his head. "Dreams are meant to be followed."

"Your mother would be so proud of you, young man. You're wiser than me in too many ways."

"I miss, Mom," said Charlie. "She's the only one who understood me."

Like a knife, the words stuck into David. He put his index finger under his son's chin and pulled his head up so that he could look him straight in the eyes. "Let's change that, Son."

The tears welled up in their eyes, David's voice cracking. "It's been a long day, Mr. Hustle. Get some sleep, and we'll talk in the morning." His dad kissed him on the forehead, a first that Charlie could remember.

After his father closed the door, Charlie put his head on the pillow. Yes, it had been a long day, and he was exhausted, both physically and emotionally, but he couldn't sleep. His mind was racing faster than it had ever raced before, quite a feat given his commonly overactive brain. His father wowed those Tigers' players, including the best of them all, Miggy. Their stunned looks would be forever etched in his mind as that home run sailed over the fence. To see Miggy slapping his teammates on the back when that 6.45-second figure popped up on the board was a lifelong memory, a gift nobody could take away.

He had to convince his father to play. What was life without dreams to follow?

The following morning, Charlie awoke at 6:30 a.m. to the sound of clanking weights in the basement. His eyes opened, refreshed after the best sleep of his life. "What the heck?" he mumbled.

David had also slept well, jumping out of bed, descending the stairs to his home gym in the basement when he awoke.

Charlie's mind began to swirl again. His dad had a beautiful swing, but he still had a suggestion or two for him. He grabbed his phone from the night table. Wow, eleven messages to respond to, including two from a new Tigers player.

He slid out of his bed and threw on some clothes and his Tigers helmet before descending two sets of stairs, arriving in the basement in time to watch his dad complete his last set of squats.

David smiled at his son. "Grab your glove and a ball, Charlie," he said through heavy breathing.

Now in the front yard, the two commenced playing catch on the perfectly manicured lawn, courtesy of the Skag Tiger Striper and Charlie's uncompromising attention to detail. It marked the first time the two played catch together, an almost unimaginable circumstance. Charlie had dedicated hours bouncing a ball off the side of the house, but his father had never joined him.

After a dozen tosses back and forth, David walked over to his son and showed him where to place his fingers on the baseball to throw a curveball, changeup, and two-seam fastball, all of which Charlie knew, but he didn't let on—he *was* instructing eleven Detroit Tigers, after all.

Charlie threw his father a few pitches, all without much success. On his fourth, David held onto the ball and jogged to

Charlie. "So, how do you feel about missing a year of school, Charlie?"

"Of course!" replied Charlie, his eyes lighting up like fireworks, the ramifications of the question setting in. Charlie threw his hands up in the air and hollered as loudly as he could, "My dad is a Detroit Tigers baseball player!" He repeated the words, they sounded so good, "My dad is a Detroit Tigers baseball player!"

David laughed. "Single-A, Charlie. Just the minors."

Ms. Jenkins, two houses down, looked up from her gardening. "Crazy kid," she said to her husband.

A Cadillac pulled up in front of their house, interrupting the mini-celebration. A tall, lanky man, dressed in a suit and tie, exited and crossed the lawn to meet David. Charlie did not recognize the fellow shaking hands with his dad. The two men disappeared into the house, a curious development, thought Charlie, taking the opportunity to spread some grass seed in an area that was becoming a touch thin.

A half hour later, David and the visitor exited the house. David looked content, or perhaps resolved, as he watched the fellow walk back to his car, open the trunk, and pull out a sign. With a mallet in hand, the realtor took a few steps and pounded the sign into the front lawn, waved goodbye to David, and drove off.

Charlie couldn't believe it. He ran to the sign, then looked at his dad, who smiled at him. Charlie looked back at the sign, For Sale.

"Charlie, I signed the single-A contract this morning and faxed it to Mr. Kilmer. He was kind enough to email me another one. My resignation letter to the law firm has also been delivered."

Charlie hugged his father, a man that was going to follow his dream, and Charlie would be there every step of the way.

"I'm to report to Lakeland in two weeks, on August 1st."

"That's amazing, Dad! You've made the right decision; I'm behind you one hundred percent."

"We have some things to discuss, young man," announced David, who directed Charlie to get into the car. After twenty minutes, their sedan pulled into Glendale Recreation Vehicle Center, just south of Plymouth, a couple blocks off of Interstate 275.

David turned to his son after turning off the car engine, "Are you okay with living in an RV while this journey is played out?"

"Absolutely, Dad!" replied Charlie, vigorously nodding his head up and down.

"I thought we could take two weeks and follow the Tigers on their upcoming road trip, arriving in Lakeland on July 31st."

"You have no idea how okay I am with that!" responded Charlie. His body tingled while he knocked three times on the side of his head.

After two hours of investigating dozens of options and some lengthy negotiation, David and Charlie settled on a sleek black-and-gold used 2009 Sunseeker Special, equipped with too many gadgets to count. It had all the comforts of home, theater seating, a bed for each, satellite television, and a fully-equipped kitchen.

They planned to leave in a week, Charlie tasked with planning their route, following the Tigers, and ensuring David had training facilities nearby. Charlie tackled his task, full of zest and a goal of maximizing efficiency—locating camping facilities close to parks, gyms, and batting facilities.

"I want good seats, Charlie," directed David, handing over his credit card. Charlie purchased all the tickets, except for two, calling in an old promise for two freebies.

"Charlie, I look forward to having you and your father at Chase Field as my guest," said Franklin McNeil, president of baseball operations for the Arizona Diamondbacks.

That evening, David asked Charlie to prepare for a guest at 7:00 p.m., refusing to identify the mystery person. After an hour of racking his brain about who would be visiting, Charlie came up empty. Thankfully, the mystery was not left unsolved for long. The doorbell rang at 7:00 on the dot.

"Hello, Charlie," greeted Rodney Kilmer, extending his hand to his young host. "I understand that you and your father are about to embark on the journey of a lifetime."

"Hello, Mr. Kilmer," replied Charlie, accepting the hand into his own. "Yes, sir. This is a dream come true!"

What was this all about? wondered Charlie. Surprise after surprise had his mind in a perpetual state of whirl, similar to the tornadoes in the movie *Twister* he had watched with Jasmine.

After accepting a seat at the kitchen table, Rodney got right to the point, "Gentlemen, welcome to the Tigers organization. David, you are an untapped talent and deserve a shot. It is my pleasure to return your copy of the contract, executed by the Tigers. Welcome aboard."

"Thank you, Rodney," replied David, taking the document into his hand.

"And now, with all due respect to you, David," said Kilmer, smiling, "what I'm about to do is the single most delightful pleasure that I've had in my life. And while I'm prone to exaggeration and hyperbole, this is not one of those occasions."

Charlie was perplexed, as was David.

"Charlie Unger, you may have the most amazing baseball IQ I've ever seen, and I've seen many in my sixty years on this planet."

"Thank you, Mr. Kilmer. I love baseball and I love the Tigers. I'm the biggest fan in the world."

"Yes, Charlie, I believe you are," agreed Rodney.

Kilmer placed his briefcase on the kitchen table, clicked it open, and removed a large manila envelope. "You have made quite an impression on the organization, Mr. Hustle. You've picked up on things that coaches with decades of experience overlooked."

Kilmer pulled his chair in closer and stared intently at Charlie. "And the consensus is that not only did your recommendations have merit, but some of them were downright brilliant."

"Thank you, sir."

"The Tigers organization considers you an unbelievable talent and wants to make you an offer."

Charlie wondered where this was going; when he heard the offer, his stomach churned, the butterflies bouncing off the walls in anticipation. Kilmer handed Charlie an envelope.

"Take it out and read it, Charlie."

Mr. Hustle slowly removed the document; he couldn't get farther than the first paragraph, he was so excited. His hands trembled, unable to believe that his dream of dreams was about to come true.

"I'm going to be a coach with the Detroit Tigers?" asked Charlie.

"Yes, if it's okay with David and the terms are acceptable. School comes first; we'll need to work around your studies."

Charlie kept reading. "You're going to pay me thirty thousand dollars a year?"

"This year, Charlie. Just to start."

"Of course I will!" yelled Charlie, who looked at his dad, relieved when David nodded his approval.

"I thought you may say that," replied Kilmer, who handed Charlie a pen to sign the contract.

Charlie rose from his chair and hugged his new boss.

"Welcome aboard, Mr. Hustle. Here's a copy of the press release going out tomorrow." Kilmer reached behind him, grabbed a suit bag, and gave it to Charlie. "Now that we have the contract business behind us, let's get to the fun part. Open it up, young man."

Charlie unzipped the bag and pulled out a new Tigers uniform, with the number 12 and the name Unger placed on the back. He immediately stripped to his underwear before putting the uniform on, causing the two men to laugh.

Charlie ran to the bathroom to look in the full-length mirror, returning a couple of minutes later. "It's perfect!" exclaimed Charlie, beaming from ear to ear. Charlie wore his uniform for three days before he agreed to let his father wash it.

"There's one more thing, Charlie," said Kilmer. He handed him a regular-sized envelope. "One of your biggest fans asked me to give it to you."

Charlie pulled out the hand-written letter:

Welcome to the team, Charlie! Thanks for your advice, and I look forward to seeing you on the field when we win the World Series.

Your friend and best student, Mad Dog

CHAPTER TWENTY-SIX

Cloud Nine

The day after the house went up for sale, Charlie had a difficult conversation with Jasmine, the excitement of the adventure in front of him juxtaposed against the heartache of leaving her behind. She came bounding across the street, her usual exuberance tempered with the sight of the For Sale sign.

"You might be gone for a year?" she repeated, questioning whether she should have torn down her wall. She plopped herself on the grass, the ramifications of what she heard sinking in. "No, Charlie. I need you here."

"We'll text every day. Every hour!" emphasized Charlie.

She looked back at him, tears making an unannounced appearance, marching through the front door of her vulnerabilities without knocking first. "I need you, Mr. Hustle."

Charlie dipped into his substantial savings the following day and purchased Jasmine a cell phone and an unlimited texting plan in her name. It required some questionable tactics, but the deviousness was worth it when he saw her relief.

"Remember, you are eighteen, Peg," warned Charlie, chuckling as he handed her the phone. She took it, feeling better they could keep in touch every day.

Charlie completed some final touches on his lawn, wishing to leave it in perfect condition for the new owner. Jasmine pitched in, raking, picking weeds with a tweezer, and edging at the curb.

Satisfied with the finished product, they both lay with their back on the grass, pleased to be spending one final day together. They shared their favorite sports stories, Charlie baseball and Jasmine football. As always, it evolved into a debate as to which was the best sport, neither of them giving an inch on the matter.

"Have you ever seen Beckham bend it, Charlie?"

"Have you ever seen a triple play?" retorted Charlie.

Agreeing to disagree, they focused their mutual attention on the sky, gazing up at the few fluffy white clouds that slowly drifted across the brilliant blue sky.

"Look, Charlie. That one looks like an elephant."

"Hmmm. Looks more like a Tiger Striper to me," replied Mr. Hustle.

Jasmine cocked her eyebrow, unconvinced. "How about that one? It looks like an airplane."

"It looks like a center fielder leaping for a fly ball, Peg."

Jasmine laughed. "Oh, Charlie, how about that one. It looks like an eagle."

"That I agree with," he replied, chuckling again. "I don't believe your dad is fond of me," announced Charlie.

"It's not you, Charlie. He's protective. There's a cloud following him around. He's never been the same person."

"I understand," came the reply.

"And you *are* a little crazy according to Ms. Jenkins and Mr. Cooper," she said, poking him in the ribs.

"There's some truth in that," he agreed, his lips curling into a grin.

"How did your mom die?" asked Jasmine, turning serious.

"Skin cancer," explained Charlie. "She had a mole on the back of her neck; she never saw it growing, hidden by her hair."

"I know you miss her, Charlie," she said softly, grabbing his hand.

"The doctor said it was growing for years, that had it been detected earlier, she could have been saved. But it spread."

"Cancer is an awful disease, Charlie."

"That one looks like a baseball diamond," said Charlie, pointing to the latest cloud drifting by.

"A baseball diamond? It looks like nothing," she replied.

"You're not looking hard enough, Jasmine."

"Maybe, Charlie."

"My mother always told me that if you can't find God, you're not looking hard enough," explained Charlie.

"My mother told me that God is everywhere," replied Jasmine. "I'm not so sure about that anymore, but God is somewhere. God has to be."

"I saw the mole growing for over a year," Charlie blurted out. "I saw it several times. I knew it was growing and didn't say a word. I didn't say a word." His voice trailed off with the admission.

Jasmine grabbed his hand.

"I could have saved her," he confessed. "How could there be a God? How could a God allow your mom and sister to die like that?"

It was the first time he'd ever mentioned his guilt to anyone, the failure to warn his mother eating at him every day. He couldn't bring himself to apologize to Heather while she was alive; now, it was too late. Explaining to someone that you could have prevented their death is not an easy conversation.

"I understand your pain, Charlie. But you didn't know what it meant."

"That one looks like Miguel Cabrera," said Charlie, pointing high to the northeast.

"Nah, it looks like Alaine Ekwe," replied Jasmine.

CHAPTER TWENTY-SEVEN

Road Trip

"On the road again, goin' places that I've never been, seein' things that I may never see again, and I can't wait to get on the road again." David pushed in the CD, rolled the window down, and belted out Willie Nelson's tune as the Ungers pulled out of their driveway to begin the journey of a lifetime.

Charlie sat shotgun, clad in his Tigers uniform, warmed by the joy in his father's voice, amazed that it was the first time he could recall hearing him sing. Mr. Hustle looked over at the driver, thankful to be with his dad; however, the pensive sadness of watching Jasmine's house disappear clawed at his attention. The two friends had said their goodbyes last night, Jasmine lacking the heart to wave him off today.

David quickly returned his son's look. "What, you don't like my singing?"

There was something different in his father's eyes, his old ones replaced with a newer, exciting version—a pair that danced with the possibilities, the kind that only come with giving it your best shot.

"It's not very good, to be honest, but go on," replied Charlie, sitting high in the cab, understanding the Unger boys were making a fresh start.

Charlie rolled down his window as they passed by Ms. Jenkins, who was out front working on her garden, turning his back toward her to show the name on the uniform.

"Charles T. Unger, coach of the Tigers, at your service!" he yelled out the window.

"Crazy kid," she retorted to her husband, shaking her head. She stood up and watched the back of the RV disappear down the street along with the large blue-and-orange sign fastened to the rear: Go Tigers!

As they made the first turn off their street, Charlie looked back at their house, maybe for the last time. As the Old English *D*, spray-painted navy blue and embedded in the perfect lawn faded from view, Charlie harbored no regret at leaving it all behind, except, of course, for Jasmine.

Jasmine was at her window, peeking through the curtains as her best friend left her, the single tear on her face confirming she was in love. "Good luck, Charlie Unger," she said, waving through the window as the RV disappeared.

For both Unger men, it was surreal, hitting the road with the horizon in front, a new beginning, and an acceptance that an uncertain future was the only certainty. David was nervous, unsure if he had made the right decision, but he was confident that it was a choice he needed to make to ensure there would be no further regret in his life. The liberation was real; to have his son beside him meant the world to him—a second chance to be a good father and earn his son's respect.

Charlie had become a burgeoning mini-celebrity, seemingly overnight. When the Tigers' press release shot across the news wires and the media discovered that the Tigers had hired a thirteen-year-old coach, Mr. Hustle was inundated with interview requests. The interest was not limited to Michigan, or even the United States, but came from across the world, as far away as China, Japan, and the Dominican Republic. Charlie quickly learned how to say baseball in dozens of foreign languages: *bankqui* in Chinese, *yakyuu* in Japanese, and *beisbol* in Spanish.

Who was Charlie Unger, the youngest professional baseball coach ever? Every baseball enthusiast wanted to know. Once the Tigers players were free to discuss the young phenom's impact on their games, Charlie's popularity increased further. Mr. Hustle accommodated as many interviews as possible from the comfort of his captain's chair, holding court with his subjects in the spirit of King Henry VIII. But Charlie saved his very first interview for a local call.

"This is KRBA 690 Detroit, your favorite stop for everything sports!" announced Nelson Green. "I have a very special caller on the line, the newest coach in the Tigers organization, who just happens to be only thirteen years old. Welcome, Charlie!"

"Good morning, Green Machine," replied Charlie.

"First things first, Charlie. I have a little crow to eat. The last time I had you on, you offered up what I thought was a hair-brained idea about King Fisher's batting woes. You said it was his new, heavier bat. I was wrong. Mea culpa, Charlie. I bow down, sir."

"No problem, Mr. Machine. Just pleased King Fisher is tearing it up and grateful I could play a part."

The two discussed the Tigers for another ten minutes, Charlie providing his views on a multitude of topics.

"Charlie, rumor has it that you have a tendency to knock three times on your head. What's up with that, kid?"

Charlie was stunned by the question, a question directed at the heart of his insecurities, an uncontrollable act that had caused him ridicule for as long as he could remember. And now, millions of people were awaiting a response.

Charlie looked at his dad for help. David shrugged his shoulders, not knowing how to help his son.

"Mr. Machine, if you see me knocking on my head, you'll know I'm thinking about something great."

"Okay, Mr. Hustle. I believe it!" replied Green, putting his head close to the microphone and rapping three times on his head. "Do you hear that, everyone? Look for Mr. Hustle smacking that big brain of his because good things will follow."

David looked at his son, nodded, and mouthed the words, "Great answer."

"One final question, Charlie. Why do you love baseball so much?"

The truth was, the game had always been there for him, in the loneliest and darkest of times. When his mother died, he relied on the excited screams from the seats, the unbridled passion, the quest for greatness to pick him up just enough to keep going. However, he decided upon another answer, also true, but succinct.

"The crack of the bat, Mr. Machine. There's nothing better than the sound of the crack of the bat."

"Amen to that, Charlie!" And with that answer, the interview was complete.

"Well done, my boy. No media training required for you," said David.

The following two weeks flew by. The Unger boys made their way west across Michigan toward their first destination, Chicago, where the Tigers took on the White Sox. The two sang every baseball song known; "Take Me Out to the Ball Game" and John Fogerty's "Centerfield" were sung so frequently, they both agreed that those two ditties would remain shelved until their arrival in Cincinnati, when the Tigers took on the Reds.

En route, David shared some of his favorite moments from high school. As a sophomore, but playing for the senior team, David hit a grand slam in the bottom of the ninth with two out to win the league championship game. The thrill of rounding the bases and seeing the excitement on the faces of his teammates waiting at home plate was a memory that was etched in his mind.

"I can still see Bobby Little's face, a bench warmer. We may as well have won the World Series, the indescribable excitement on his face, Bobby jumping higher than I had ever seen him leap before. The energy that was thrown over me when they mobbed me at home plate was a feeling that I've never felt again."

Then, in his junior year, while patrolling center field, a ball was hit deep over David's head. He drop-stepped to his left and knew he had an excellent route to the ball. Feeling the warning track under his feet, he took two steps and leaped as high as he could, stepping on top of the home run fence and springing into the air, the ball falling into his glove for the third out.

"My feet must have been ten feet off the ground, Charlie. As I jogged back in, every single person in the park was on their feet, clapping, including the other team, including the guy that hit it."

"Wow, Dad. I wish I was there."

"Charlie, it was at that moment that I truly understood what good sportspersonship and respect for the game meant. My opponents respected the game and respected that catch more than winning. I will never forget it."

Charlie nodded, taking it all in, making mental notes on every word out of David's mouth.

"Remember, Son, no individual is bigger than the game. Never forget it."

When David pulled their new home on wheels into the campground the first night, near dinner time, after five hours on the road, Charlie felt full inside, the feeling having nothing to do with their midafternoon meal at Steak 'n Shake.

David couldn't believe that his son had found an RV park with a batting cage. After a meal of Kraft Macaroni & Cheese and hotdogs with S. Rosen poppy seed buns, David took some swings. Still in his uniform, Charlie carefully stood by, taking notes and providing instruction.

Now that Charlie was on the payroll, he had access to all the Tigers' internal data and scouting reports. When Mr. Kilmer sent him a password, he began salivating at the possibilities. How would he ever get any sleep?

David was swinging the bat well, but there were significant differences between a batting cage fastball and professional pitching, but he could still focus on his swing mechanics.

They took in the Chicago White Sox afternoon game at Cellular Field the following day, a 4–1 win for the Tigers. Charlie started with a bacon-cheddar pretzel dog in the first inning, paired with a juicy Vienna beef hot dog topped with nacho cheese. He downed a chicken parmesan sandwich in the fifth, topped with mozzarella cheese and served between a warm garlic ciabatta bun. Finally, in the seventh, to celebrate a Miggy dinger, Charlie ordered a thinly sliced rib eye steak specialty, tossed in a pico de gallo sauce, all served on a hoagie roll.

That evening, back at their home on wheels, David and Charlie sat in lawn chairs underneath the RV canopy. Several

Chicago fans strolled over and provided some good-natured ribbing to the out-of-towners. When they discovered Charlie's connection to the Tigers, autograph seekers lined up for signatures and photos, many that ended up on social media that night. Every one of those fans thanked Charlie and knocked three times on their heads before they left.

Once the Ungers found themselves alone, the two enjoyed the gentle cracking of the campfire with iced tea in their hands.

"How does it feel to be a celebrity, Charlie?"

"Everything is happening so fast. Hopefully I'm liked because of me, not because I'm a Tigers coach."

"Anyone who knows Charlie Unger in here," offered David, pointing to his son's heart, "will love him. I promise. You're an amazing person. Someday, everyone will know it."

David became quiet as he sipped on his tea, jiggling the ice cubes around in his glass, the tiny blocks of ice quickly melting because of their proximity to the fire.

"What are you thinking about, Dad?"

David smiled softly and tossed a baseball up into the air, catching it with his bare hand on the way down.

"It's strange, watching those pros play today, knowing I will be playing professional ball in nine days. It's not the same as the show, but it's still pro ball."

David tossed the ball over to Charlie, which dropped to the grass when he failed to catch it. They both laughed.

"That's why I'm the coach," explained Charlie. Charlie's mind drifted to Peg, how they laughed when he dropped her football when she tossed it to him. It prompted him to send her a quick text to say goodnight.

"Dad, you have world-class speed, even at your age. You'll be playing at Comerica Park soon. I feel it in my bones. I'm as sure as anything that I've ever been sure of before."

David nodded his head, but he knew the odds were not with him. The odds were terrible, and at his age, they were worse than awful. His heart told him that the goal of this journey was about playing further than single-A ball, but his head leveled with him, told him the cold, hard truth. This was a long shot, the only reasonable view.

"I love summer, Charlie," said David, taking in a deep breath of the campfire smoke and late-season scented lilacs that were scattered throughout the park.

Charlie looked at his father and shook his head. "Summer is great, but fall is the perfect season. Yes sir, October—when the postseason begins; that's when legends are made."

The following morning, up before the sun, the RV hit the road, heading toward Cincinnati for a late-afternoon game. Luckily, when they arrived, they found a spot to park in the stadium parking lot, where they joined scores of other tailgaters under the sunshine. After signing twenty autographs and devouring a beef brisket lunch, courtesy of another Tigers fan, David and Charlie headed into the game.

Later that night, after a Tigers 3–2 loss, Charlie's dejection over the loss was replaced with surprise after discovering that he now had over six thousand followers on his Facebook page, and two thousand likes from his afternoon post. Maybe he was becoming a celebrity?

"How about we watch *Bull Durham* on the satellite TV?" suggested his father.

Charlie responded in a split second, "Of course."

So the boys sat down on the couch, popped some popcorn, and watched *Bull Durham*, a movie that was entirely inappropriate for a boy of Charlie's age.

Charlie loved *Bull Durham*, a movie about the minor-league baseball team the Durham Bulls. When it was over and they readied themselves for bed, Charlie looked over at his dad and quoted the movie, "You see, Dad, baseball is a very simple game. You throw the ball. You catch the ball. You hit the ball. Sometimes you win. Sometimes you lose. Sometimes it rains."

"Charlie, I'm recommending that the newest coach to the Detroit Tigers comes up with something more sophisticated if you want to keep your job," suggested David, winking.

Charlie looked at his dad, "If it wasn't so complicated, it would be simple."

"Who said that, Yogi Berra?" asked David.

"No, I did," laughed Charlie, throwing a pillow at his father.

Suddenly, David was distracted by the television. He stood up and cranked the volume as images of rioting in downtown Detroit crossed the screen. The violence and destruction were escalating as racial tensions bubbled over. Reverend Baptiste repeated his calls to boycott professional sports, including the Tigers games.

In the next segment, Mad Dog Madison was interviewed, the reporter asking his views on the call to boycott.

"I'm a black man in a white man's world. It's time for change in America, and something needs to be done now. Not tomorrow. Not next week. Now." Luis walked away without directly answering the question.

217

Charlie and David looked at each other, worried and concerned.

"I'm sure that everything will get worked out, Charlie," said David with a sigh. "Don't worry."

"Dad, Jasmine told me that she had never been called the N-word until she came here."

Horrified, David looked down at his son, pausing to formulate his response. "Wow, I'm sickened to hear that. I don't know what to say."

They both had the same thought: baseball didn't seem quite as crucial while watching the carnage in Detroit.

Two days later, the two headed off to Atlanta to see the Tigers take on the Braves for a series. Then, they were off to Phoenix, Arizona, to the Diamondbacks series. Franklin McNeil treated the Ungers like kings, going well beyond a couple of complimentary tickets. The good-natured president spared no expense, rolling out the red carpet for his visitors. He put them up in the presidential suite at the Waldorf Astoria for the weekend and provided David full access to the team's practice facilities.

The Ungers watched each game with their host in his luxury box, equipped with an extensive buffet. Whether it was the poblano cheesesteak, beer cheese bratwurst, or the Danzeisen Dairy milkshakes, Charlie left each game comfortably stuffed. His father, needing to remain in game shape, stuck to low-calorie options.

McNeil was aware of the hoopla surrounding Charlie's new position with the Tigers and peppered him with questions about his own players.

"Why do you think George Kennedy is having control problems?"

Mr. McNeil offered Charlie a job by the end of the weekend, Mr. Hustle reminding him that he was now under contract. McNeil laughed.

"Of course, Charlie. Or should I call you Mr. Hustle?"

"Either is good, thank you."

"Have you spoken to Pete Rose about that nickname of yours?" asked McNeil, referring to the original Charlie Hustle.

Charlie responded without missing a beat, "I wouldn't bet on it," causing McNeil to double over with laughter, aware of the MLB's concern with Pete Rose having bet on baseball games.

"Charlie, my boy, you are one of a kind. Brilliant and funny."

McNeil took it in stride when he and Charlie were featured on the oversized stadium scoreboard. A chant emerged, "We want Charlie! We want Charlie!" apparently protesting McNeil's refusal to fire the embattled Diamondback manager, Perry Childs.

Charlie didn't want to, but he couldn't hold back. On full display on the stadium screen, he knocked three times on the side of his head, afraid that his face would begin turning crimson red with embarrassment. Instead, the crowd erupted with pleasure, at least half the crowd responding by knocking on their heads. Even McNeil partook by knocking, causing Charlie to giggle.

The Tigers won two out of three in Arizona to continue their march up the standings, finding themselves third in their division. Phoenix was the Ungers' final stop before heading off to Lakeland, Florida, to join the single-A minor club team.

After checking out of the Waldorf Astoria, the last leg of their journey now in front of them, the nerves came knocking on David's door as they pulled onto the interstate.

"It's getting real now, Charlie. I've got to show up and play some ball, some good ball. What if I'm a big flop and this was all a waste of time?" Charlie's response had David considering which of them was the adult in the vehicle.

"Waste of time? Are you kidding me? It's never a waste of time to follow your dreams. Dreams make life tolerable. Following your dreams makes life worth living."

David nodded his head. He agreed, but his heart and mind had conflicting messages.

"Dad, what did the great Babe Ruth say? You know, the Great Bambino, the Sultan of Swat."

"I know who he is, Charlie!" came David's reply, complete with a roll of the eyes.

"Never let the fear of striking out hold you back. I believe that," explained Charlie, gazing out the window. Mr. Hustle watched a group of kids playing stickball in a sandy lot as the RV whizzed by, smiles on their faces and identifiable twinkles in their eyes from fifty yards away. The dust kicked up as one of the kids stepped over a jacket, doubling as home plate, raising his hands in celebration. "Dad, this adventure will not work out unless it's fun. That's the key."

David was quiet, embarrassed that he was leaning on his son to show strength and character, traits that Charlie had inherited from his mother. Not a day passed since his wife's death that he didn't recognize that Charlie would have been better off if it was him, rather than Heather, who had died. It was a hell of a thing to accept.

The RV whizzed by billboard after billboard, primarily personal injury attorneys in search of the maimed. Were there enough injured people to support all of those lawyers? wondered Charlie. Then they passed a giant billboard: Jesus Will Save Your Soul.

"I think there are as many Bible thumpers as attorneys, Dad," scoffed Charlie, pointing at the sign, hoping to remove the pensive look from his father's face and replace it with laughter.

But David did not laugh, shame sinking its grappling hooks into him and climbing aboard. What message had he imparted on his son? It wasn't decency. It wasn't respect. Heather's faith had navigated her through an illness that robbed her of everything, except her dignity. How could he have been so cruel?

"Charlie, I was wrong. Everything I said was wrong. Out of respect for your mother, let's never use that phrase again. I don't have all the answers, but I should never have said those things." His voice trailed off.

Silence ensued for a few minutes, reflection dominating. David pressed rewind on his life and paused at every regret, necessary before pressing onward. A familiar glaze formed over his face, identical to the one that occurred so often in the kitchen as he sipped on an awful cup of joe.

Charlie focused on his mother, a warm feeling colliding with the unimaginable guilt stuck in his soul. Mixed together, it was impossible to untangle.

"Agreed, Dad," replied Charlie finally, the pair satisfied with their understanding.

"Can we make fun of lawyers though?" asked Charlie.

"Definitely lawyers," replied David, smirking. "They deserve it!"

David pulled off the highway, carefully meandering through the parking lot, squeezing the RV into the Dunkin' Donuts drive-through. Charlie ordered his favorite, chocolate dipped with sprinkles.

"And, you, sir?" asked the teenager through the window.

"Small black French vanilla, please," he ordered, memories of his wife's favorite washing over him.

Two days later, the Unger boys rolled into Lakeland, Florida, mid-afternoon, the day before David was to join his teammates for an extended homestand. Charlie filled the drive by communicating with Tigers players and sifting his way through all the Tigers' data. He also began writing code for a new app that he was developing to provide team coaches instant access to any stat on their phones.

After securing their rolling home at a local KOA park, the Ungers strolled four blocks and made their way to a local fair. Not wanting to spoil the dinner of barbequed steak and baked potato that his father promised later, Charlie settled for a light snack of deep-fried ice cream.

The highlight, however, had David knocking down six milk bottles with one throw of a baseball, eleven times in a row, which eventually drew a chanting crowd, "One more time! One more time!" Charlie envisioned Jasmine wowing the bystanders back in Plymouth; he bet Jasmine could knock them down eleven times as well.

After his father's performance, which the carny said was a record, David returned to the RV for an afternoon nap. Waffling, he reluctantly permitted Charlie to remain for one more hour after promising to return to the camp by 6:00 p.m.

Charlie wandered around and played a few games of darts and Whack-a-Mole. Drawn to a vendor selling deep-fried gummy bears, he remained disciplined, thinking of the rib eye steaks marinating in the fridge. As he left the gummies in his rearview mirror, Charlie knew exactly where he would end up, identifying the destination as soon as he entered the grounds with his father.

After traveling a few hundred feet, Charlie came to a stop, carefully studying the sign now in front of him: Communicate with the Afterlife—Medium Services. Charlie tentatively stepped to the tent door and peeked in, déjà vu washing over him while he scanned the room.

Cool air from within the mobile structure struck his face, relieving the sweltering heat. Strange, because there was no evidence of an air conditioner or fan. Old photos, some black-and-white, sat atop a rudimentary shelf in the corner. Charlie believed that he recognized some of them, celebrities perhaps. Framed certificates, and awards of some type, rested beside them haphazardly, consistent with the transient lifestyle of someone who was never in one spot more than a few days. Quiet and creepy, thought Charlie, the hairs on the back of his neck springing to attention. Relieved the room was empty, his hand began to close the door, but a hoarse female voice interrupted him.

"I'll be right there, sweetie."

Seconds later, a petite lady with a cane in her left hand appeared from the back, swaying side to side on account of an arthritic left hip. She smiled through her pain, deep wrinkles giving away her membership in the century club. Her thin white hair had not seen a brush today. Charlie wondered if she had a glass eye, the pair not moving in unison.

"Come in. Sit down, young man," she instructed encouragingly.

Charlie opened the door and tentatively stepped in, trepidation harnessing his movement. Once fully in, she encouraged him, "Come on now. Sit down."

Her visitor sat down in a rickety wooden chair, the creak and wobble giving doubt to its structural soundness, Charlie now questioning his light snack.

"How can I help you, young man?" she asked, knowing the answer. Charlie wasn't the first lost soul to open her door, although this was the first teenager in years.

At least she didn't refer to him as Mr. Hustle, thought Charlie. "I'm not sure, to be honest," replied Charlie nervously, a falsehood precipitated by his uneasiness.

"Fifty bucks for kids," she said.

Charlie stood up, pulled out his wallet, and laid five $10.00 bills on the table.

"Let's start with your name then."

"Charlie Unger."

"I'm Elaina. Do you know what a medium is, Charlie?"

Of course, he did, nodding up and down.

"May I take your hands?" she asked.

Taking his silence as tacit approval, the old woman took Charlie's hands into hers and looked directly into his eyes. The warmth of her rough palms became hot, their hands melding together. It felt good, comforting, but be he didn't know why. It was somehow different than Marlene.

"Charlie, why are you here, dear?" she repeated.

The answer was simple, "I want to speak to my mom."

Elaina nodded. "I see. Are you here with anyone?"

"No."

"There are no guarantees," said Elaina, a warning that troubled Charlie, his fifty bucks already scooped up off the table.

"I understand," he replied faintly, dryness in his mouth setting in.

"Just relax." She smiled at him. "It's not a test."

His eyes remained fixed on hers, Charlie nodding his head up and down slowly. What would Polaris think about all this? This was no time for rational, logical thought.

"Can you see my mother?" blurted out Charlie, his mind racing fast.

Elaina closed her eyes and held Charlie's hands tightly, but did not respond.

"I'm not sure, Charlie, but I don't think so. I'm receiving a message of twins? Does that mean anything to you?"

Charlie didn't know any twins. He racked his brain but he was certain that it meant nothing to him.

"No, Elaina. I'm positive."

The medium remained silent for several minutes, a trance enveloping her. Finally, she addressed her young guest again. "It's still there, the twins. I'm definitely seeing twins. I could be wrong, but I don't think so."

Charlie didn't know what to make of it, but he felt like exploding, the disappointment throwing his excited anticipation out the door. He looked down at his watch; it was 6:02 p.m. "Dang it. I'm late, Elaina!"

Charlie hustled back to the park, kicking himself for getting fleeced of fifty bucks, but more importantly, for allowing his hopes to rise. Duped by another charlatan. Polaris would not be impressed.

When he opened the RV door, breathing heavily with sweat dripping off his face, Charlie was thankful to find his father napping on the couch. The nap morphed into an all-night sleep, ensuring David would be well rested for his big day with the Flying Tigers.

Sunday morning arrived. After a breakfast of bacon, eggs, and freshly squeezed Florida orange juice, the two headed to the stadium where manager Lou Park greeted the duo and sat them down in his disorderly office. Generally a friendly man, Park had a reputation for going ballistic when plans went off the rails. Earlier in the year, he threw every last bat from the dugout onto the field when his team made three consecutive errors. It was that untamed temper that had him stuck managing in the minor leagues for the entirety of his career. Every year for the last ten, he announced it would be his last, but he couldn't shake the game.

Lou shook hands with the thirty-six-year-old rookie forced upon him by Rodney Kilmer. "Welcome aboard, David," he said through a forced smile.

It was ridiculous, in his opinion, that he was taking on a ballplayer at that age who was beginning his career, another one of Rod's special projects. He was in his final year anyway. Kilmer was pretty excited about the guy. "Lou, give him an opportunity. He's the real deal!" emphasized Rod on the phone that morning. Park had heard it before.

Lou saved his genuine excitement for Charlie. "Hello, young man," he said, extending his huge bear-sized paw, his hand matching his bear-sized body.

"Thank you, sir," replied Charlie, gripping the bear paw back tightly. Lou squeezed back even tighter. Neither let go, and the contest was on. Lou came to his senses when he saw the grimace forming on Charlie's face, appreciating the mismatch. However, he was impressed that Charlie even took him on.

I like this guy, thought Charlie, as Lou released his clench.

"David, you will see Dr. Parker for a physical at 1:00 p.m. Your gear and uniform are in the clubhouse. I hope you're okay with number eight. I've asked Frank Little, our trainer, to show you around. Our pregame warm-up is at 5:00 p.m., and game time is 7:00 p.m. tonight."

"Thanks, Lou, I'm excited to be here."

"So, Charlie, are you as brilliant as they say?" Lou had heard the rumors for weeks, that a young phenom corrected Mad Dog's swing and a handful of others that kicked off a torrid run for Detroit. Lou was skeptical of the claims. Admittedly, the Tigers were on a great run, and only three games out of a wild card spot heading into the last month of the season, but how could this teenager be responsible? Some noses were out of joint; no Major League coach wants to be outshone by a teenager. But Charlie Unger was considered a rock star by Kilmer and Earley.

Charlie considered Lou's question. He wondered who "they" were. Apparently, humility was an admirable quality. His mother had told him so, and she was a brilliant mom.

"I believe so, Mr. Park." It was the best he could do, remaining humble and honest.

Lou laughed. "I appreciate honesty, Charlie. I think you and I will get along just fine."

CHAPTER TWENTY-EIGHT

The Great Divide

Luis Madison sat down with William Baptiste and his wife for Sunday dinner. As Georgina placed the pot roast, pork-filled dumplings, and butternut squash on the table, the ball player knew that more than the food was on the menu. He recognized the strain in the reverend's eyes, having witnessed it many times growing up. The three of them routinely shared a weekly meal, except when the Tigers were on the road. The Baptistes were his family, raising him from a baby and supporting him through some difficult teenage years.

The two men were incredibly close, more than a typical father and son relationship. However, the reverend's call for a boycott of the Tigers strained their relationship, given that Luis was very loyal to the organization that employed him. Over the last fourteen years, the Tigers had been very good to him, including drafting him out of college despite some run-ins with the law. Kilmer and Earley always had his back; he considered them friends. Mad Dog was not inclined to cause the club any harm, loathing the possibility.

Kilmer came to Madison when Baptiste began his very public campaign to boycott, "Luis, you've got to rein him in," pleaded Kilmer. "This organization is not racist. The community needs the Tigers in these tough times. It's how fans escape."

It was true. Luis did not consider the organization racist, but that did not prevent him from being caught in the uncomfortable middle of a brewing dispute. And now, his team was on one heck of a tear because of its excellent play over the last twenty games. The city of Detroit was excited at the possibility of a playoff berth; the enthusiasm was palpable on the streets, those wearing Tigers garb increasing as the Tigers marched up the standings. Many of Luis's teammates had reminded him that the organization didn't need Baptiste's distraction. Luis agreed.

Mostly, he and the reverend stayed away from the subject, but that was about to change at the dinner table.

"Luis, I don't like this divide between us. Trust me, I don't want to hurt you, but I feel very strongly about what I'm doing. My moral compass directs me to speak out and lead our community."

"Nobody is closer to me than you, William," replied Luis, shaking his head sideways. "From the moment I ended up on your doorstep until this very day, you've been there for me. I trust you more than anyone."

"Then join me. Stand by me, and let's make change happen!" exclaimed Baptiste, grabbing Mad Dog's arm.

"It's not that simple," replied Mad Dog. "I respect what you're doing, and I agree that change is needed. But most police officers are good and decent. Most people are good and decent. The Tigers have been great to me."

Baptiste paused before responding. "The ramifications of our struggle are not always easy. Search your heart, and you'll know what's right, Luis. The people of Detroit look up to you. They'll follow you."

"That's my concern. It's not black-and-white, William."

"Right and wrong are always black-and-white. Justice is black-and-white. What are you afraid of, Luis?"

Luis shook his head, knowing nothing he said would sway his godfather from his convictions; he wasn't sure he even wanted to sway him. The man's stubbornness could be frustrating, but the commitment to his beliefs was admirable.

"Luis, fear makes the wolf seem bigger than it is. What are you afraid of?"

They were family, and they loved each other, but there would be no meeting of the minds today on boycotting the Tigers, although they agreed the pot roast and dumplings were delicious.

CHAPTER TWENTY-NINE

High Flying

In David's first game as a Tiger, the Lakeland Flyers took on the Tampa Tarpons at Publix Field. While Florida's humidity had everyone wiping their brows, the heat was overshadowed by the excitement permeating the air, the unique variety that baseball brings. Anything can happen in a game—at any time, a fan may be treated to something spectacular.

Charlie thought of his dad's catch in high school, leaping onto the top of the fence with the power of a mountain cat, stretching out and robbing his opponent of a home run. How Charlie wished he could have seen it. Every witness to that catch was still thinking about it, sharing the memory whenever the great game of baseball came up. Had they seen a better catch since? Doubtful. Don't turn your head for an instant while watching, at any level, or you might miss a once-in-a-lifetime play.

The eighty-five-hundred-person stadium was sold out—completely packed, adding to David's angst. He didn't expect to be in the starting lineup and was relieved when Lou posted the lineup on the dugout wall, confirming he was on the bench. David hadn't even practiced with his teammates yet, and here he was sitting on the bench with them. His fellow players were friendly enough, but there were a few grandpa-type comments. Some specimen of a man nicknamed Robocop smiled at him and asked if the trainers should place an oxygen tank on the bench. It was good-natured, but it reinforced how far-removed David was from the comfort of a courtroom.

Lou pulled #8 aside and told him that each player was striving to make it to the show. "Make no mistake, David. Each of these players sees single-A as a stepping stone to the bigs. Each of you stands in the other's way."

Lou invited Charlie onto the bench during games, an unexpected invitation that garnered further attention to the boy wonder. "You're on the payroll, Mr. Hustle; you might as well be on the bench helping any way you can." I might need some advice, Park thought to himself, chuckling.

The front-row seat was a pleasant surprise to Charlie. It wasn't Comerica Park, but it was a professional ballpark, and Charlie had the best seat in the house. When he took the field, he sat down on the bench, tilted his head back, closed his eyes, and took a deep breath through his nose. Novertdortis. Cut grass from an actual ball field smelled better than from his front lawn, somehow. He breathed in his airborne elixir, the magical cure-all far more effective than anything found in a pharmacy.

Charlie was in pregame demand, the power of the uniform filling him with confidence as he shook hands with fans. He answered questions, signed autographs, took selfies, and did what he did best—talked baseball.

Mr. Hustle didn't expect his father to play in his first game; however, he had no idea that Kilmer had given Lou Park some specific instructions to get Unger some playing time quickly.

In the eighth inning, with the Flyers down by two and a man on first, David received the call to pinch-hit. "Unger, you're in for Lewis," yelled Parks.

Oh, boy, thought David, not expecting to be brought into the game. He popped off the bench and grabbed his bat, catching Lewis with his peripheral vision shaking his head in dismay at the substitution. David focused, trying to batten down the nerves gaining the upper hand, but he was sure his wobbly legs undermined any attempt to exhibit confidence.

"Isn't there a senior's league somewhere, Coach?" asked Lewis.

Park ignored Lewis and looked at David, "Relax, Unger, and let it rip."

David nodded slowly, his heart pounding faster than he could ever remember. Having eight thousand fans stare at you as you walk to home plate is not something one can prepare for. There hadn't been an opportunity for the team to ask David about a walk-up song, so the Flyers' entertainment technician took it upon himself to choose a song: "Grampa's Got Game," by the Oldtimers. His teammates chuckled on the bench, the laughter discernible to the rookie, as the lyrics shot out through the speakers. Even Lou smirked, believing he had seen it all before today.

Charlie began breathing slowly, trying to calm himself. His father had dropped everything, exchanged one life for another, and taken a glorious leap of faith. He couldn't wait to hear the crack of the bat, to see every doubter become a believer in front of his own eyes. Park was gazing down the bench when he witnessed the newest coach knock three times on the side of his head, bringing a scrunched face and squint from the manager. Park put his palms out. What the heck was that? he wondered.

David stepped up to the plate as the music blasted, the stomping of the crowd's feet keeping pace with the song's pounding. *Grampa's got game; once you see me, son; you'll never be the same; yes sir, get those young legs ready; be prepared to run.*

David dug in, twisting his cleats into the dirt.

"Are you lost?" asked the twenty-year-old catcher. "The old age home is down the street."

"Strike one," yelled the umpire as a fastball sailed down the middle of the plate without a swing.

"You can do it, Unger!" yelled Charlie. Mr. Hustle looked up to the blue sky to pray, and then realized the ridiculousness of such action, shaking his head in disgust for violating his scientific principles.

"Strike two," yelled the umpire as a nasty slider caught the edge of the outer corner without a swing.

Charlie tensed up. This was not looking good. Use that magical swing of yours, Dad, he thought to himself.

"Are you ever going to swing that bat, gramps?" asked the catcher, chuckling and looking back at the umpire, who responded with a snort and a smile.

David focused, telling himself he would not go down on a called third strike. Swing at anything close, the cardinal rule in baseball.

The pitcher wound up and released the ball. David watched it come out of his hand and saw the spin, indicating a two-seam fastball. Except, it was a change-up. That juicy-looking pitch, heading straight down the middle, was still two feet from the plate when David swung, the ball hitting the dirt just in front of home plate. He was so far out in front of the pitch, he dropped to his right knee, missed the ball, and looked like a fool.

The hometown crowd groaned in disapproval. David's head slumped in disappointment as the excited fans went quiet, except for scattered, disappointed murmuring. Many looked at each other with a wince, an expression that said, "Uh, oh, this rookie won't work out."

"Damn it," whispered Charlie, forgetting his promise not to swear. It dawned on him that he and his father had spent so much time on swing mechanics, they had failed to discuss the mental part of the game. What kind of bloody coach was he? He shook his head, discouraged and vowing to do better.

David walked back to the dugout, head down. He was met by icy silence at the bench; no, "You'll get 'em next time," or any other word of encouragement. Lou shook his head slightly. David knew exactly what he was thinking, "What the hell was this guy doing here?" It had been forever since he had played ball.

David was thankful when he did not get another at-bat in the ninth inning, pulled for another pinch hitter. After the game, David showered and exited the clubhouse as quickly as possible. What had he done? What the hell had he done, quitting his job and selling the house?

He stepped out into the parking lot where Charlie was waiting for him. "It's only one at-bat, Daddio! No biggie. We'll get 'em tomorrow!"

David and Charlie began the half-hour walk back to the RV, Charlie encouraging his father, David having none of it.

"What am I doing here?" asked David, the rhetorical question hanging in the thick humidity. Neither of them spoke another word during their return. The two pulled up lawn chairs around a roaring campfire with a snack and iced tea upon their arrival. The hypnotic flames warmed the pair and melted the tension.

Charlie finally broke the silence. "It's hard to beat a person who never gives up," stated Charlie matter-of-factly.

David looked up from his drink, which he was staring at. "What?"

"Yes, sir. Babe Ruth said that. The Bambino. The Sultan of Swat."

"It's not that simple, Charlie."

"It's exactly that simple," replied Charlie. "That's the beauty of those words."

David looked at his son and shook his head, confident that his son didn't understand. Two more minutes of silence went by when Charlie began to chuckle.

"What's so funny, mister?"

"It's something Jasmine always says to me."

"Well, what is it?"

"Fear makes the wolf bigger than it is. Her mother always said it."

David nodded.

"So, what are you afraid of, Dad?"

"What makes you think I'm afraid of anything?" responded David, looking up from the fire.

"Besides those shaky legs walking to the plate," said Charlie, smirking.

David laughed. "I thought my legs were going to collapse. What am I afraid of? Giving up my livelihood for a pipe dream. Looking like a fool. Did you hear all the fans laughing at my pathetic at-bat? But my greatest fear is continuing to be a poor father, to set the wrong example."

Charlie sat back in his lawn chair and put his hands behind his head. He considered his words carefully. "I wouldn't change this road trip for anything, for a million houses, or a million dollars. Hasn't your decision already been worth it?"

David appreciated his son's words, but it was hard to shake his perception that he had made a colossal mistake.

"Even if we head back to Plymouth tomorrow, this has all been a success, Dad."

David was weary of his son acting as the parent in their relationship.

"Never let the fear of striking out hold you back," announced Charlie.

"I know. I know. The Bambino," replied David.

"Bingo, Dad. I've got one last quote for you. I'll always be proud to stand by a man who dusts himself off and steps back into the batter's box after being knocked down by a brush-back pitch."

"Let me guess, Charlie, another Bambino quote."

"No, Dad, a Charlie Unger quote. It's an original."

David looked at his son, concerned that he could not meet his son's standards; it was a difficult notion to consider. Believing in an unattainable dream and letting his son down frightened him to his core.

After a further half hour of utter silence, the two Ungers prodding at the logs occasionally, David spoke, "Do you have any advice for tomorrow?"

"Of course, I do!" Charlie said, loud enough to draw the family's attention at the adjoining site. He missed Ms. Jenkins's scornful stares, strangely. "I've been waiting for you to ask."

The two of them got to work strategizing. "You struck out on three straight pitches today. You're playing Tampa again tomorrow. Their pitchers will have been chuckling at your plate appearance, convinced that you couldn't hit a beachball thrown down the middle. Trust me, you will receive a first-pitch fastball right down the middle tomorrow. Be ready to crush it."

"If I get to play. That's a big if. And if I don't hit it?" asked David.

"When you think a fastball is coming, be ready to hit the curve."

"What?" asked David.

"It's a hitting philosophy, Dad. In high school, you could get by on pure talent. These pitchers are too good. It's a chess match."

"Okay, I'm listening," replied David.

"Think like a pitcher. Hitting is timing. Pitching is upsetting timing. Pitchers use different locations, different speeds, and different pitches to upset your timing. You need to stay back for as long as possible and give your eye a chance to see the pitch and speed. Be patient."

David softly patted his son on the head, "Thanks, Son. Let's see what happens tomorrow. Exactly when did you become an adult? I must have missed that."

"One last piece of advice, Dad. Keep the walk-up song! I love it." Charlie began to sing, "Grampa's got game, once you see me son, you'll never be the same, yes sir, get those young legs ready, be prepared to run."

David was unaware there was almost no tomorrow. After the game, Lou Park was on the phone with Kilmer, cursing at him for sending him a little league player. Rodney understood and did trust Park's opinion. Maybe he did jump the gun, given that David hadn't played organized ball in such a long time. But what he'd witnessed at Comerica Field was special.

One at-bat, even a terrible one, was insufficient to cut the cord. "Give him one more game, Lou, and then we'll talk. Be nice to the kid, though, we're keeping him!"

Early the following day, both Charlie and David awoke at 8:00 a.m. When David stepped into the shower after breakfast, Charlie left a note and took the opportunity to walk back to the fair when it opened. He made a beeline to Elaina's, hoping she was available and accepting customers. Slowly poking his head into the tent, he was pleased to see her sitting there, alone, drinking a cup of steaming tea.

Elaina looked up and gave Charlie that soft smile of hers, as welcoming as a warm hug. Charlie stepped in, "Hello, Elaina. I brought money."

"Come sit down and put your money away, dear."

"Can you really speak to the dead, Elaina?"

"Yes, I can, Charlie. It's not the same as calling someone on the telephone. I see images that I have to interpret. Sometimes it's easy; sometimes it's difficult. When the physical body dies, the energy of the soul is released."

"I don't believe in God, Elaina."

"What do you believe in, Charlie?"

Charlie stared at her, tired of life's difficult questions.

"I don't know." He paused. It was true; he didn't know. "I believe in my Detroit Tigers."

"I'm a Marlins fan, but, hey, that Miguel Cabrera guy is pretty good," said Elaina, pretending to swing a bat.

Charlie laughed. "He's the best hitter ever!"

"Tell me about your mother, young man."

Charlie looked down at the floor. The change in subject caught him off guard, his emotions always close to the surface. Unexpectedly, the tears flowed, meandering down off his cheeks and onto the floor. Grief dripped off his face, marking its territory on the dirt floor below.

"Oh, honey. I'm sorry." Elaina stood up, pulled her chair close to Charlie, and hugged him.

"I miss her," mumbled Charlie through his tears. "I'm a peculiar fellow. She loved me as nobody else could have, and she's gone. Gone forever. I need to talk to her one more time. I need to apologize."

Elaina poured a glass of water and set it in her visitor's hands. "She'll speak to you when its time, Charlie. In my experience, when a loved one doesn't communicate, it's because their spirit wants you to hear from someone else first. They step aside for your good."

Charlie's head bobbed up and down. "I'm not aware of any scientific proof that a human can speak to someone in the afterlife."

Elaina laughed. "That's because science is not advanced enough, Charlie. Science hasn't figured out human consciousness, but we have it."

That's what Michael Star had said to him, recalled Charlie, remembering his advice at Reverend Baptiste's house. Charlie let the comment settle in, and then put a checkmark into the God column.

Elaina took his glass and set it on the table before taking his hands. Those rough and wrinkled hands of hers felt softer today. After a few minutes, she spoke. "I'm seeing twins again, Charlie. It's very clear. Crystal. Are you sure it doesn't mean anything to you?"

"I'm sure, Elaina. I really am." He shook his head, the disappointment repeated from a day earlier.

"Why don't you ask your father?"

"Hmmm. He doesn't know I'm here."

"I see," replied Elaina, who wiped the final tear that appeared under his left eye.

She continued to grasp Charlie's hands and focus. "I'm still seeing twins. It's strong. I'm not getting anything else, Charlie. I'm sorry, it's not your mother."

Charlie nodded. "It's okay. Thank you, Elaina. I better go, but might be back." He dashed out of the tent, running at top speed back to the RV. Was she a charlatan? He didn't think so; she didn't ask for payment today.

Charlie arrived at the campsite as his father was stepping out of the house on wheels. "Where have you been?"

"Just for a walk. I needed to think," a response that David questioned, but he couldn't think of where Charlie could have been, so he let it be.

"Listen, let's hurry, Mr. Hustle. I need to be at the park in an hour."

When the two arrived at Publix Field, David was shocked to find his name posted as the starting center fielder. Lou had decided that if he was going to send his rookie packing, he would at least play him a complete game and give him a proper opportunity.

Charlie cheered internally, watching those gazelle-like legs effortless take his father onto the field. He was as surprised as anyone that David was starting, thinking his dad would have his keester glued to the bench today. He hadn't wanted to share that opinion last night around the campfire, his father already carrying all that gloom around.

Charlie looked down the third base line and smiled when he saw a young boy holding a sign above his head, Unger the Ageless Wonder!

"Go, Unger!" screamed the fan. The crowd applauded the team as the starters made their way out to start the top of the first inning. His father looked confident, shoulders back, head up, and throwing to his fellow outfielders with pinpoint accuracy. He did not resemble the defeated man slumping in front of last night's fire. Charlie snuck a quick photo of David, inconspicuously, and texted it to Jasmine.

David caught a lazy fly ball in a 1-2-3-out first inning for the Flyers, slightly calming his nerves. Not surprisingly, David was placed ninth in the batting order, a spot generally reserved for the least effective hitter on the team. When he stepped into the batter's box in the bottom of the second inning with two out and men on second and third, he could feel the disagreeable looks from his teammates and fans. Everyone knew he shouldn't be there. David focused on his son's advice as he readied himself at the plate.

"Surprised you're still here, gramps," questioned the catcher, causing the umpire to chuckle. David barely heard the ribbing, concentrating on the pitcher. He didn't hear his son yelling at him in support either.

"Unger, the ageless wonder," yelled Charlie, standing up, excited in anticipation.

David's walk-up song pounded through the speakers. *Grampa's got game, youngsters 'bout to die of shame.*

The twenty-year-old pitcher on the mound, Sandy Jarvis, drafted third out of the University of Michigan, set himself. He was taking a 10–2 record into the game and was expecting a promotion to the organization's triple-A team next week. The always confident and sometimes cocky player looked toward home plate for the sign. Jarvis nodded, agreeing to the pitch that he and the catcher had discussed before the game.

The two had shared a pregame chuckle over the foolish old guy and his inept plate appearance the day before.

David took a deep breath as Jarvis set himself on the mound and began his windup. He watched the ball leave the pitcher's hand and begin its approach to home. Jarvis had been given the sign for a low fastball strike, but he elevated it slightly, arriving just under David's beltline. David took that moment, frozen in time, peeled back the four corners of his soul and retrieved every buried frustration, disappointment, and regret, transferring them squarely onto the surface of the oncoming ninety-three-mile-an-hour fastball.

When the pitch was ten feet from home, David began his swing, placing every desire and dream onto the end of his bat, forcing a showdown against the incoming ball, now carrying all his baggage.

A cannon went off in Publix Field. Well, that's how those in attendance explained it. Most described it as a sound never heard off a baseball bat, a crack so loud it turned every head in the packed park toward home plate, even those at the concession stands.

Crack! Sure, the warm air and slight breeze heading to left field aided the ball, but even incoming hurricane winds wouldn't have kept it in the park. It was still rising as it sailed over the left-center fence, traveling 456 feet. The center fielder didn't even bother to move when David struck the ball, an obvious no-doubter.

Lou Park jumped to his feet, "What the hell!" he whispered, his head following the ball all the way.

The snide and resentful comments stopped at the crack of the bat, any future pejoratives flushed away as they watched the ball leave the field of play.

"Holy crap," yelled first baseman Frank Keen, stepping out of the dugout in amazement, bringing his teammates with him.

Charlie went wild, jumping up and down. Like yesterday, Lou looked down at Charlie and observed the kid knock three times on his head. Maybe it was because of the excitement—Park never explained why—but he followed Mr. Hustle's lead, lifted his hand, and rapped three times on the side of his ball cap. Three million YouTube views of Park smacking his head occurred over the next twenty-four hours; Charlie's Facebook followers topped one million by the end of the same period.

David rounded third base and saw every one of his previously uninterested teammates standing at home plate, waiting for him. He wondered if he might cry, every hair on his body standing on end. He held it in until he saw Charlie at home, his boy's eyes wider than humanly possible, his son's feet higher than that body of his should have allowed for. It was all too much. By the time he joined the celebration, he had to wipe a few tears away.

Lou, who had not once joined his players at home plate over his career, joined the celebration at home, raised his hand, and gave David a high-five.

The home run kicked off an eighteen-for-forty run for David at the plate, a sizzling .450 batting average that turned heads throughout the Tigers organization.

Two days after David launched his monster home run, *Sports Center*, a national television sports show, featured David, the oldest minor-league rookie in the league's history. It was also determined that David's home run was the farthest ever struck at Publix Field. Suddenly, he had become a local celebrity in Lakeland.

An enterprising teenager took full advantage of David's rising popularity, purchasing a used T-shirt heat press off Kijiji for $125. He then bought one-hundred white T-shirts from a local discount clothing outlet. Finally, after designing an attractive logo, he took four hours to press it on all one hundred shirts. The last step was striking a deal with one of the souvenir vendors who had a stand outside Publix Stadium. They agreed on an equal split of the profits.

"Grampa's Got Game" T-shirts were everywhere after a few days. Those first shirts sold out in a day, and Charlie had to head back to the discount store and purchase five hundred more. It wasn't quite as lucrative as his investing algorithm, but the quick profits sparked many ideas in the budding entrepreneur. Besides, seeing his dad's face on all of those torsos was terrific. Charlie kept one for himself, something to wear when he wasn't in his Tigers uniform.

GM Kilmer was pleased with the success that David Unger had found in Lakeland. Likewise, he was thrilled with the analytics and observations that the youngest coach in Tigers history had provided. Charlie and Rodney spoke two or three times a week to discuss the players on the big-league team.

"Tim, we have to get this kid up here full time," remarked Rodney to his boss while seated for their weekly meeting. "We're in a playoff race, and we need every advantage."

CHAPTER THIRTY

Divided Loyalties

Reverend Baptiste organized a rally in front of Detroit's City Hall on the Sunday of the final weekend of August to protest police brutality. The passionate and often bombastic man had gained respect because of his extensive role in community development over the decades. He was revered in the black community as a person of principle who walked the talk. In for a pound, in for a penny.

Unwavering commitment to a cause became a frequent a source of conflict in the Baptiste household. His wife loved his passion, but her husband never walked away from a fight, regardless of the personal costs. William considered himself a warrior, battling black oppression and discrimination. He determined that personal sacrifice was required to defeat the enemy, and it was not for someone else to step up and take on the risk; it was his responsibility, a stance that had thousands of followers willing to do anything for him.

By 3:00 p.m., six hundred people had assembled at the rally, a figure that was exponentially swelling as the minutes ticked by. The anger and frustration in the black community had been building like a tidal wave over the years; it was cresting when Baptiste took the microphone.

The thirty Detroit police officers tasked with ensuring order became uneasy as they quickly became significantly outnumbered. Order would be near impossible to maintain should the protest escalate beyond a peaceful gathering.

In support of his godfather, Mad Dog attended the rally but with mixed emotions. His attendance was sure to attract attention from the press and his employer, but he felt a responsibility to the black residents of his community, and indeed the United States. Racism was a troubling issue in America, an ugly blight on the great country. Despite his success, the journey had had many barriers, the color of his skin the most formidable. Luis had borne the painful sting of racism far too often, his status of professional athlete failing to protect him. Last week, while walking alone, he watched as an oncoming white female on the same sidewalk slightly clutched her purse and crossed the street. Thirty seconds later, he turned around to observe her cross back, now that he was well past her. When he approached the reverend at the rally, this incident was on his mind.

"God bless you for coming, Luis."

"Of course," replied Mad Dog, squeezing the man who had raised him.

By 3:30 p.m., Mad Dog was thankful that he had attended, the solidarity with his brothers and sisters reinforcing the importance of the gathering. Privilege had sometimes delayed his perceived urgency to take action, the crowd's energy reminding him that their cause was righteous, his reservations dissipating. The chants, signs, and speeches created a festive atmosphere, but the mission was serious.

At 3:43 p.m., one of the protesters, now consuming his ninth beer, threw an empty beer bottle at Officer Robertson of the 14th Division. When it struck the side of Robertson's head, he dropped to the pavement like a sack of potatoes, instantly darkening the atmosphere. Several of the knucklehead's friends, who were just as inebriated, cheered at the sight of the fallen officer.

Reverend Baptiste and Mad Dog, a hundred feet away from the violent act, became outraged at what they had witnessed, neither of them condoning such behavior.

"Oh my God," declared Baptiste through a frown, blood now gushing from the fallen man's head.

"This is exactly what the movement doesn't need," exclaimed an exasperated Mad Dog, turning to his godfather, his reservations seeping back in. "I don't want to be associated with this, William!" declared Mad Dog. "This is not why I'm here!"

The two concerned men rushed over to check on the downed officer, pushing their way through the crowd, arriving to find him surrounded by his colleagues, who were attending to him.

"Is he okay?" asked Mad Dog.

"Get the hell back!" ordered a snarling beefy officer, sticking a baton directly into Mad Dog's chest, shoving him back with all his might.

"Hey, easy, man!" yelled Mad Dog, surprised and angered by the officer's response.

"We only want to ensure he is okay," exclaimed Baptiste genuinely, offering his empty palms to signal their lack of aggression.

"Get your black asses out of here before we make examples of both of you," growled Officer Pendleton.

"Hey, screw you!" screamed Mad Dog, stepping forward, unwilling to retreat from the racial belittling. In a flash, storm clouds of anger moved in; Pendleton felt the oncoming push of the crowd in support of Baptiste and swung his baton with full force, hitting Mad Dog in the midsection, sending him to the pavement. Pendleton raised the club again. As any father might, Baptiste came to Luis's rescue, punching Pendleton in the side of the face, preventing the baton from landing a second time.

Seeing their leader in the middle of a scuffle, a hoard of Baptiste supporters advanced to protect their leader, sending all officers in the vicinity to join their colleagues. The spectacle sent the unconfrontational scurrying away, the remaining clamoring for the challenge. The brawl was on.

Standing on the lawn in front of city hall, one attendee took it all in. Learning from her best friend, she had concocted an excuse, taken the bus, and arrived at the rally after three transfers. She had to be there, a desire burning strong from the instant she was called the N-word and mocked because of the shade of her skin. Realizing she had traded oppression on one continent for another, the righteous fire was lit, fanned into a raging inferno when Luis Madison hit the ground.

An hour later, four officers and six protesters were hospitalized, twenty received first aid on-scene, and ten were locked in jail cells, including Baptiste and Madison. Baptiste had been locked up briefly several times before, resulting from peaceful protests. However, Mad Dog was extremely shaken by the experience, the disturbing howls and clanking metal of the cells forever etched into his memory. He was also livid, seething from the way he had been treated by the Detroit Police and what he considered an unlawful arrest, stripped of his dignity and freedom.

Not surprisingly, the ugly confrontation and the accompanying arrests of Baptiste and his godson became not only a local story, but also a national and international story. Every Detroit television and radio station led with Mad Dog's altercation, his nickname providing easy fodder for media soundbites.

"Mad Dog Madison will be missing tonight's game. Why? Because a judge is keeping him locked in the doghouse after the player found himself embroiled in a riot yesterday. Thoughts? Is he setting a poor example? Is he letting down his teammates, who are gunning for a playoff spot? I want to know." The Green Machine used the two hours of the show to discuss Luis, the lively discussion somewhat split in perspective.

Two days later, William and Luis walked out of jail, courtesy of bail, but facing serious criminal charges of inciting a riot and assaulting a police officer.

How many other black men had sat in a cell, unlawfully, just as he had? The rhetorical question swirled in the ball player's mind, appreciating that his celebrity status afforded him no protection.

Earley was inundated with requests to comment. Years later, he admitted that his initial statement constituted the worst mistake of his professional career, talking without having all the facts. If only he had waited to speak to Luis first, the trajectory of the following month would have been different. Unfortunately for the president, the initial media reports had Mad Dog in the middle of a violent protest where a police officer was hit in the head with a beer bottle. And, with this incomplete understanding, he provided an ill-advised response to a reporter.

"We are disappointed that Luis Madison was involved in such an altercation with the Detroit Police Department and that an officer was injured. The Tigers organization provides its full support to the men and women in blue that protect our streets."

"Will Mad Dog be disciplined by the Tigers?" came the follow-up question.

"No decisions have been made yet," replied Earley.

Earley's statement was repeated hundreds of times over the next twenty-four hours on radio, television, and in print, all of which further enraged Madison.

A day later, Mad Dog stood by Reverend Baptiste's side at a press conference, calling for a boycott of the Tigers games. His previous reluctance was exchanged for resolve, fortified by a baton to the stomach and a lack of support from his employer. Luis offered his explanation, "What happened to me at the hands of the Detroit Police would not have occurred if I was a white man. It's time I played a role in shining a light on racism in this country. Effective immediately, I will not be playing for the Detroit Tigers and urge everyone who demands change to boycott Detroit Tigers games."

Earley and Kilmer watched the press conference from Comerica Park, Timothy's face becoming beet red with anger listening to Mad Dog.

"How could he do this to us, Rod?"

Rather than reaching out to his player, in an attempt to calm matters, Earley's emotions got the best of him. He was outraged himself.

"That son of a bitch! That ungrateful son of a bitch! Rodney, we have been nothing but good to the man, and this is how he repays us."

"Maybe you should talk to him, Tim?" suggested Rod.

Earley shook his head. "Not a chance! Stop his paycheck. Maybe the loss of a few million dollars will make him reconsider."

Earley considered Mad Dog's call for a boycott a slap in the face to an organization that had always supported his career. "How could he do it? We're only two games out of a playoff spot. How could he do that to his teammates, Tim?"

A day later, Kilmer realized that the Tigers' issues ran deeper than Mad Dog Madison. He nearly fainted when he learned that all seven of Mad Dog's black teammates were joining the boycott.

"Shit," said Kilmer, processing the development, completely caught off guard that all of them would risk everything, including a chance at a post-season berth.

This action was unprecedented in professional sports history, the Tigers organization caught flat-footed as this crisis unfolded. Mad Dog was a beloved Detroit sports hero, a rags-to-riches story that resonated with the community— growing up in an orphanage to become a successful professional baseball player.

When Earley discovered what had actually occurred at the rally, he publicly apologized to Mad Dog and reached out to him, but it was too late to push back the tide of the movement. The black community and many in other marginalized communities supported Mad Dog and his call to boycott, although it was not unanimous. Sentiment was split in Detroit and the nation.

The Tigers organization held an emergency board meeting to discuss the public relations disaster threatening the season. The team took out a full-page ad in the *Detroit Free Press* apologizing to Mad Dog and confirming their support for the black community and diversity.

One other important decision was made—seven players from their minor league teams, four of them black, were called up to fill the vacant positions. But those four black players refused to report, expressing their solidarity with Mad Dog. As a result, the Tigers had no choice but to call up seven non-black players.

CHAPTER THIRTY-ONE

Grampa's Got Game

After going two for four in a Flying Tigers' 3–2 win at Publix Field, David exited the shower. A diving catch with two out and the bases loaded in the ninth inning saved the game and contributed to the rookie's growing reputation as an excellent outfielder.

"Gramps," yelled assistant coach Hank Phillips. "Lou wants to see you in his office." David embraced his new nickname. He now starred in a local television ad for a Lakeland old-aged home, where he endorsed its comfortable living conditions, teasing viewers that he would be moving in the following year.

David hurriedly dressed and hustled to Lou's office.

"Come in, David," beckoned Lou, waving him in.

David plunked himself down in front of Coach Park's desk.

"You're going to the show, David."

David's eyes widened. "What?"

"They're down seven players. Rod called five minutes ago. Robocop is going too."

"But me? What about the guys in double-A or triple-A?"

"These decisions are made at the top. Although, Rod asked me if you were ready."

"What did you say?"

"I told him the truth. I have no bloody idea, but you would be one of the seven if it was my decision. Oh, and Charlie is expected to join the coaching staff on the bench."

David knew about the mess in Detroit, but he had never considered that the chaos would result in his ascension to the big leagues. After all, he was just a single-A ballplayer. "I don't know what to say, Lou."

"Don't say anything, David. Make us proud. Grab this opportunity because, honestly, at your age, it's a miracle it's coming your way. You're hitting .462 and catching everything in sight. You deserve a shot."

David met Charlie in the lounge, digesting the unexpected news as he greeted his son. He was about to become a Major League player for the Detroit Tigers, too inconceivable to comprehend.

Lou's comments to the aging rookie were half-truths; however, he reasoned nothing was gained by expressing his reservations to the rookie. While David was playing fabulously, a resume containing a few weeks' work at single-A was woefully inadequate to prepare a player for the Majors. A handful of more qualified black players had already declined the promotion. Earley was desperate and betting that David and Charlie would provide some excitement and positive publicity to a team in need of good press.

"We're going to the show? We're going to the show?" Charlie asked the question twice, slowly, not believing the message transmitted from his ears to his brain.

"I can't believe it either, Son."

The pair cleaned out their lockers, and Sherpa-like, made their way back to the RV with their overloaded bodies. They were both ecstatic, but their excitement mellowed as they discussed the circumstances bringing them back to Detroit. They loved Mad Dog and respected the stand he was taking, but was it really their issue? While it felt wrong to capitalize on the tumult, how could they say no? After a lengthy discussion, David arranged with the camp superintendent to store the RV for another month, and then the two caught a taxi to the airport to catch an 8:00 p.m. flight.

The Tigers' next game was scheduled for Sunday, three days later, at Comerica Park. Charlie was pleased to have the few days off because he had some sleuthing to do. He required answers to some nagging questions. Fortunately, their house had not sold yet, allowing them to return to their home.

When their plane touched down in Detroit, they took a cab directly to the stadium and met with Earley, Kilmer, and current Tigers head coach, Dwayne Mornington. The mood was solemn, the trio clearly distressed about the social unrest, boycott, and player defections. The organization was under a microscope, making it difficult to celebrate the Tigers' impressive play of late.

"Gentlemen, we are excited to have both of you here. I wish it were under different circumstances. There are four games left in the season, and we're a game out of a wild card playoff spot," explained Earley.

Rodney appeared as though he hadn't slept in forty-eight hours. "Guys, the stadium was half-empty last night, down from the sellout crowd two nights earlier. Almost all white faces in the stands. The two of you need to discuss whether Charlie should be on the bench in this environment. There's a lot of anger out there. The community is divided."

"Oh, there is no question. This is my dream!" replied Charlie. "Nothing will keep me off that bench!"

"We'll talk about it, Charlie," said David, grabbing his son's shoulder.

Back at the house, Jasmine came bounding across the street as a taxi driver dropped off the Ungers, wrapping her arms around Charlie, "I've missed you, Mr. Hustle!"

Charlie was excited to see Jasmine, not expecting to be reunited so quickly. The excitement did not extend to his lawn, crabgrass invading on three undefended fronts, and most concerning, a brown spot that looked suspiciously like a grub investigation.

"I know, Charlie. But you can repair it!" encouraged Jasmine, eying the botanist extraordinaire survey the insidious onslaught against perfection.

Charlie ushered Jasmine into the house, grabbing her hand and pulling her down the basement stairs while his father ascended the second floor for a nap.

"I need your help!" he pleaded, Jasmine appreciating the look of unabated intention in his eyes.

David had forbidden his son to contact his parents, a painful chapter that he wished to keep in the past. Charlie understood, and took no delight in defiance, but his curiosity—his desire for answers—was overwhelming. He had never met his grandparents, even once, and that didn't sit right. Sure, they hadn't treated his father well, but many years had passed. Maybe they were different, perhaps older and wiser? Or maybe they were miserable, wretched goblins who deserved their segregation. To Charlie, the truth was preferable to the unknown.

Jasmine helped Charlie rifle through old boxes, securely taped and stored in a basement closet. "Look for anything that has the names Gerald or Helen Unger on it, Jasmine," directed Charlie.

The two emptied box after box after box with no results, the pile of papers resembling a mini-Mount Everest, until Jasmine pulled the last paper out of the second last box. "Here, Charlie," said Jasmine, handing him loan papers.

"Gerald Unger, born June 5, 1941. Helen Unger, born April 9, 1944. 388 Pike Avenue, Livonia. A quick Google search confirmed what he hoped for, "They still live there, thirty years later. Wow!" exclaimed Charlie.

"What are you going to do, Mr. Hustle?"

Two hours and three buses later, Charlie pushed the doorbell on a modest, outdated bungalow in a quiet Livonia neighborhood. Charlie heard footsteps approaching the door. The door swung open. An elderly lady with snow-white hair and reading glasses hanging on the end of her nose greeted him. Charlie scanned every feature, but nothing suggested he'd received 25 percent of his DNA from her, at least physically.

"Hello, young man," she greeted gently. "Can I help you?"

Charlie decided against blurting out, "Hi, Grandma!" but, nevertheless, proceeded with the direct approach. "My name is Charlie Unger, David Unger's son."

The soft smile disappeared faster than Punxsutawney Phil on a sunny day, along with the color in her face. Her neurons fired rapidly, shaking her from a comfortable afternoon, never once contemplating this situation. Her mind felt around for the playbook, finally accepting one did not exist. She would have to wing it, her silence creating time to contemplate.

"Sorry, what did you say your name was?"

"Charlie Unger."

"Gerald!" she yelled, cranking her neck toward the living room, seeking backup. "You better come to the door."

Ten seconds later, a man nearing eighty arrived at the door, his scowl and aggravated brow highlighting his irritation. Again, no evidence in the soured puss suggested Charlie was a descendant.

"What do you want, boy?" asked Gerald, zooming past the pleasantries and idle chit-chat, offering his ill temper in their place.

"I'm Charlie Unger, your grandson."

It was Gerald's turn to embrace stunned silence, his cranky visage wiped clean by the introduction. Without saying another word, Gerald pushed the door open wider and waved the visitor in. The three of them took a seat in the living room, furnished in '70s decor but impeccably maintained. Helen brought them sodas.

"I wanted to meet you," explained Charlie, taking a sip of his Coke.

"Does your father know you are here?" asked Helen, not questioning the veracity of the young visitor's pretense.

Charlie shook his head. He explained how he had lost his mother and that his father had switched from lawyering and was about to play for the Detroit Tigers.

Helen and Gerald listened intently. The fallout with their son was heartbreaking, but Gerald Unger was as stubborn as they came. He had promised himself that he would eventually connect with David, but the months turned into years and then decades. Then, it became just too long, the shame and hard-headedness blocking any sensibilities.

Helen clasped her hands together. "Charlie, it's a pleasure to meet you. You appear to be a wonderful young man. It's unfortunate that we've not been around to see you grow up. I tried many times to meet with David early on; however, he rejected the idea."

Gerald raised his head, confused and irritated that he was hearing of his wife's attempts for the first time.

Helen looked at Gerald, a subtle look, asking if it was okay to tell the youngster. Gerald nodded his approval. Helen turned back to Charlie, "We should be telling David this directly, but you have a right to know too. You see, honey, we are not David's biological parents. We adopted David when he was a baby."

Meerkat-like, Charlie's head popped up, moving back and forth between his hosts, digesting Helen's revelation.

"We couldn't have children of our own, Charlie, so we adopted. We took home this beautiful baby boy—your father," explained Helen, grabbing her visitor's hand and leaning in. "We have so many regrets, Charlie."

"But then, who?" mumbled Charlie, staring at Helen with a quizzical look. "Who are my real grandparents?"

"We don't know, Charlie. That information was never shared with us."

Charlie asked several more questions, trying to gather as much information as possible, a fruitless investigation about Charlie Unger's lineage, a dead-end of answers. Helen offered that David's adoption was arranged through New Beginnings, an adoption agency located on Ford Drive in Detroit at the time.

Charlie accepted Gerald's offer to drive Charlie home, but once they were on the road, Charlie asked to be driven to downtown Detroit, which Gerald reluctantly agreed to.

Gerald asked many questions about David during the drive, including his burgeoning baseball career, strange for a man who hated the game.

When they finally pulled up at the corner of King and Davidson, Charlie hopped out of the car, but not before Gerald grabbed his arm.

"Charlie, please tell your father I'm sorry."

Charlie nodded and responded, "It would be wonderful if you told him that yourself."

Gerald waved as Charlie stepped away onto the curb. Smart kid, he thought, watching the boy disappear around the corner.

Mr. Hustle walked three blocks, intent on arriving at 411 Ford Drive before 4:30. A quick Google search confirmed New Beginnings remained at the same location. At 4:29 p.m., he pushed the front door open, immediately met by a pleasant young woman who told him to return with an appointment because they were about to close. However, Charlie had never suffered from a lack of persistence.

"Please, please! This is so important," pleaded Charlie, managing to push a single tear out of his eye for full effect. He bowed his head in dejection, further yanking on those heartstrings.

The young woman sighed, provided a quick smile, and then asked Charlie to wait for a minute while she excused herself. Two minutes later, she returned and had him follow her to a back office where he was greeted by Jennifer Stonehill, the agency's executive director.

Charlie quickly explained the condensed version of how he was searching for his grandparents.

"Charlie, we have stringent privacy requirements and protocols that govern how information is released by persons seeking information about their biological relatives. I will take a peek to see if there are any records," she said as she began typing into her laptop. Her eyes darted back and forth, a clear signal that she had found something.

"Did you hear that, Ms. Stonehill?"

"No. What, Charlie?"

"Someone just knocked on the front," replied Charlie, looking back through the open office door.

"I didn't hear anything," replied Jennifer, who got up, exited the office, and headed down the hallway to investigate.

As soon as she left, Charlie jumped up and maneuvered around the desk to view the laptop screen. He pulled his phone out, took a photo of the screen, and then quickly jumped back into his chair, barely ahead of Jennifer's return.

"There's nobody there. Are you sure you heard something?"

"I must have been mistaken. Sorry."

Jennifer continued reading. When she was done, she returned her focus to Charlie and handed a pamphlet to him. "Take this and read it. It explains the entire process. A friendly warning: not everyone wants to be found. I don't want you to be disappointed."

"Thank you, ma'am. I appreciate that you've stayed past closing time." And with that final exchange, Charlie left Ms. Stonehill, exited the building, and returned to the sidewalk on Ford Drive. He immediately pulled out his phone and stared down at his latest photo.

CHAPTER THIRTY-TWO

Taking a Stand

Charlie turned the key to the off position after finishing the last stripe. It felt good to be back on the Tiger Striper, rehabilitating the neglected front lawn. He threw his head back and closed his eyes. "Novertdortis!" he yelled with all his might, his favorite smell powering his voice, followed by a turn of the head to see if Ms. Jenkins was working on her garden. The disappointment of her absence came as a surprise, as was Mr. Cooper's closed curtains and any evidence of the cantankerous man's presence.

Charlie turned the striper back on, and immediately shut it off, wishing to hear the purr of the motor one more time. "Well done, boy!"

Charlie watched as Jasmine pushed her front door open and headed toward him, her powerful legs whisking her to his side within seconds, not a hint that she was out of breath. She put her arms around him, her affection saying more than any words could ever accomplish. Only one other person ever had that ability. He looked down at the shiny metal object in her hands.

"You brought your own tweezers?"

"Hey, we need to get this lawn into tip-top shape, Mr. Hustle."

"Yes, we do!" replied Charlie.

"So what did you find out this afternoon? Did you find your grandparents?"

Charlie explained the afternoon events, pulling out his phone and showing her the photo.

Jasmine slowly read the adoption summary, turning back to Charlie when she was done, "Wow. What are you going to do?"

"I'm going down there first thing tomorrow morning."

"Does your dad know?"

"No. I don't want to distract him with his big day coming. He needs to focus. Distraction is the enemy of performance." Charlie's mind was swirling. He and his father would be on the bench for the Detroit Tigers in two days, and he was busy chasing down the truth.

"My dad receives two tickets to each home game. He wants you to have them for Sunday," explained Charlie, knowing that Jasmine wouldn't miss his debut on the Tigers bench for any reason.

"You must be excited," she replied in an unusually subdued manner, reluctant to share some news with Charlie.

"My dream is coming true, and you'll be there to see me take the bench. It means everything to me."

Jasmine bowed her head and stepped toward Charlie, shaking her head slowly, not immediately looking him in the eye. "About that, Charlie, I won't be able to come."

"What? Why not?" he asked, concerned. "If it's about your father—"

She cut him off, "It has nothing to do with Papa."

"Then, what, Jasmine?"

"I support the boycott. I support Reverend Baptiste."

Charlie was quiet, caught off guard, hurt galloping in.

"My family was targeted in Cameroon because we spoke English. My mother died because she stood up for her principles. There are many great things about your country, I understand that, but there's also racism. Baseball is just baseball. Football is just football. They're games. Racism is real life. I'm going to respect the boycott."

Baseball is just a game. Charlie repeated her statement twice in his head. How could she say that to me?

"Fear makes the wolf bigger than it is. That's what my mom said, Charlie."

"And what are you afraid of, Jasmine?"

"I'm afraid of losing my best friend. I'm afraid of letting my mother down, of not respecting her legacy. She gave up her life to do what was right—to protect me. What's going on in this country is no different than in Cameroon. I'm afraid of not doing the right thing."

Charlie stared at her, taking in her plea, trying to understand her position. He raced through his mental Rolodex of Confucius sayings, wanting something to help him make sense of this disappointment. He was angry, but unsure if he had the right.

"Say something, Charlie. Please."

But Charlie didn't say anything. Instead, without responding, he turned around, retreated to his house, and disappeared.

CHAPTER THIRTY-THREE

The Issue Is Black and White

Charlie awoke at 7:00 a.m. the next morning, having barely slept, Jasmine's position on the boycott dominating his thoughts. That was an impressive feat, given the previous day's discovery that his dad was adopted, and that he was taking the field with his heroes in two days. The hamster wheel of rumination revolved at maximum speed.

He needed to be downtown by 8:00 a.m., too early for a bus, so he summoned an Uber, which he met at the end of the street to avoid his father's detection. He would have preferred hopping in the car with Jasmine, but he did not extend an invitation. Just a game. The words trivialized his very being. How could she say that to him?

Traffic was light, the ride only taking a half hour before reaching his destination. Who was David Unger's father? It's all Charlie could think about.

Exiting the Uber at the corner of Reynolds and George Washington Boulevard, Charlie looked up at the grand, century-old building and its ten steps leading up to the hand-carved double front doors. He realized the trip would have been easier with Jasmine at his side.

Charlie stood there, looking down at his phone and the adoption summary. Finally, after gathering himself, Charlie made his way to the front door, pushing his doubts aside. Maybe this wasn't a good idea, he mused. I'm probably the last person he wants to speak to, given I'm a Tigers coach. It would be simple to reverse direction, retreat down the steps, and be home before his father awoke.

Charlie stepped to the door and pushed the doorbell, the loud chime from within heard outside. He again thought about making a run for it, but his feet were now in quicksand.

The door swung open.

"Right on time, Charlie," said the man gently, providing an unexpectedly warm smile. "I always pegged you as the punctual type." He extended his hand, and they shook. How could such a man of principle, a fierce and uncompromising advocate, have such gentleness and kindness?

Charlie smiled back, relieved at the lack of tension.

"Come in, young man. I'm very curious why you arranged this meeting."

Charlie followed his host down a long hallway with fifteen-foot ceilings, light reflecting off the glittering chandeliers. They arrived at a library, warm from a roaring wood fire.

"Sit down, Charlie, and relax. Can I get you something to drink?"

"No thanks, sir."

Charlie scanned the room, gazing over the bookshelf and numerous photos hanging on the wall, most with Baptiste and someone else. "The new paint job looks good, Reverend."

"Get up, Charlie. Take a look at them," Baptiste said, referring to the photos.

Charlie raised himself and made his way to the wall closest to him.

"That's Martin Luther King Jr., a Baptist minister, Nobel Peace Prize winner for fighting racial inequality, leader of the American civil rights movement until his assassination in 1968."

"Why was he assassinated?" asked Charlie.

"Fighting injustice creates enemies," came the reply.

"And this is Desmond Tutu, a South African Anglican cleric, anti-apartheid and human rights activist. Mahatma Gandhi here, leader of India's movement for independence from British rule. Always nonviolent protests. Assassinated in 1948. And Nelson Rolihlahla Mandela, political activist dedicated to deconstructing anti-apartheid in South Africa. Served twenty-seven years in prison for his efforts. Eventually became president. I have all these as reminders of what true conviction means, of what real sacrifice is, of what it means to have real courage."

Charlie retook his seat, having a better understanding of his host.

The reverend bent down and looked his visitor in the eye. "You don't have to be an adult to make a difference. Courage is not reserved for adults."

Charlie nodded his head, taking the advice in, depositing it away for further assessment.

"Okay, young man. Tell me what brings you here?"

Charlie handed him his phone with the adoption summary. After two minutes, Reverend Baptiste gave his phone back to Charlie. "Does your father know?"

Charlie shook his head. "I discovered it yesterday."

"How did you get a copy of this document, Charlie?" came the question, William knowing full well the legal confidentiality requirements of the sensitive information.

"I'd rather not say, sir," he replied, wondering if he could be arrested and wind up in jail for his devious act, perhaps as long as Nelson Mandela.

The reverend looked back at him suspiciously. "The Lord does move in mysterious ways sometimes. Charlie, give me a few minutes please. I need to check something."

"Of course, sir."

The minutes ticked by until a half hour passed, the delay elevating Charlie's already-present uneasiness. Where was the reverend?

Suddenly, the door opened, "Hello, Charlie."

Startled, Charlie jumped to his feet. "Mad Dog! What are you doing here?"

"William called me, told me to come right over."

Five minutes of discussing batting theory followed, Luis and his new coach enjoying each other's perspective.

The door opened again; this time Baptiste entered, followed by another man, which shocked Charlie.

"Dad! What are you doing here?" he exclaimed, his face turning white, not easily accomplished for the already-pasty kid.

"I believe that is a question more appropriately put to you, Charlie," replied David, unimpressed that the reverend had called him and asked him to come immediately.

"I called him, Charlie. I had to," explained William, before sitting Luis and David down beside him.

"What's this all about?' asked David.

"Gentlemen, I'll get straight to the point. In 1982, my wife and I were asked to attend St. Joseph's Hospital. Our attendance was not unusual. A young girl was giving up her newborn twins for adoption. We took in several children each year, some who were eventually adopted out, and some that remained here for their entire childhood, like Luis."

"And what does that have to do with me? I'm baffled," admitted David.

"I remember the day clearly," replied Baptiste. The obstetrician had completed his final day, delivering the last babies in his career. He was animated, excited, telling me that in all his years of practicing medicine, he had never seen it before."

"What was it?" asked Mad Dog.

"Mom and Dad were black, but one twin was black and the other was white. The doctor had a technical name for it. It's rare."

"Again, Reverend, I'm lost," said David, scrunching his eyebrows.

"David, one of those boys was Luis. The other one was you."

"What? What?" exclaimed David, now scrunching his entire face. "No, no, there has to be a mistake. There has to be. What are you talking about?"

"Charlie, show your father the adoption summary. David, look at the date of birth."

David slowly read the document. "Mary Helen Green—mother, born January 12, 1966; Trent Higgins—father, born August 6, 1964; David Thomas Higgins, son, born July 14, 1982."

"David, you were adopted by the Ungers. I remember them. I pleaded with them to take you both, but they refused. Mr. Unger was emphatic. He said a black boy had no business in a white family."

Baptiste went on to explain that their father, Trent Higgins, was in prison for a deadly confrontation with a police officer, their sixteen-year-old mother believing she could not raise children at her age.

"Your mother died in a terrible car accident two years later. I don't know what became of your father."

Charlie looked at Mad Dog. "You're my uncle."

Luis nodded. "It certainly appears that way. "And we're brothers," he said, looking at David, trying to absorb the news.

"Why didn't you tell me that I had a brother, William?" asked Luis.

"I'm bound by the confidentiality legislation as well. I've struggled with my decision, Luis."

"What is it, Charlie?" asked William, seeing a strange look on his face.

"When I first met Mad Dog, he was out celebrating his birthday on the same day that me and my dad were out celebrating his birthday."

CHAPTER THIRTY-FOUR

Hustle In, Hustle Out

"We have a special caller on line two, Charlie Unger, also known as Mr. Hustle. Charlie Hustle, welcome back to KRBA 690," offered the Green Machine.

"Thank you, Mr. Machine."

"Reports have it that you will be on the bench this afternoon with your father in a crucial game for the Tigers. How do you feel?"

Two nights had now passed without any meaningful sleep. Charlie was exhausted, but his mind was clear.

"It's a dream come true, Mr. Machine. A dream of a lifetime. A wonderful, unbelievable opportunity. I can't think of anything more special than taking that bench with my dad and the best baseball team in America."

"How do you feel about the boycott, Charlie?"

Charlie paused. He thought of Jasmine, losing her mother fighting oppression in Cameroon. His reply was not at all what he had carefully planned. Instead, he looked deep within his heart. "I'm not sure if I support or don't support the boycott. I guess that's something for each person to decide. But I will not be sitting on the bench for the remainder of the year."

"Charlie Unger!" exclaimed Green. "Why would you do that?"

"I'm doing it for my best friend, Jasmine, and for Mad Dog Madison. I'm doing it for everyone who has been called the N-word."

It was a decision that hurt—that tore at his every fiber. Oh, how he wanted to sit on the bench with his father, with all those great Tigers players, and to smell the air of Comerica Park. Novertdortis.

When Charlie couldn't fall asleep the night before, he read Nelson Mandela's autobiography, *Long Walk to Freedom* and, watched a documentary on Martin Luther King Jr. He couldn't shake the words Reverend Baptiste had shared as he marveled at those civil rights heroes on the wall, "I have all these as reminders of what true conviction means, of what real sacrifice is, of what it means to have real courage."

The Green Machine had one final question. "What advice do you have for kids starting in the game of baseball?"

Charlie thought for a moment. He smiled, thinking of Jasmine, standing on his front lawn with him, giving him his silly nickname. Finally, he answered, "You can't control everything in life. I couldn't control my mother dying. But she taught me that I could always control my attitude. When you get to the ballfield, if you always follow this advice, you will be successful." Charlie paused for effect and summed up the best he could, "Hustle in, hustle out."

CHAPTER THIRTY-FIVE

The Bigs

Nothing racks the nerves more than a rookie's first plate appearance in the Major Leagues. Add in a playoff race, the media frenzy toward a thirty-six-year-old rookie, a divisive boycott, and the drama of a son who had joined the boycott, this became no ordinary first at-bat. The world had its eyes on Detroit, the tension thicker than a Sleepy Hollow fog.

David and Charlie had a long discussion about his son's decision not to join him on the Tigers bench. They agreed to disagree.

"I'm proud of you, Charlie, for the decision that you've made. I respect it. I'm not sure the city of Detroit can handle two Ungers missing these last few games."

"Dad, I'll get another chance. But I need you to play; it helps make this tolerable."

David did not believe in using the game as leverage for social change. While he was sympathetic to Baptiste's goals, the game of baseball should remain pure, he reasoned.

David stepped to the plate in the eighth inning as a pinch hitter. "Scab." "Backstabber." "Racist." David pushed aside the many insults from the last twenty-four hours, hurled at him by people who did not know him. Thankfully, he also had supporters. "Grampa's Got Game" shirts dotted the stadium, a warming antidote for the vitriol surrounding the team. David declined all media requests out of respect for the boycotting players, unwilling to contribute to the volatile atmosphere.

David's media interest paled compared to that generated by the Tigers' youngest coach. The marketing prowess of America was on full display. Within hours after it was announced that Charlie "Hustle" Unger would be on the bench, he became a global sensation. T-shirts with Charlie's face and "Mr. Hustle" were everywhere. The boy genius saturated social media, including Mad Dog's clip explaining how Charlie gave him the swing tip. Charlie received widespread credit for single-handedly turning the Tigers season around.

Once Charlie advised the world he would not be joining the Tigers, T-shirts with "Hustle In, Hustle Out" became extremely popular. However, Charlie's stance attracted many detractors, the biting criticism hurtful to a boy attempting to do what was right. Many messages on his Facebook page now included hateful jabs about his weight and his autism.

Prior to his announcement on Green Machine's radio show, Charlie arrived for an early morning national television show proudly wearing his uniform to wild applause. Mr. Hustle participated in a game called Stump the Genuis. Charlie was peppered with baseball trivia questions. After correctly answering six questions in a row, a caller thought he had Charlie stumped.

"What happens if a ball becomes stuck in a catcher's or umpire's mask?"

Charlie thought for a few seconds, scanning through the Rolodex in his brain. "Nothing happens . . ." The caller interrupted and began to tell Charlie he was wrong, but Charlie cut him off at his first syllable, "Nothing happens, unless there are players on base. Rule 5.09(g) Runners advance one base if a pitched ball lodges in the umpire's or catcher's mask or paraphernalia."

"Correct, Mr. Hustle. You're too good!" replied the caller.

Even Mad Dog, who was watching the show, smiled ear to ear, watching his nephew answer the questions and generate interest in the game.

As David stepped to the plate for his first at-bat, the Tigers were down 3–2, bases loaded with two outs. The Tigers remained a game out of a wild card playoff spot. Coach Mornington wanted a right-handed hitter to face the lefty on the mound. Giant George Mason, a six-foot-four, 240-pound pitcher, stared at David.

The brief fissure in Charlie and Jasmine's friendship had been repaired, the two of them having an extended conversation about social justice and racism running through a complicated America. The pair sat with Luis and William in the reverend's library, all of them agreeing that the boycott did not apply to watching the game on television. Charlie was nervous, wishing he was at the game, but at peace with his decision. Still, it was unbearable not to be at Comerica Park to witness his father's first Major League plate appearance.

Charlie knew Mason had a crazy, nasty slider in his repertoire that broke so hard it made accomplished hitters in the game look foolish.

As David put his feet into the box, he remembered Charlie's advice, "Dad, if you see the spin of the slider and the pitch looks good, it isn't. It's going to drop out of the zone just before the plate."

The fans were on their feet, stomping and clapping. Here he was, playing at the highest level of baseball. He had dropped everything to follow his dreams, and this moment could never be taken away from him.

The Giant's first pitch was a "welcome to the big leagues" two-seam fastball that registered 102 miles per hour on the radar gun, his fastest of the season. The Giant was pumped up and throwing heat.

"Strike one!" screeched the umpire.

Then came a nasty slider that looked like it was right down the heart of the plate. David's eyes opened wide and he took a mighty hack, only to see the ball dip nastily onto the dirt in front of the catcher.

"Steeeeeerike two," yelled the umpire, pumping his hand in the air.

All the players on the Tigers bench groaned, seeing the rookie start with two strikes against one of the best relievers in the game. Only Charlie knew that zero players had ever reached base against the Giant this year when he started with two strikes and no balls against the hitter. That was precisely zero out of twenty-four players that started with two strikes. The odds were dismal. In fact, the odds were less than dismal. There was a zero percent chance that David would reach base, statistically. Charlie had memorized every helpful stat and a few that were simply interesting to know, in anticipation of the season-ending series against the Yankees. He took his job seriously.

David wasn't thinking about odds or statistics as he stood in the box for the third pitch. He was as focused as he had ever been, pushing all the noise out of his mind. It was just him and the Giant, and he wasn't scared. Rather, he felt a calmness come over him.

That next pitch came in, a slider, and it looked perfect, heading right down the middle. David kept the bat on his shoulder.

"Ball one," said the umpire as the ball cut outside off the plate. David took a quick look back at the dugout.

"Ball two!" yelled the umpire, on an almost identical pitch.

David fouled off the next two pitches before the Giant threw another ball to make it a full count. The fans remained on their feet, the rhythmic clapping and stomping music to Charlie's ears. The place was wild. Everyone on the Tigers bench was now on their feet, only Charlie knowing that his father's odds had now increased to 32 percent, improved, but still not great.

David immediately recognized the fastball coming in. When a major league pitcher releases the ball, their hand is only fifty-five feet from home plate, and it takes less than half a second for the ball to reach home plate. David immediately recognized it as a borderline high pitch. As the saying goes, when you have two strikes, swing at anything close, but David held back and let that ball sail into the catcher's mitt. It was pure agony waiting for the call, the park briefly hushing, waiting on the umpire. David held his breath and looked back.

"Ball four!" yelled the umpire, setting off an explosion of cheers from the fans and the Tigers bench. David was credited with an RBI—run batted in—in his first at-bat. That ninety-foot trot down to first base was satisfying, not because the tying run came in, not because fifty thousand fans were cheering for him, but because he didn't let the fear of striking out hold him back.

Charlie was beside himself with glee. He couldn't stop cheering, seeing his own father standing on first base with the crowd screaming in delight, both Mad Dog and William slapping him on the back. Mad Dog began clapping, knowing how his newfound brother must be feeling.

When Brian Mays hit a walk-off home run in the ninth for the Tigers to seal a 4–3 victory, it capped off a magical night that both David and Charlie would remember forever.

That evening, David, Charlie, and Jasmine celebrated at Tigers Time. With a french fry hanging from his lip, Charlie couldn't shake the excitement from his face. "Wouldn't it be awesome to see your face up on these walls someday, Dad?"

"Easy, Son. I've had one at-bat in the bigs. But it was a thrill."

"Your on-base percentage is one thousand," replied Charlie, raising his eyebrows. "And we're tied with the Yankees now, three games to go. Oh, I wish I was on the bench, Dad."

"Excuse me," came a voice from an elderly woman approaching the table. "May I have your autograph, Mr. Hustle?" She held out a baseball and a pen. "It's for my grandson. All he does is think about baseball. He wants to be just like you."

Charlie grabbed the pen and signed the ball without reservation. "Thank you, ma'am."

"Thank you," she replied, offering some final comments. "Mr. Hustle, I don't know a lick about baseball, but I know when someone puts others ahead of themselves. And that's what makes this signature so valuable." The woman began walking away, stopped, and turned around to look at Charlie. She knocked three times on the side of her head. "Knock it, then rocket. It's so cute. My grandson hits his head, then shouts those words when his favorite Tiger is batting, when he's hoping for a home run."

"Knock it, then rocket," repeated David, when the autograph seeker had stepped away. "I like it."

Charlie was about to return to his fries but couldn't; eight further customers had lined up, pens in hand, and Mr. Hustle would oblige with a smile and a handshake.

CHAPTER THIRTY-SIX

Tiger Fever

In the next two games, both wild affairs that required extra innings to determine the outcome, the Yankees and Tigers split, leaving them tied in the standings with one game to go. Unlike the fan composition in David's first game, there were decidedly more black faces in the crowd for the next two games, a curious development.

Several interviews took place prior to the games, providing some insight into the change in behavior.

A sixty-year-old black man looked into the camera and explained his position. "I did support the boycott. I still support it, I suppose. But I've changed my mind about attending. The Tigers need our support too. They're a great organization. Look at the fans. Look at the excitement. The city of Detroit needs baseball."

"What changed your mind, sir?"

"Charlie Hustle changed my mind. God bless that kid for sitting out."

The city of Detroit and the entirety of the United States was abuzz with the rookie sensation affectionately known as Grampa. He had walked four times, had been hit by a pitch twice, and had eight hits in his first fourteen plate appearances, without recording an out.

A carnival atmosphere surrounded Comerica Park on the final game of the season, a playoff berth requiring a win. Every bar and restaurant in Detroit with a television was packed, lines reaching the streets. Drivers honked their car horns and hung Tiger pennants from their windows, proudly displaying their team's blue, white, and orange colors.

Given his hot bat, David was inserted second in the batting order up and placed at center field on the defensive side. To the crowd's delight, David drew two walks in his first two at-bats, but failed to score, a pitching duel unfolding. Both Yankees pitcher, Frank "Zinger" Zettle, and Tigers pitcher, Jimmie "Cannon" Cranston, were throwing gems.

When David came to the plate in the sixth inning, with the game tied at zero, he fouled off four pitches, the count eventually becoming full. David did the unexpected on the next pitch, following the coach's sign and catching the Yankees and all fifty thousand fans off guard. He had been given the bunt sign, dangerous because a fouled third-strike bunt is considered a strikeout. But the Tigers needed baserunners, and the first base coach, Donnie Staub, saw the Yankees' third basemen playing extremely deep.

David laid a beauty down the third base line, the ball slowly rolling, a foot within fair territory. With David's blistering speed, no chance existed to throw him out, David hitting the bag before the third baseman even reached the ball. Unfortunately for the Tigers, David wasn't advanced past first base.

"Wow, Charlie, that's seventeen plate appearances and seventeen times on base for your dad," said Mad Dog, getting up from his chair and grabbing a cola.

"Seventeen. Seventeen. Why does that number mean something?" Charlie pulled out his phone and began his search. "Of course!" he screamed. "Seventeen is the MLB record! Piggy Ward in 1893 with the Cincinnati Reds and Earl Averill Jr. with the Dodgers in 1962. Both of them reached safely on base in seventeen consecutive plate appearances. Dad could break the record if he gets another at-bat and reaches." Charlie looked at Jasmine, then at Mad Dog, and finally at Reverend Baptiste. They all carried the same thought.

Mad Dog looked at Baptiste. "The kid needs to be there, William. It's his dad."

Baptiste was pensive. He looked at the other three, all of them waiting for a response. "I'll grab my keys; let's go!" replied the reverend.

Road congestion was awful, slowing their advancement. Successfully traveling the five blocks in time was in doubt.

"I hope we make it in time!" exclaimed Charlie. "Turn on the radio, please."

Charlie wasn't the only one who'd figured out that David Unger had matched the MLB Record.

The radio play-by-play announcer, Morris Freedman, let everyone know. "Well folks, it's on the stadium screen. David Unger has just tied the MLB record for safely reaching base in seventeen consecutive at-bats. It's an obscure record; there has been no media coverage on the possibility that the record could be reached today. Wow. All I can say is wow. He's only had seventeen trips to the plate in the Majors. I'm not sure how to describe what we've seen. Amazing. Incredible. Stupendous. Unbelievable. Pick an adjective, folks. Any of them will do."

"Faster, Reverend," pleaded Charlie. "I don't want to miss it if he gets a chance."

The radio announcer continued, "The Yanks have two out in the top of the ninth. Bases empty. Baserunners scarce today. Cleanup hitter Calvin Bright is at the plate for New York. Here comes the windup. Uh oh. That's hit hard. That's hit deep." The stadium went quiet as the crowd watched the ball sail toward the four hundred-foot sign, visions of a playoff sinking. Every Yankee jumped out of the dugout, preparing to celebrate.

David had a bead on the ball as soon as it came off the bat. He used his world-class speed and raced to the wall, pushing his body to the very limit, never taking his eye off the white spherical object. He felt his foot hit the warning track, knowing he was closing in on the wall, taking two more steps, and then a desperate leap. His left foot landed halfway up the wall; David pushed hard again, soaring higher, allowing his right foot to step on the top of the wall. One last mighty push sent David higher than any player had been in Comerica Park; many later said it wasn't humanly possible. David stretched his glove hand, catching that ball twenty feet off the ground, an ice cream-cone catch, the ball caught, but the top of it still sticking well above the top of his glove.

As David hurtled back to the ground, the crowd remained quiet, everyone carrying the same concern—would his impact with the ground knock that ball from his glove. David landed with a thud, trying to protect the exposed ball by cradling his glove underneath him, his body coming to a rest, the umpires racing to him to determine the ball's final resting place. The outfielder laid momentarily, the wind knocked out of him, the fans joining him by holding their collective breath.

Veteran umpire George Smith arrived first to observe David stick his glove hand in the air, the ball now precariously extending three quarters out of the glove; but it remained. Smith raised his right arm to signal an out, the crowd erupting with the power of Mount Vesuvius. Left fielder José Martinez and right fielder Barry Jones ran to David, embracing him, congratulating him.

"I have just witnessed the best catch in the history of the game," screeched Freedman, jumping to his feet as he watched David sprint back to the dugout. "Goodness, we'll be talking about that play until the end of time."

"The boycott is over after today," announced the reverend. "The regular season will be complete. I think we've made our point. I really do."

"Yes," hollered Charlie, first hugging Mad Dog and then Jasmine. "Faster, Reverend! Turn the radio up louder, Mad Dog!"

Mad Dog had never heard the announcer, Freddy Freeman, more excited. "And here we are in the bottom of the ninth. Two out. Bases empty. A zero–zero tie. This is what we've been waiting for! David Unger has stepped from the on-deck circle and is walking toward home plate."

"Oh my God. Faster, Reverend. I need to see my dad! I need to see him hit!"

"I'm trying, Charlie," replied William, maneuvering in and out of traffic in a questionable fashion.

"I can't hear myself think it's so loud in the stadium, folks," announced Freedman. "I've never heard it this loud in the stadium. Ball one! New York's pitcher, the Giant, missed low and inside with his first pitch, producing no swing from Unger."

"Come on, Dad," pleaded Charlie, clasping his hands in prayer.

"Ball two," announced Freeman. "Unger is ahead in the count, folks. The Giant will have to bear down now."

"You can do it, brother. Come on," said Mad Dog, closing his fist and shaking it.

David stepped into the batter box, focused on the Giant. Surely, I'm getting a strike to hit with this count, he assumed.

"Ball three!" yelled the umpired when the ball sailed high, his voice competing with a crowd that went berserk with excitement after the call.

"Well, this is a first, folks," announced Freedman. "The Giant has lost his control and will have to come with a strike now, or risk putting Unger on first. Every fan is on their feet. They're clapping twice and then knocking three times on the sides of their heads. I've never seen the crowd partake in such a gesture before. They're also chanting something. I can't make out what it is, but Unger has stepped out of the box. I believe he wiped a tear from his face."

"Dad, you can do it," said Charlie, his voice softening, knowing precisely what the crowd was chanting.

"I've figured out what the crowd is chanting," explained Freedman. "'Mr. Hustle.' Yes, it's clear now. They've put it on the stadium screen. They're chanting, 'Mr. Hustle,' exaggerating every syllable. Unger is having some difficulty composing himself."

"Back in the box," ordered the umpire, the delay extending too long.

It was all too much for Charlie. He was a genius, but was also a boy who wanted to be at his father's side.

David admitted later that what he did next was not good sportspersonship; the moment controlled him, the thought of his son breaking his focus. After taking his sign from Coach Staub at first, he stared out at the pitcher and yelled, "Give me something!"

The provocative challenge made the Giant seethe, Unger showing him up on the grandest of stages.

"What the hell are you doing, Unger?" yelled Coach Mornington from the bench. "Take your walk!"

Mornington flashed the take-a-pitch sign to Staub at first base, who relayed it to David. He touched his chest, left ear, and then the right arm, which was the indicator. He then tapped the tip of his baseball cap, the sign David was to follow.

David readied himself, his eyes glued to the Giant who was intently staring back at the batter, a snarl across his face. The chanting continued; clap, clap, "Charlie Hustle." Clap, clap, "Charlie Hustle." David took one hand off his bat, knocked three times on his helmet, and then looked back at the catcher and said a few words, barely audible over the stadium's noise.

The reverend pulled onto Adams Avenue and parked in front of the Detroit Athletic Club. "Charlie, get out and run. It's your best chance! I'll never get any closer; the street's jammed."

Charlie hopped out and started running toward Gate 6, reserved for Tigers staff. He wasn't convinced he would be allowed in, possessing no ticket. Rumors had it that Kilmer was so upset when Charlie did not take the bench that he ripped his contract into so many pieces that it resembled confetti when he threw it across his office. Charles T. Unger may very well be considered persona non grata.

Miggy's home run plaque came into Charlie's view, ten feet in front of him. Normally, he would have stopped and rubbed it for good luck, but the urgency afforded no time today. Instead, he continued at his top speed.

Suddenly, Charlie stopped before he reached the plaque, two paces before he would have crossed over the bronzed plate on his way to Gate 6. Several in the vicinity looked up, hearing a clap of thunder, confused by the clear blue cloudless sky. Charlie wasn't confused, the sound of that crack stopping him dead in his tracks, three feet in front of Miggy. He knew he was too late, even before the roar began, the crowd speaking a language requiring no interpretation. The ground shook under his feet, a rumbling that had never before been felt around Comerica Park. Sixteen nearby residents called 911 within minutes, reporting an earthquake, their misinterpretation rushing them to their phones.

Charlie was never fooled. He had heard the crack of the bat from home plate. Louisville. Maple. No doubt existed.

Luis, Jasmine, and William joined Charlie in the middle of the busy road, ignoring the honks from drivers who they now impeded, the beautiful singular roar of the crowd drowning out all other noise. The excitement of the crowd was undeniable.

Two seconds removed from the crack, the four of them understood the fuss, although it felt like minutes.

Charlie looked up to see a ball coming over the left-field brick wall, a huge moon shot on the same line as Miggy's. All eight of their eyes followed it down from the stratosphere, where it landed well into the concourse, taking a gigantic bounce and then sailing over the metal gates before landing on the asphalt of Adams Avenue.

The ball rolled across the road with some speed, crossing over Miggy's plaque directly toward Mr. Hustle. Charlie bent over as it approached him, reaching out, but then quickly pulling his hand back, allowing it to roll through his legs, his stunned expression remaining.

The foursome turned around to watch it roll to the curb, coming to rest in front of the Athletic Club. Every car on the street came to a stop. Drivers and occupants alike jumped out and started cheering, all of them congregating around the ball in a giant circle, divine intervention the only explanation for why not one of them picked up the ball.

Charlie slowly walked over to the group, the circle parting like the Red Sea as he approached, bent over, and picked up the home run souvenir, 512 feet from home plate, 11 feet farther than Miggy's historic shot. The roar from within Comerica continued, an unrelenting and unabating appreciation for David Unger's first home run in the Majors, a blast that put him into the record books by reaching base eighteen consecutive times.

Charlie placed the Rawlings ball into his left hand, unblemished, except for one giant dark smudge. Staring down at the ball, his fingertips soon resembled the shade of that magical white sphere. He loosened his grip, allowing the blood to return, memories washing over him, some that he welcomed, and others that were tougher to hold back than a man in rage. After a brief clash between the two, the warm images took control and blanketed the cold losses that he had suffered with a wave of goodness.

Two checkmarks for the Bible thumpers, he reasoned, cocking his head up and looking to the heavens. Charlie raised his arms and screamed until there was no air left in his lungs, "He did it! My dad did iiiiiiiiiiiiiiiiiiiiiiiiiiiiiit!"

CHAPTER THIRTY-SEVEN

He Who Knows All the Answers

"It's got 641 horsepower under the hood, sir. Fast as a cheetah, zero to sixty in 2.8 seconds. Sleek, with the curves of Marilyn Monroe."

"She's a wonderful machine," came the reply from the man, pulling a black handkerchief from the front jacket of his tailored suit. "Hey, Sam. Do you mind getting me a coffee? Two sugars and one milk."

"Of course, sir," replied the salesperson.

"And a double chocolate biscotti while you're at it."

"Yes, of course."

The gentleman of exquisite taste circled the machine a few times, appreciating the German engineering. Damn, he would look fine in the car, feeling the wind in his hair, becoming one with the two thousand pounds of metal.

Sam returned with a coffee and biscotti. "I'm sorry, sir. There was no double chocolate left. I brought you raspberry."

"I'll take the coffee but pass on the biscotti," the man replied, casting indignation and a frown upon the salesperson.

"I can tell by your suit, sir, that you enjoy the finest things in life. Armani, is it?" asked Sam.

"It is. One hundred percent virgin wool. Fits like a glove. I could have knocked the tailor's block off though. Pricked me right here," he said, pointing to a tiny red dot on his wrist.

"How disappointing, sir. I'm sure it was terrible."

"Does it come in metallic blue?" he asked Sam.

"Yes. And canary yellow, midnight black, thermal orange pearl, lime essence, papaya spark, stealth gray, and for the traditional, baby powder white," explained Sam.

"Oh, white's a nonstarter. My complexion will wash out with white, Sam."

"Metallic blue is suitable for a man of your stature, or stealth gray. Powerful colors. Gray is in stock at the dealership. The vehicle could be registered and licensed within the hour."

"Yes, Sam. Stealth gray. Definitely stealth gray."

"Owning a Porsche 911 Turbo says a lot about the man who drives it, sir. But I don't need to tell you that," said Sam, smiling, keeping his contempt under wraps.

David Unger gazed around the showroom, the wide-spread pampering of the well-heeled customers on display, hefty commissions in the balance. Maybe it wasn't ideal timing for such a purchase, so soon after his wife's death.

An hour later, David was the proud owner of a Porsche 911, stealth gray.

"Mr. Unger, here are your snakeskin racing gloves, complimentary, of course. Oils in the hand will denigrate the leather on the steering wheel. We recommend wearing these gloves."

"If you have children in the car—"

David cut the man off, "No kid of mine is getting in this car! Not with this price tag."

Friday night, sun in the west, David topped 120 miles per hour barreling down Highway 67. He felt the power. The $120,000 bonus from work paid for half of his new toy—the spoils of success; he couldn't be more pleased with his success.

He turned off the highway and onto Devils Line, taking the curves, pushing the German engineering to its fullest capabilities. David kept his foot on the pedal, accelerating, moving the speedometer into the red zone.

It had been a long week, a long day, up at 4:00 a.m. every morning to arrive at his law office by 5:30 a.m. He did not look forward to tomorrow, two depositions and a pleading to complete. Truthfully, he didn't look forward to any morning.

The sports car rumbled, the gravel and uneven shoulder shaking the chassis, but still, David's foot remained on the gas pedal. The barrier failed to hold the car, the wood shattering, pieces propelled in every direction, the turbo engine taking the automobile off the shoulder. When all four wheels left the ground, the Porsche now airborne, David closed his eyes, the weightlessness providing a moment of freedom.

His eyes remained closed as the car struck a full-grown juniper tree, searing it in half, the impact destroying the moment of quiet. The seatbelt kept him secured in his seat, his chest a bull's-eye for the steering wheel, pushed in by a mangled front end.

Minutes later, David felt the energy draining from his body. And then it went dark.

And then there was light, beautiful, inviting light that welcomed David. His vision was clear, his thoughts cleansed, a clarity enveloping him that was previously unknown.

"Is it really you, Layla?"

"It is, my love."

He recognized her smile. He knew her shape. But it had to be a mistake. "I don't believe it. No, I don't believe it. It can't be you." He never wanted anything so badly, but he must be mistaken.

"I'm right here, my love." She moved closer and extended her arms toward him.

He scanned her frame, inspecting every last inch of her body. She was wearing his favorite outfit, a silky beige top and a tight black skirt. The diamond earrings he had given her for Christmas dangled from her ears.

"I wore them for you, Coco. I know how much you love these clothes."

"You are gorgeous, Layla." He reached out and ran his fingers through her long hair. "Thanks for keeping it long. It looks the best on you."

"I know," she said, laughing. "I thought about cutting it, but I wanted to keep it the way you like it."

"It's so soft," he whispered, moving in closer. He put his face into her hair and took a deep breath. He breathed in every last inch of her, and it was intoxicating. He wrapped his arms around her and squeezed. She reciprocated.

"God, you're beautiful, Layla. I'm never letting go."

"Oh, Coco, it's so good to see you, but you can't stay."

"Why? Why? I don't want to let go!"

"I can't stay, Coco. You can't stay."

The tears streamed down his face. "Please, Layla. I don't want to go."

She gently pushed him back and wiped away a tear slowly running down his cheek. "We'll see each other again. I promise, okay? But for now, I have to say goodbye."

"I don't want to say goodbye. I want to hold you forever."

"David, it's not your time. We'll see each other again. Can't you see that now?"

"I can, my love, but I don't want to leave you. I want this to last forever."

"I'll be waiting here for eternity. Now, return and take care of our son. He needs you."

"But, Heather."

Heather put her fingers on his lips to stop him from saying anything further. "Goodbye, my love."

David reached out for her, but she was gone.

"Sir! Sir! Mister! Wake up!" yelled Thomas Sanderson at his unresponsive patient, now lying in the ditch, pulled free from the crushed vehicle. "Wake up, sir!" Adrenaline surged through the paramedic's body as he attached the adhesive defibrillator pads to the man's chest. The paramedic had been in this position dozens of times, trying to save someone who was not meant to be saved, who had no chance of returning. No pulse, and a lack of oxygen destroying his tissues indicated that the end was now. But it was his job, his moral responsibility, to do everything he could, for as long as he could, to save his patient.

One never becomes accustomed to someone dying in front of you, each time leaving a little more scar tissue on the ability to remain carefree. Thomas pushed the button on the battery-operated portable unit, sending an electrical current into the man's chest.

Thomas grabbed David's left wrist. "I've got a pulse!" he yelled to his colleagues. "Let's load him!"

"David!" yelled Thomas again. "Wake up!"

David opened his eyes, staring at the man who had saved his life, David's warmth replaced by the cooling evening air. "Heather, where is Heather?" David asked, barely audible, barely understandable.

"You've been in a car accident, David. We're taking you to St. Joseph's Hospital."

FINAL CHAPTER

Bottom of the Ninth

It was a fantastic sight, the throngs of fans surrounding the parade route in downtown Detroit, excitement dancing in the air. After the final win of the regular season propelled us into the playoffs, the Tigers continued on an amazing run. Baptiste called off the boycott, allowing all the regular players to return, the call-ups no longer necessary. I retired on the eve of the playoffs to the chagrin of Charlie and millions of fans. Kilmer and Earley begged me to stay on, but I would have bumped a regular player down to the minors. I had learned something about decency and was not prepared to do it. Besides, one further at-bat would have threatened my perfect season. My occupation remains as attorney-at-law, employed as an in-house lawyer for the Tigers, Earley offering me the position once my ball career had ended.

Charlie took the bench for the Tigers and was part of an incredible run culminating as World Series Champions. When the World Series ring was presented to my son, it completed him in a way I can only describe as esoteric, Jasmine at his side, clapping for his accomplishment.

One might have expected the players to receive the most cheers as we meandered our way around the core of the city, but the loudest applause was reserved for the youngest coach in MLB history. The parade was to last one hour, covering five miles, but it took six hours to complete the route. Every Detroit resident skipped work that day to celebrate with us, the congestion reducing our movement to a crawl, the consequences of an estimated one million wild and fanatic fans. Robocop and I were invited to participate in the parade, despite our lack of participation in the postseason, a kind gesture that I will treasure forever.

We Love You, Charlie and Nothing Is Faster than Mr. Hustle were typical of the signs on display. Grampa's Got Game was popular, too, with scores of fake white beards affixed to people's faces, but nothing compared to the public adoration of Charlie Unger.

Since my memorable home run, I've often been asked about swinging on a three-ball, no-strike pitch, when conventional wisdom dictated trying to work a walk. It's a delicate explanation. I've stuck with the same story, taken the mea culpa from my back pocket, and apologized for messing up on the signs. It was my fourth game with the Tigers and I became confused. Andrew Ford, the catcher for the Yankees, raised public doubts about the tale I told.

"Oh, he was swinging away," Ford said confidently. He took a hand off his bat, knocked three times on his head, and then turned around and said to me, 'Knock it, then rocket.'"

I've denied saying those words, perhaps a misunderstanding attributable to the raucous Tigers crowd.

What came over me? A desire to give Charlie a gift that he so deserved, something to prove that dreams can come true. Mission accomplished, I figure, my gift paling in comparison to the most important one—Jasmine Bouba wrapping her arms around him and whispering her love for him.

Despite my denial, the words "Knock it, then rocket" became folklore, fans of the game comparing it to Babe Ruth's famous calling of his home run by pointing his bat toward the home run fence.

"Charlie! Charlie! Charlie!" they chanted, knocking on their heads, when the parade car he was riding in drove by,

Jasmine at his side. Standing on several flatbed trucks, the rest of us waved and danced, championship smiles on our faces.

Charlie had become a hero, a symbol of baseball IQ brilliance. It's difficult to describe how I felt about my boy, but pride was undoubtedly the best description. Unbridled, unmitigated pride. Seven thousand, two hundred letters and one hundred thirteen thousand congratulatory text messages found their way to Mr. Hustle. Every misfit kid in the United States who had been ridiculed or bullied contacted Charlie. I was sure of it. Charlie read and responded to every last one of them, our kitchen resembling a United States Postal sorting station.

A week of World Series celebrations for Charlie included thirty-six radio and podcast interviews, twenty-one television appearances including *Good Morning America*, the *Today Show*, and the *Tonight Show*.

When Stephen Colbert asked Charlie to describe his favorite memory from the year, he pulled up his shirt and showed his Tigers tattoo to the camera. My Charlie was brilliant, mature beyond his years, but he was still a kid, and that felt good.

The live studio audience burst out in applause, my shocked look contributing to the laughter. It was the first time I had laid eyes on the Old English *D*, inked in navy blue. Charlie kibitzed with the host, the game of baseball providing a sanctuary for his usual awkwardness. I cannot agree that baseball is just a game for this reason alone.

The Tigers organization was emphatic that Charlie remain with the team, promising to work around his school schedule. Charlie would have done it for free, but they extended a healthy signing bonus. Mr. Hustle agreed, signing on the dotted line. What else would you expect from someone who had Tiger blood coursing through his veins?

My boy pushed me to be the best that I could be—to follow my dreams. More importantly, he helped make a broken man whole again.

Charlie and I decided to celebrate our World Series victory at Disney World. We had to retrieve the house on wheels, so it made sense, first flying into Lakeland to retrieve our RV before traveling across the state to Orlando. When Charlie wasn't giving interviews from his captain's chair, or studying game video in preparation for next season, we dreamed big and sang songs. We sang "Grampa's Got Game" until we were both utterly sick of it. Then, we would belt it out one more time.

We'd finished riding Space Mountain when I saw it under his left ear, a dark irregular-shaped patch the size of a dime. It was an area where the sun could reach, but it was awkward to apply sunscreen properly. My heart sunk, its familiarity striking me with a sledgehammer, my boy's recent claims of feeling some aching in his right leg bringing on a quiet panic.

Three weeks later, when biopsies confirmed melanoma, the news was dire; the cancer had metastasized to Charlie's bones. Charlie endlessly researched all treatment options; his spreadsheet included the modalities and the odds. Several rounds of radiation and chemotherapy slowed the cancer, but the aggressive and deadly cells were unstoppable. The boy fought with all his might, with every last ounce of strength that he could summon from his body. Through it all, he stared at the ring on his finger, a reminder that odds could be beaten. When he couldn't report to spring training, he received a giant get-well card signed by every member of the Tigers organization.

. When treatment was no longer an option, I placed Charlie in the hospice wing of St. Joseph's Hospital. Charlie had one last wish.

"I want to see one final World Series, Dad."

It was August 17, 2019, and I was doubtful he could make it. Of course, Mr. Hustle surprised me one last time. I still hadn't learned not to underestimate him.

Forty pounds lighter, and with no appetite, Charlie opened his eyes and smiled when I turned the television on for game one of the 115th edition of baseball's Major League World Series.

Jasmine was at his side every day, arriving after school and staying until the end of visiting hours. William and Luis arrived every other day, reading scriptures and discussing faith. Charlie hadn't talked too much about his beliefs as his final months approached.

I finally told Charlie about the thirty seconds that changed everything—my outlook, my relationships, and how I viewed humanity. It's an experience that does not easily come up in casual conversation, natural segues limited. Of course, detractors and cynics exist; there was a time I was one of them.

When I explained my near-death experience after my automobile accident and that I had crossed over and communicated with his mother, Charlie's eyes lit up—a twinkle appeared. I could see his brilliant brain processing my news through his unique prism, one that allowed the logical in, refracted the nonsensical away, and deposited the ambiguous into a repository for further assessment. Where would he place this?

"That's an awful lot of checkmarks, Dad," he finally said, clutching a nearly finished Michael Star book in his hand, *God and Gravity*.

Layla and Coco were secret pet names my wife and I had given each other. They also served as code if one of us was in any danger, the use of the name alerting the other that they were in peril and required help.

After the Washington Nationals secured their first World Series championship, I knew it wouldn't be long. Twelve hours later, I put my ear to Charlie's lips.

"It's the bottom of the ninth, Dad," the weakness barely allowing his lips to move.

I put my arms around him and grabbed him, too choked to say a word. I knew it was the end, but I couldn't believe that he was leaving. "I love you," my words coming out as a squeak. "It's okay to go, Son," I said, placing the home run ball bestowed on him by the benevolent baseball gods into his hand, the smudge remaining. Charlie made me sign it the day I hit it.

Charlie cracked open his right eye, nothing more than a tiny slit. "Dad, did you know there are 216 stitches in a Major League baseball?"

"I do now," I replied, destined to learn something new from Charlie right to the very end.

I put my ear back to his lips. "I'll say hi to Mom for you."

I trembled, the emotional pain overwhelming me.

"Fear makes the wolf bigger than it is, Dad." And Charlie closed his eyes for the last time.

The undertow of loss ripped me out to sea, where I flailed for weeks. I was ready to sink, the albatross of grief hanging around my neck, my ability to tread water waning to a dangerous level. I considered letting my head fall beneath the surface, but a ghost grabbed my shirt, held me up, and whispered in my ear, "Life is like baseball; when you expect a fastball, be prepared to hit the curve." The next day I was introduced to Darlene, Jenny, and Kevin at a bereavement group.

Every October 31, Jasmine, Luis, William, and I meet at Tigers Time, sharing our memories of Charlie and a Mr. Hustle Hamburger, which remains on Micky's chalkboard—fried onions, hot peppers, and sauteed mushrooms, served on a Pepperidge Farms sesame seed bun.

Jasmine eventually completed Harvard Law, graduating cum laude. This had followed her four years at the University of Notre Dame where she had played soccer for the Fighting Irish on a full scholarship. Her mother would have been proud.

Jasmine could have gone anywhere with those credentials, but she decided upon a position with the Michigan Coalition for Human Rights. Her eyes twinkle when she discusses the vital work she is embarking on. It's a look you cannot fake.

Reverend Baptiste tracked down a few articles about my father from high school. They called him the Dragon Slayer. It wasn't clear why, but it sounded impressive.

Fifteen years after my last game, I mingled at a cocktail party. I had become a baseball footnote by then, having never returned to play the game. However, a bronze plaque with my name is embedded on Adams Avenue, eleven feet farther from home plate than Miggy's. During a pleasant conversation with a woman who had no idea who I was, one of my many witty comments drew laughter from her. Before responding, she raised her hand and knocked three times on the side of her head.

"Brilliant, David, but you are no Charlie Hustle."

The irony was almost too magnificent to withhold from my new acquaintance, but I refrained. Instead, I knocked three times in return, memories washing over me, some that I welcomed, and others that were harder to hold back than a man in rage. I replied with a smile on my face, wholeheartedly agreeing with her, "You're damn right I'm not. He was a much better man."

THE END

About the Author

Stephen Roth is a Canadian lawyer who resides in the charming and captivating city of Stratford, Ontario, Canada, home of the world-renowned Stratford Festival. Influenced and inspired by the numerous artists, writers and actors that have called Strafford home, including esteemed writer and former resident, Timothy Findley, Stephen used a COVID-19 slow down to switch from writing legal briefs to penning his first novel, Innocence on Trial.

The Perfect Season, inspired by the French-English strife in Cameroon and his family's love for the Detroit Tigers, is Stephen's follow up book.

Stephen is currently working on the biography of Calgary's incredible Stephen Deng, a "lost boy" displaced from his home at age 7 by the horrific Sudanese civil war.

Printed in Great Britain
by Amazon